THE TENTH MANTLE BEARER

NIERGEL CHRONICLES
BOOK THREE

D. I. HENNESSEY

arkHarbor press

www.arkharbor.press

ISBN 979-8-9859336-4-2 (Paperback Edition)

ISBN 979-8-9859336-5-9 (Hardcover Edition)

Version 00004252026

arkHarbor press, www.arkharbor.press

info@arkhsc.com

DEDICATION

In grateful tribute to life-changing Grace.

'Godly sorrow is the bridge upon which God's mercy travels... it is the thoroughfare of Grace.'

CONTENTS

NIERGEL

NIERGEL

(Welsh: 'Nirgel,' pr. Near--ġ-el – Mysterious Secret)

"In the time of my favor, I heard you,
and in the day of salvation, I helped you."

~ 2 Corinthians 6:2

WOUNDED

J eff lies wide awake in his bed on Saturday evening, unable to sleep despite a long, strenuous day that should have left him near collapse. Closing his eyes, he takes another deep breath and lets it out slowly. Trying to use the controlled breathing technique that is the best cure for insomnia, he knows. At least the best one that doesn't resort to sedatives — or CHET's knock-out strobe.

Given the day's events, his elevated heart rate and stress level are not surprising. He relives the harrowing ordeal of the recent attack, noting that the Borgia's near victory was much too close for comfort.

While considering the continued danger that their enemy poses, his mind is drawn back to his uncle's challenge — his Quest. That thought soon triggers a flurry of memories about the secret Tower Lab and his uncle's fantastic avatar. His conversations with the avatar replay in his mind as clearly as a recording — especially the avatar's words as he was leaving the Tower on the first night they met. The words stir him uncomfortably as they surge through his mind again with an unnatural force...

"I must warn you...." the avatar had called after him. *"The battle you are about to wage is unlike any you have ever known — it will demand spiritual strength and no small measure of God's help ...without that, you will surely fail."*

Trying to still his anxious mind, Jeff lifts the Bible from his bedside table and opens it again to the handwritten note from his uncle Barrymore. His uncle's words have comforted him through all the stress and danger of the past few weeks.

Dear Jeffrey,
May you find here all that your heart desires.
'You will seek Me and find Me when you search for Me with all your heart.'

HE DOESN'T HAVE to turn to the verse his uncle quoted... he has memorized it. It still stirs his heart as it repeats in his mind for the hundredth time.

'I know the plans I have for you' — the Lord declares —' plans for your welfare, not for disaster, to give you a future and a hope. You will call to Me ... and I will listen to you. You will seek Me and find Me when you search for Me with all your heart.'

It has certainly been true that Jeff has been protected. He recalls a flurry of scenes, from EB's arrival on his doorstep until the previous night's events, every one of which could have ended differently. It could have ended *him.*

'You will call to me....'

Those words seem to ebb and flow repeatedly, like waves lapping against the shore. As irrational as it seems to him, they are strangely comforting. They conjure memories of his young parents kneeling beside his bed with him in prayer as a child. The world has surely become complicated since then, he bemoans regretfully. If only life were that simple.

Releasing a deep breath, he closes the Bible and lays it down with a yawn. This time, his exhaustion finally overcomes him, and he drifts into a deep sleep.

HUNAHPU IS surprised to see Jeff wearing a suit when he joins him for breakfast on Sunday morning.

"Don't look so surprised," Jeff says as he catches his great-grandfather's surprise. "I have a whole closet of these."

Hunahpu nods with a smile and sips his coffee, waiting for Jeff to explain.

"I figured it couldn't hurt to sit through one chapel service," Jeff concedes. "Showing some gratitude seems only fitting after yesterday. I have to admit that it could have gone a lot differently."

Hunahpu winks at Isabel, who is gesturing toward Heaven with a joyous expression. She comes from behind Jeff's chair to fill his coffee cup, smiling broadly.

"It looks as if you slept better last night," Hunahpu observes.

"Well, I guess you could say that, once I'd passed out from exhaustion."

Jeff sets his coffee down and looks into it as he thinks silently. Rather than revealing the personal struggle he was having last night, he decides to change the subject.

"I GUESS you heard about the intelligence report on the Borgias' new ships. Do you think they really have a spacecraft?"

Hunahpu accepts his breakfast plate from Isabel as he straightens to consider Jeff's question.

"It is surprising, I will admit. We had seen no indication before now that they had been testing such a capability. If it is true, then I suspect we will hear of it soon."

THE SOUND of ABBI's voice greeting a new guest interrupts their discussion.

'Good morning, Mr. Billingsly.'

"A beautiful mornin' i' tis," EB says as he enters the kitchen.

Isabel fills a waiting teacup and saucer and delivers it to the table as he sits down.

"What's this?" EB gasps as he takes a seat, catching sight of Jeff in a Sunday suit. "Are ye preparin' fer a photo shoot?" He winks at Hunahpu with a knowing smile.

"I know, it's a shock... I get it," Jeff shrugs. "Don't expect it to be a habit."

"Well, what we expect and what God gives can sometimes be surprisingly different," EB replies mysteriously. Huanhpu hides a smile of his own behind his mug of coffee as he comprehends EB's meaning.

Jeff's eyes shift back and forth between them as he takes a sip from his mug. He fully understands that EB is suggesting it is Jeff himself who may ultimately be the one surprised. He feels a familiar tug as a nagging thought flashes to mind once again: 'You will call to me....' He decides to shift the topic back to something more comfortable.

"We were just talking about the intelligence report... about a possible spacecraft," he says to EB.

"Aye. I was speakin' with Bear about it jus' before arrivin' here," EB reveals, referring to Berenger Bern, their head of aerospace operations. "He's quite worried about what he's seein', without a doubt. The intercepted list of materials looks nearly like one for our own Space Birds."

"Does he think they could really be building one? Wouldn't they need to test things first — before building a whole ship?"

"Ye'd think so, most surely. If they've been testin' engines or proto-types, they've done a good job o' hidin' 'em."

"Could they be using the island base off Greenland?" Jeff wonders. "Maybe their testing has been underground."

"I suppose it's possible," EB concedes. "Although ye'd expect there to at least be some sign of equipment or material deliveries. Nothin' like that has been seen in the nearby shipping ports."

Isabel politely interrupts their conversation with deliveries of breakfast plates to Jeff and EB, diverting their attention to something more pleasant.

"HEY, WHAT'S THIS?" Eugenia says with a smile as she sees Jeff accompanying her grandfather and Hunahpu on their way to the Chapel. Jeff answers with a shrug and subtle smile. He's actually enjoying the effect that his surprise attendance is causing.

Eugenia takes her grandfather's arm in hers as they walk together.

"I love this chapel," she says, mainly for Jeff's benefit, looking up at it as they approach.

Jeff takes in the sight. 'Chapel' seems to him like an odd name for the impressive structure — it is more of a cathedral. He just nods to her that he agrees, giving her a quick smile. His fondness for his friends adds to the comfort Jeff feels as he enters the grand sanctuary. He is beginning to get a feeling for why they love it so much.

JEFF IS WARMLY RECEIVED at the Chapel by Reverend Abbott. Word spreads quickly that he is there, and he is soon greeted with enthusiasm by many others as well. The friendly greetings are warm and sincere, and the service seems simple and genuine, not the kind of stuffy church formality he expected. By the time the service has ended, the morning has given him more to think about.

MONDAY MORNING...

Jeff is feeling a renewed eagerness to continue his fight training, sensing the difference Eugenia's lessons are making. After a month of workouts, he is definitely feeling stronger and has more endurance. More of his training time is now spent on familiar routines and the exercise equipment, leaving his muscles sore, but at least he isn't being beaten up, as he likes to remind himself.

Entering the gym, he walks toward his usual starting point on the spinning cycle, but Eugenia blocks his path, throwing him a long stick that matches the one she holds in her other hand. He watches as she expertly twirls the five-foot pole — first in front of her and then over her head, making it sound like a helicopter, before planting its end on the mat with a loud thud.

The beckoning motion she makes with her other hand means 'bring it on' — Jeff hates it when she does that. He does his best to raise an attack but is instantly knocked off his feet with a blow to the back of his legs. He looks up from the floor at Eugenia's long pole poised inches from his nose, realizing the pain she could inflict if she wanted to.

She helps him to his feet and begins her lesson.

"Today we start weapons training," she declares, stating what is already obvious. "We'll begin with the Dragon Pole — *luk dim boon Gwan,* she says, naming it as she lifts it above her head. It's a deceptively simple weapon," she admits, looking it over as she holds it horizontally in her hands, "its proper use is an extension of empty hand training, but with triple the difficulty of balance, precision, strength, and endurance."

Oh great, Jeff moans to himself, admitting that he has only just begun to master hand-to-hand.

"This is a crucial step in your progression to lethal weapons," she adds, nodding toward the rack on the wall. Jeff gulps, thinking about the dangerous possibility of facing her with one of those in her hands.

As odd as it seems, that thought makes him appreciate her training even more. He silently acknowledges that it is a great gift she is giving him in dedicating so much of her own time… time that must be precious given the size of her other responsibilities. Most people in her position would surely have left it to someone else to train a novice like him.

He is beginning to realize that there could be more to his feelings for her than he has so far allowed. The idea of inviting her to dinner comes to his mind — he has never taken EB and her up on their invitation, after all.

WHILE HE IS APPRECIATING HER, however, he manages to miss the instructions she has been giving him. The next thing he knows, he is flat on his back with a red welt on his forehead from Eugenia's pole. She lands from her airborne spin and runs to him with a look of concern on her face.

He looks up at both of her images kneeling beside him as they slowly come together again.

"You were supposed to crouch and block with your pole!" she gently chides him.

She helps him to his feet, but he is too dizzy to stand. The welt on his head is quickly growing into a large bump.

"Just lie down over here," she directs, helping him to a stack of mats; "I'll get some ice."

He is lying down with a towel full of ice on his head when the doctor arrives with a pair of EMTs, escorted by EB.

"Thanks…" Genie says sincerely to her grandfather. She is looking shaken as EB wraps his arm around her shoulders.

"No worries," he answers dismissively, "he's a tough one; this'll be a good lesson to him, no doubt."

The doctor finishes checking Jeff's heart, breathing, and eye dilation, quizzing him with a barrage of questions, and then walks back to Eugenia and EB. "He appears just fine, but he'll have a bit of a headache for a few hours," he reports. "Someone should keep an eye on him for any sign of concussion; that would be any dizziness, disorientation, memory loss, nausea… that sort of thing."

"I'll see to it," EB readily volunteers.

"Good," the doctor nods, "I've left him instructions to take Aspirin or his choice of pain medication — six or eight hundred milligrams should do it. He'll be back on his feet soon enough."

"Thank you, Doctor…." Eugenia says appreciatively.

"That's quite all right," the doctor replies kindly, "no harm done; you can rest assured of that."

The interns help Jeff to his feet, and he holds a hand to his head to still the sudden throbbing.

"We'll get him back to his apartment," the doctor offers as they walk him out.

EB turns back to Genie, who is still feeling terrible. "If yer lookin' to win a man's notice, perhaps ye'd best avoid beatin' him over the head quite so literally," he jokes, watching her worried expression soften into a smile. "I'd say a sparrin' helmet would be a good idea," he suggests with a smile as he pats her on the shoulder. She smiles back sheepishly and shakes her head in agreement.

⌘

2

WHAT'S THE MATTER

J eff has to miss his Dibjet training for the day, which honestly wounds him more than Eugenia's blow to the head. He spends the morning in a recliner in his sitting room with EB and Hunahpu to keep him company. Isabel dotes over him to the point that he has to politely ask her to stop, but she still pokes her head in every fifteen minutes to ask EB in a whisper whether they need anything.

By midday, he seems to be feeling much better and is beginning to bristle at being confined. He is out of his chair and pacing the room, noticeably frustrated.

"Well, go ahead and ask me if you want…" he challenges his older friends in a tone that reveals his irritability, "I know you're wondering how it's going with my…" (he pauses, looking for a word other than Challenge or Quest) "…my Heritage!" he finally blurts, expressing exasperation.

"I suppose by now I should be in the home stretch!" He waves his arms as he speaks, revealing his frustration over the limited progress he has made.

His wise counselors share a glance and look back at Jeff sympathetically. Neither of them will speak openly of the Quest. Jeff accepts their queue for discretion and sits back down in surrender, running a hand through his hair. "Fine," he sighs, acknowledging their silent admonition, "…but I have to admit it feels like I'm at a dead end."

Hunahpu looks at him with an expression that conveys an immense degree of wisdom — as if he can read parts of Jeff's soul that even Jeff doesn't understand.

"That is good… That is very good," he says while nodding his head as if diagnosing an ailment.

Jeff looks at him, confused.

"You have come to the end of your own path," Hunahpu explains, "…**now you can begin**."

Jeff has never heard anything so deflating in his life — he feels his stubborn determination suddenly ebb away as his Great-Grandfather's words repeat in his head:

…now you can begin.

As discouraging as it is, the thought is also strangely liberating.

Jeff scans Hunahpu's face with a searching look in his eyes and then leans back in his chair with a hand to his chin, staring out the window.

THE OLDER MEN sit quietly as Jeff ponders Hunahpu's meaning. Suddenly, the room's silence is interrupted by a chime from EB's O-P. He reads the waiting message and opens the linked report, reading it without speaking as a look of grave concern forms on his face. EB hands the tablet to Hunahpu, who quickly reads it, then offers it to Jeff.

The report is marked **Top Secret**; below the heading is a link to images — Jeff taps it and selects the first image, opening it to fill the screen. Glancing at EB and Hunahpu, he quickly leans forward in his seat and 'pushes' the image to the room's large monitor, where it quickly fills the screen. It is an image of a ship against the black background of space. Jeff recognizes its uni-wing shape and partially transparent surface.

EB explains what they are seeing in a concerned voice. "We have confirmation of a Borgia spacecraft; this picture was captured from one of our satellites just this morning. This does indeed mark a significant advance in their capabilities."

"Can they threaten our assets in space?" Jeff asks.

"Ours and anyone else's," Hunahpu responds honestly.

Jeff sits, processing the information for a minute, then looks up.

"This ship looks surprisingly similar to our own Space Birds. Do you think they're developing these advances by themselves?"

"Who else could they be getting them from?" EB asks curiously. "No one else has this technology but us."

"Hmmph..." Hunahpu intones, leaning forward in his seat, answering Jeff insightfully. "You have a point... I confess I hadn't considered it."

"You mean a mole inside Hastleworth?" EB says in surprise as he catches on.

"Think about it," Jeff suggests, "How did they know how to defeat the castle's defenses so easily last weekend and use the elevator shaft to target the underground lab? Azeem knew exactly where to find the descent pod's shaft to the control bunker, and he knew I'd be there. It was like they knew our greatest vulnerabilities and exploited them as if they'd carefully planned and practiced for it."

Jeff silently recalls that the avatar said their enemy only copied what Hastleworth did. "What if they aren't just copying our ideas—what if they're duplicating stolen designs? There were some here who were loyal to Katkeruus, right? ...what if some of them are still here?"

EB and Hunahpu look at each other, realizing that Jeff seems to have information about Katkeruus that neither of them has shared with him. Both quickly conclude that his knowledge must have been picked up in his pursuit of the Challenge.

"It makes perfect sense; I don't know why I hadn't seen it sooner," EB admits as he grips his chin distractedly, "but what about their anti-gravity weapon? They couldn't have copied that from us — we'd never devise such a thing!"

"No, but you said Barry anticipated it," Jeff reminds him. "Who else knew about his concerns?"

The older men sit thinking... "Many..." EB answers as Hunahpu agrees. "The risk was known by the engineerin' teams in all three centers... Peru, here and at CNAL."

"None of those in Peru would aid our enemies...." Hunahpu assures them, "...I know all of them personally; they remember too well Katkeruus' vicious attack."

"I feel the same about Loch Harnan," EB says confidently.

"Then we need to warn Berenger," Jeff says with a concerned look.

"This is too sensitive to entrust to communications channels," EB notes, "...we should meet with Berenger in person. I'll prep a Dibjet for us." He is deep in thought as he excuses himself and departs in a rush.

"You two go ahead," Jeff suggests to Hunahpu, "there's something more I need to take care of here."

Hunahpu nods knowingly and looks into Jeff's eyes with a kind expression, "...Listen to your heart as well as to your head," he counsels quietly. "The mind may answer *what* and *how*...but the heart must tell you *why* ...and *when*."

He places his hand on Jeff's shoulder and pats it, then makes his way out.

Jeff is left standing alone, lost in thought. The events of the past month race through his mind — the wisdom of Hunahpu's advice has been unassailable, he admits. What's more, the old man's comments about the evidence of an ancient global flood have proved shockingly true, and Jeff is forced to concede that he is likely right, as well, about the impossible odds of life's DNA code occurring accidentally.

Most unsettling of all, however, are the words of caution that the avatar had spoken — they continue to repeat in his mind:

"...the battle you are about to wage is unlike any you have ever

*known — it will demand spiritual strength and no small
measure of God's help ...without it, you will surely fail."*

Jeff is standing in the same place five minutes later when Isabel appears in the doorway.

"Will the others be joining you for lunch?"

He glances at her distractedly... "N-no, no, they won't," he answers without elaborating.

AFTER TOYING with his lunch briefly, Jeff excuses himself: "I think I'll go upstairs to my room for a while — just for an hour or so," he says to Isabel.

"Of course, sir..." she responds with a hint of concern. "Do take care of yourself — I'll make certain that no one disturbs you."

He feels a little guilty about misleading her — he hadn't technically said he was going to sleep, but he thanks her politely without correcting her perception and makes his way upstairs. He locks the door as he enters his room, then immediately takes the elevator to the Tower.

THE AVATAR GREETS him as he enters.

"What additional questions do you have? There must be many more for which you seek answers."

Jeff considers the question and realizes that this time he doesn't know where to start. "My Challenge. The Ring and Scepter..." he begins, as his attention is refocused on the mission he has been given, "...what are they made of — why is it impossible to destroy them?"

"It would appear that their origin is not of this earth," the avatar answers mysteriously.

"Not of this earth?" Jeff repeats, "...you mean, they're alien — from another planet?"

"Not another planet... another dimension," the avatar corrects. "Perhaps we should begin with the beginning...."

The large monitors on the wall are filled with images of an open ocean.

"...Water ...our planet is covered with it. You have likely been taught that vast quantities of it were deposited here by comets over millions of years."

Jeff simply nods in agreement, wondering what this could possibly have to do with the ring and scepter.

"That theory is astonishingly inadequate to account for the earth's massive oceans, based on purely objective calculations of our oceans' volume and the rates of evaporation in a theoretical young planet.

"What you must assume instead is that water — or at least an elemental form of it — was not added to the earth, but rather was its source — its origin ...the essential material from which all else was derived."

Jeff looks at the avatar suspiciously as he listens.

The screen shows a sophisticated animation of interacting atoms... Hydrogen and oxygen, with their atomic weights, along with a complex soup of other elements, in a chaotic mix.

"It is estimated that the entire mass of observable matter that exists in our universe could once have consisted of a chaotic mix of matter and energy, much like a liquid form. It can be estimated that a sea of condensed energy and matter containing the fundamental building blocks of all we see in the universe would have occupied a space approximately two light-years across. All of the observable universe shares this same elemental mix, as if it were spawned from a single elemental source; ...this single ocean of matter."

The monitors switch to a display of the Ring and Scepter, as the avatar continues....

"Yet, the elements from which the ring and scepter are derived are wholly different from our universe — their elements cannot be identified."

"I take it, then, that my uncle analyzed them?"

"Indeed... heat and chemical testing ... X-ray, electron micro-scope, and electro-spectral analysis ...All of that and much more," the avatar confirms.

"...Are the findings available to study?" Jeff asks anxiously.

The room's screens fill with tables and graphs depicting the results of those tests. Jeff stares at them with an amazed expression.

"These are incredible! How is this possible? ...Look!" he says, pointing at the charted results on different screens, "...heat, cold, radiation, wavelengths of light and sound, all known gases... even blunt impacts — they had no effect whatsoever ...none of the chemical agents produced any effect at all — it's like the artifacts weren't even there." Jeff feels a sudden despair as he quickly concludes the same thing that his uncle had — "Even a hydrogen bomb couldn't touch these things!"

The avatar stands quietly as Jeff's mind races. Then a new series of results fills the screens....

"These readings were measured when the items were in the presence of the Shepherd's Staff," the avatar explains.

The measurements were dramatically different — though still not enough to materially damage the ring and scepter, they appeared to resonate unusually, almost like a glass crystal reacting to high-frequency sound.

"That must be how the Staff interfered with their powers," Jeff observes. "They were somehow destabilized. Couldn't Uncle Barry increase the Staff's effect? ...enough to shatter them?"

The avatar shakes its head; "He tried extensively — nothing worked."

"What about simulations? Is there enough data to predict their limits?"

"The Staff does not appear to emit any detectable power at all; neither its position nor its proximity made any measurable difference."

"But there must be a limit to the distance at which it can work," Jeff suggests, "if that's true, then proximity must have some effect."

"That's the odd thing," the avatar offers, "it's as if any line of sight is all that's needed."

"You mean the Staff needs to have an unobstructed view of the objects?" Jeff clarifies.

"Not the Staff itself… the bearer of the Staff."

Jeff considers that in surprise; a sudden thought hits him: "The power of the Staff is in the one who wields it…" he says distractedly.

"Interesting hypothesis— what makes you suggest it?" the avatar asks.

"…W-what?" Jeff says, jolted from his momentary distraction. He considers the words he has just uttered and looks at the avatar with a disarmed expression. "…I'm not sure, but it seems like the one who uses the staff… channels its power somehow. You said that it could only be used by someone who had been chosen by it, right? So, the user is the important variable.
"You already knew that, didn't you — uncle Barry came to the same conclusion."
The avatar nods silently.
Jeff rubs his forehead and plops himself into a chair, deep in thought. "What I don't understand is …how did Uncle Barry know that the Staff would select me? Is it only because I'm the last one left?"

"There were many factors," the avatar answers, "that one, perhaps, being paramount."

"What made him think I'd be any more successful than he was?" Jeff asks in wonder.

"He couldn't be sure, of course, but it was his greatest hope and prayer."

"As remarkable as their powers appear to be, we know that the ring and scepter follow natural laws, though they may be different laws than those that we know. It stands to reason that the Staff adheres to those laws as well."

Jeff looks at the avatar as the implications of his statement dawn on him. "The Staff is from the same place as the ring and scepter? From that other dimension?"

"Whether it be the same or not, we cannot say, but its origin was certainly not in our space and time. And for a reason that we do not understand, its use of those laws appears to be especially tuned to your unique heritage."

Jeff stares at his O-P lying on the counter in front of him as he considers what the avatar is saying, remembering the way each O-P is created for a single individual. He looks back to the avatar as the thought hits him: "It's like the Staff has been *keyed* to recognize our family."

"More precisely, a specific member of your family," the avatar corrects.

"Has it ever selected more than one person? ...at the same time, I mean?"

"It appears that there can be only one," the avatar answers poignantly.

Jeff considers that thought quietly for a minute, then looks up curiously. "If that's true... how did the Staff know that Uncle Barry had died?"

⌘

3

ENEMY REVEALED

Location: CNAL (*pronounced: Sen-all*)
Cronk **ny** Arrey Laa (*Manx, meaning: Hill of the Day Watch*)
- *Hastleworth's secret underground aerospace base.*

A red light is flashing on the Dibjet's control panel as EB disengages the autopilot and expertly maneuvers their craft for its underwater approach. They wait as the secret facility's sentry station acknowledges their access request, and an interior scan of their cabin confirms their identities.

The radio reports their access confirmation:

Clearance approved...

A large section of rock in the sheer underwater cliff face splits apart in front of them, revealing a gigantic steel door that is opening just behind it; EB smoothly moves the Dibjet forward into the dark passageway, entering a long tunnel as the doors seal behind them.

Only the ship's lights illuminate the pitch-black passageway until they approach a wide pool at the far end, with light flooding down from the surface above. The Dibjet breaks the surface and maneuvers into one of the empty docking bays, which is lifted from the water as the large bay platform rises and locks into place.

Berenger is waiting for them as EB and Hunahpu climb out of their ship.

"Isn't Jeffrey with you?" he asks in surprise, "...I assumed when you arrived unannounced that this was an introductory tour."

"Jeff has some urgent business to attend to back in Loch Harnan," EB explains.

Berenger's face grows serious: "Then your business here must be extremely urgent as well," he notes, looking back and forth between them.

EB looks around at the docking crew and other workers within earshot, "...Might we have a word — somewhere quiet?"

"Y-Yes, of course...," Berenger answers somewhat nervously. He waves toward the entry hall and then walks briskly to keep up with the pace of the older men's steps as they urgently start out. "We can talk in my office...," Berenger offers as they emerge into the hallway.

"It's such a lovely day... I don't believe Hunahpu has seen a view of the Six Kingdoms," EB suggests instead.

"All right... Certainly..." Berenger agrees with an increasing sense of alarm. EB is suggesting that they go to the lookout tower; it is an isolated structure that is seldom used these days. He can't help agreeing that a more private place for conversation could not be found.

THEY TAKE a short elevator ride from the docking level to the facility's main concourse. Then Berenger leads them past the executive office suites, without stopping to greet anyone, ...to a little-used elevator near the center of the underground complex. As soon as they are all inside, he presses the button marked "Surface." The elevator rises for more than a minute before finally stopping to open into a plain concrete bunker; just in front of them is a metal staircase leading up to a single reinforced-steel entry door. Berenger unlocks it with his card badge, and the three men emerge into what appears to be a drafty basement space. A small roofless construction elevator cage stands in front of them, with daylight flooding through the opening above it.

Berenger opens the metal gate that serves as its door and closes it behind them as the others enter, then presses the top button, making the cage jerk awkwardly upward. A brisk wind whips against them as they rise into the open air, past the barren-looking hilltop's surface and upward for another twenty meters until the cage has entered the deserted lookout post perched above. The neglected windows are dirty but offer a breathtaking view nonetheless, standing atop a large hill that rises nearly 500 meters above sea level, with sheer cliffs dropping to the ocean below.

"HERE WE ARE…," EB says, getting Hunahpu's attention. "Over there in the north can be seen Scotland …the land there to the west is Ireland …down there to the south is Wales …and there, of course, England. The land here beneath us is Mann."

"Then I count only five kingdoms," Hunahpu observes, "…where is the sixth?"

"Above us, my friend," EB explains, pointing at the sky with a smile, "…'tis the kingdom of Heaven. If they are nothin' else, the Manx people are a poetic lot."

Hunahpu slaps EB's back and erupts in a boisterous laugh that makes the other men smile despite the gravity of their intended conversation.

AS THE LAUGHTER SUBSIDES, Berenger looks at his colleagues with renewed concern. "I know you men didn't come just for the view — no doubt you have a great deal to keep you otherwise occupied… what's this all about?"

EB unzips the small backpack on his shoulder, pulls out his tablet-sized O-P, and props it against a window. "Chet, please raise Jeffrey for us, will you?" he requests.

A moment later, Jeff appears on the screen from his office desk; "Hello, gentlemen," he says in greeting. "...Where are you?" he adds as he notices their surroundings.

"We couldn't risk using normal communications, even if encrypted," EB explains, "...we have to assume that even Berenger's office may not be secure."

"You suspect someone has bugged my office!?" Berenger exclaims in surprise. "This is a top-secret facility!"

"It's worse than that, I'm afraid," Jeff begins. "We have reason to believe there may be a spy embedded deep within our operations."

"A spy!? ...Here?!"

"We must admit it is only conjectured at this point," EB explains, "but it may be the only explanation. Our enemy has been duplicating our most sensitive technologies at an increasing rate. Their apparent designs not only have the same capabilities as ours, they even look alike."

Berenger sinks to sit on a metal storage box in the center of the room, deep in thought. "The space wing..." he says in recognition as he recalls their most recent intelligence report.

"Think about it," Jeff encourages, "who has access to those designs?"

"No one... that is, the complete designs are never stored together in one file system. Components are manufactured in isolation, and there is no way for individual teams to know all the contributors ...no one has access to the full design. ...Except..." he says with a look of alarm.

He looks up at the others with a worried expression... "Our head of engineering, Dylen McGloughlin, has the same access as mine."

"We must proceed carefully," EB advises, "it's possible that only his credentials have been compromised... he may be unaware of the breach."

"How can we be sure?" Berenger asks earnestly.

"We must tell him," Hunahpu says a bit mysteriously. He looks at the others, recognizing their struggle to understand his meaning. "If he is unaware, then word that our secret designs have been compromised will not frighten him."

"...But if he reacts...," Berenger says as he understands.

"If he truly is an embedded operative, he could be hard to crack," EB notes with experience.

"Perhaps I could be the one to ask him," Jeff volunteers. He looks at EB with a subtle hint in his eye as he continues, "...Chet can facilitate another call via your O-P for us."

EB understands what Jeff is suggesting but doesn't reveal it to the others. The O-P is designed to decode billions of physical mannerisms per second — it can detect cues that are far too subtle for human detection... or human masking. "An excellent idea," he quickly agrees.

"Well... alright... if you feel that's best," Berenger concedes. "I'd like to be present if you have no objection."

"Of course, by all means, you should certainly be there," Jeff assures him.

AFTER ENDING their conference with Jeff, EB puts his O-P back in his backpack and then turns to look at the horizon again.

"It truly is a spectacular view, isn't it?" he says as he folds his arms and gazes out the window.

"Extraordinary..." Hunahpu agrees, standing beside him and gazing at the remarkable 360-degree view.

Berenger doesn't respond... he's deep in thought.

"Don't be too hard on yourself," EB says to him, "none of us suspected."

"It's not just that," Berenger confides; his expression is ashen looking: "Dylan may know where the ring and scepter are hidden — he helped to design the security that protects them."

EB and Hunahpu look at one another with grave expressions.

"We need to warn Jeffrey!" EB exclaims. "He should secure them immediately."

"But we don't know how to find them," Hunahpu points out. "Even if we did… it's too dangerous — Jeff mustn't face them before he is prepared," he warns.

Berenger thinks aloud… "The risk would be letting Dylen warn his contacts that we're on to him — we have to avoid raising suspicions."

"I agree," EB nods, "but how do we take him into custody without tipping our hand?"

"By not taking him into custody," Hunahpu offers, "…not technically, anyway. We must bring him back with us to Loch Harnan."

"Under what pretense?" EB asks.

"None will be needed," Berenger answers, "If I send him, he'll go. I'll tell him that your engineering team needs his help; it won't be difficult to convince him."

"It's settled then," EB says. "Ye'll both return with us today on our ship."

"I really can't, I regret to say," Berenger apologizes, "there's too much going on here - I don't know how I could get away…."

"I'm afraid I must insist, my old friend," EB says with a saddened expression.

Berenger understands that he hasn't yet escaped being a suspect himself. He simply nods his head acquiescently; "I understand," he says with a sigh, "the sooner we clear this up, the better.

EB AND HUNAHPU follow Berenger to his office and sit waiting while Dylen is summoned. The surprised Director is taken aback upon seeing EB and Hunahpu sitting there.

"Mr. Billingsly, Sir…" he says, shaking EB's hand, "…Sir…" he adds, greeting Hunahpu. "To what do we owe the honor?"

"Rather serious circumstances, I'm afraid," EB says as Berenger looks on and swallows nervously. "We require your help on an urgent matter back in Loch Harnan — a critical Defense initiative."

"Yes…," Berenger cuts in; the serious tone of his voice is unmistakable. "We're terribly sorry to trouble you on short notice, but it appears that the research division has hit an obstacle that requires your assistance most urgently."

"What sort of obstacle?" Dylen asks in surprise.

"I'm afraid we're not at liberty to discuss it here," EB answers quickly.

"Would it happen to have anything to do with a certain set of unusual objects?" Dylen asks with a grin that suggests he is pleased with himself for being privy to one of the company's greatest secrets.

Berenger furrows his brow with a look that reveals his regret for trusting Dylen with such sensitive information. They don't bother answering his question.

Berenger clears his throat; "We have to leave at once... We'll be traveling with them on their ship."

"Right now? But I was just in the middle of... I'll need to pack a bag..." he stammers in surprise.

"No need to worry about that," EB assures him, "We can outfit you with anything you need."

"Well... can I collect my laptop and briefcase? I'd like to at least grab a jacket for the voyage," he says with an imploring expression.

"Certainly..." Berenger assures him, "Collect whatever you need. We'll accompany you to your office on our way out."

Dylen swallows noticeably as Berenger places a hand on his shoulder and motions toward the door.

The men watch Dylen carefully as he collects his things; EB notices him slipping a thumb drive into his pocket. He doesn't say a word, simply noting the fact.

Dylen looks at his watch and presses the button on its side to update the display. Just as he does, a small chirp from EB's O-P draws his attention, and he slides it from his jacket to glance at the screen; *GPS beacon detected*, it alerts. EB casually taps the "BLOCK" button below the message, instructing the O-P to block the watch's signal, and then drops it back into his pocket. Any doubts as to Dylen's involvement are quickly fading in his mind.

⌘

4

CUSTODY

As they'd planned, Berenger and Hunahpu keep Dylen engaged in casual conversation at the gate. At the same time, EB goes on ahead and sets up his O-P to appear as if it is one of the ship's standard monitors. When they follow him inside, EB directs Dylen to the prescribed seat and seals the ship's door.

They quickly get underway as EB pilots the Dibjet back through the underwater tunnel and into the deep water of the Irish Sea. As soon as they have cleared the tunnel, Berenger quietly signals the base to order a complete lockdown; no one is permitted to enter or leave the base without his clearance.

Finally, in the open sea, EB flips the ship's controls to autopilot and spins his seat around to join the others in conversation. Just as he does, the monitor in front of Dylen pings several times.

"Ah... appears to be a call from LH," EB notes as he taps the answer button, taking the opportunity to move into a rear seat behind the others.

Jeff's image appears on the screen directly in front of Dylen's seat.

"Mr. Sutherland, Sir!" Dylen responds in surprise. He looks at Berenger and the others, taking note of the company he is in. "Well, this must be an important mission! Mind telling me what this is all about?"

"Hello, Dylen. Thanks for your help," Jeff says in greeting. He gets directly to the point. "I'm afraid we've had a serious breach in security."

Dylen swallows with difficulty: "A breach, Sir? What kind of breach... exactly?"

Jeff glances at the readings displayed below Dylen's image on his own O-P, noticing that they have turned red almost instantly.

"We're hoping that you can help us determine that," Jeff answers truthfully without revealing the O-P's insights.

"Y-Yes certainly..." Dylen agrees uncomfortably, "...what can I do to help?" He looks around at Berenger and the others, exaggerating his willingness to help.

"It appears..." Jeff says, waiting for Dylen to look back at him on the screen, "...that your security ID is being used to access extremely sensitive information — we have reason to suspect that this information has fallen into the hands of the Borgia."

"M-My ID?" Dylen stammers, visibly shaken, "I-I assure you... I've had nothing to do with anything like that... there must be some mistake!"

Jeff's O-P displays 99.999% confidence that he is lying. He taps his screen, sending the conclusion to EB's display — it pops up below Dylen's image in the corner of their screen.

The moment he sees it, Dylen reaches for his seat belt and tries to jump from his seat but finds that his lap belt and shoulder harness won't unlatch — the more he struggles, the tighter they become.

"I'm truly sorry about this, Lad," EB says as he comes up behind Dylen and presses a hypo-gun against the side of his neck, then pulls the trigger; it renders him temporarily unconscious.

"I HAD CHET DO A LITTLE INVESTIGATING," Jeff says as EB's screen fills with images of documents and bank transactions. "It appears that Dylen has been opening clandestine accounts under various aliases — all of those on this list have been traced back to him."

The account balances are shown in a long, scrolling list that ends with a final tally of more than one hundred million Euros. All of the funding transfers originated from accounts associated with the Borgia syndicate.

EB removes Dylen's watch and quickly searches his pockets, retrieving the thumb drive. As he had suspected, a pat down discovers a small revolver holstered to his ankle.

He holds the watch up to his O-P for a scan, and a schematic of the inner workings appears on the screen. It emits an ultra-low-frequency GPS beacon that the O-P is jamming and contains several other unusual microdevices.

"Looks to be Borgia technology," he observes, "let's have a closer look at that back at the lab." He powers it off and slips it into a secure container.

Next, he places the thumb drive into a port on the O-P...

"Looks like it's encrypted... needs a passcode to unlock it," EB notes, looking at Jeff.

"Go ahead," Jeff agrees, "you don't have to ask me -- you're the one with unrestricted access," he reminds his older friend. Jeff had restricted his own O-P's ability to carry out brute force attacks to override the security of other computers, leaving only EB's unit with that capability.

"Right..." EB recalls, "...just keeping it on the up and up," he adds with a smile.

"Chet, unlock this thumb drive for us if you please."

The drive's contents are displayed on the screen in a few seconds.

"Those are plans for the energy shield!" Berenger exclaims upon recognizing what it contains.

"This one appears to be the formula for hampering an anti-gravity feedback loop," EB notes.

"Can we be sure he has no accomplices?" Hunahpu asks, suddenly breaking his long silence.

They all look at Berenger, who hangs his head in a discouraged gesture. "We had better do a full investigation," he suggests sadly.

"Chet," Jeff instructs, "trace the bank accounts connected with those transfers that Dylen received. See if any payments have been made to anyone else."

"That will require overriding the security for a number of private bank accounts," Chet informs him.

"I concur with Jeffrey's request," EB adds quickly, "please proceed."

"Acknowledged… the security protocol is authorized," Chet confirms.

"Do you think he'll talk?" Jeff asks, looking at Dylen asleep in his seat.

"That may depend on whether he fears for his life or the lives of loved ones," Hunahpu answers thoughtfully.

"Don't be ridiculous! We would never threaten him with physical harm! …Right?" Jeff protests, hopefully.

"It's not us," EB explains, "Extortion is practically an art form to the Borgia. They don't take kindly to traitors."

"We can keep his arrest secret for a few days," Berenger suggests, "that may give us time to flush out anyone working with him before they're driven underground."

"Good idea," Jeff agrees, "EB, maybe you can use his laptop to open some lines of communication in his name… see what you can find."

"Right! I'm on it!"

"Does he have any family… anyone needing protection?" Jeff asks with concern.

"No wife or children," Berenger confirms. "His parents passed some years ago.

A chirp from Jeff's O-P draws his attention. "I need to go," he says, "keep me posted if you find anything."

The others agree and sign off.

"Do you think we should have warned Jeffrey about Dylen's connection with the Ring and Scepter?" Berenger asks with concern.

"Until he is prepared, the less he knows about their whereabouts, the better," Hunahpu argues.

AFTER ENDING his call with EB and the other men, Jeff sits quietly in his office, thinking. There is no telling how much damage Dylen has done; not only that, if the Borgia have been able to recruit their chief of aerospace engineering, it seems likely there could be other recruits as well.

He finally remembers the alarm chime from his O-P and looks down at the details, tapping it to open Chet's image.

"Brandish is requesting your presence in his Lab," Chet informs him.

"I'm on my way."

JEFF IS LOST in thought as he rides the elevator alone from the castle's lobby to the deep underground lab. It finally comes to a stop, forcing him to refocus his attention on his surroundings as the door opens. He steps into the underground research lab, holding the elevator door open for one of the young engineers; she thanks him with a shy smile that briefly brightens the otherwise dour mood.

Brandish, the lab's engineering chief, approaches him the instant

he enters. Noticing the bump on Jeff's head, he grows concerned —
"Are you alright?" he starts to ask.

"Yes, yes, I'm fine," Jeff quickly assures him, "just a training accident, nothing serious."

"Ah... Eugenia, eh?" Brandish says with a knowing smile; he nods
sympathetically, feeling sorry for asking.

"Well, we have some exciting news to report..." he says, changing
the subject, "Do you have a moment? ...follow me."

He leads Jeff into a narrow room as long as a bowling alley and
shows him a large white table containing a collection of mirrors and
microwave transmitters. A group of engineers in white coats is busy
making adjustments and taking measurements. He realizes that the
table is positioned at one end of a target shooting range. The long
room's walls and ceiling are covered with thick noise-deadening
material.

They gather around as Jeff arrives and assesses what he is seeing.
Brandish explains, pointing to a shielded compartment at the far end
of the range: "That target is protected by an anti-gravity curtain...
similar to the one used in last week's attack.

Anti-gravity is quite different from actual gravity," he continues to
explain. "It works as a pushing force; rather than pulling on objects, it
literally throws them upward. The anti-gravity weapon we witnessed
the other day produced a focused beam of incredible force — I believe
we have been able to replicate it."

He nods to a marksman standing nearby with a high-powered
rifle, giving him the signal to fire. The expert marksman takes dead
aim, firing off four rounds, but the target remains untouched.

Brandish presses a button, drawing the target containment toward
them. All four bullets are embedded straight upward into its ceiling
panel.

"You see, conventional weapons are quite ineffective against the
anti-gravity curtain."

He returns the containment, waiting for it to lock into place, and
then draws Jeff's attention to the components on the table.

"This prototype weapon is designed to calibrate itself to the energy signature of the anti-gravity wave. It will oscillate its laser and microwave energy in phase with the wave, allowing it to pass through."

Brandish hands, Jeff a pair of dark safety goggles, and then gives the signal. An instantaneous burst is emitted from the weapon, and Jeff sees the target instantly shatter, completely destroyed.

Jeff nods appreciatively. "How quickly do you think this can be deployed?"

"Quite soon," Brandish assures him, "the manufacturing has already begun."

"That *is* good news... excellent news!" Jeff says to everyone standing around. "Congratulations on the great work - it's truly impressive!"

He turns to Brandish as he lowers his voice. "Can we have one installed as a defensive battery on the castle?" he asks hopefully, "... how large will the working version be?"

"It's already in the works, sir. It will be discrete."

Jeff smiles, overhearing the first bit of truly good news all day. He pats Brandish on the side of his shoulder as he thanks him. A glance at his watch reminds him that he had better be going; EB and the others will be returning soon.

Just as he does, a chirp from his O-P signals an incoming message. "If you'll please excuse me..." he says to Brandish, turning to walk back toward the hangar deck; he slips his earpiece into his ear and answers the call.

"WE'RE ON THE FINAL APPROACH," EB informs him.

"How is our guest?" Jeff asks.

"Still resting comfortably. We have something interesting to report from our search of his laptop."

"That's great," Jeff says sincerely, "we can go over it when you arrive. We need to be careful until we know what we're dealing with... or whom."

"I completely agree," EB answers.

"I'm at the hangar now," Jeff adds, "...I'll wait for you here."

"Roger that. Be with you momentarily," EB confirms as he ends the call.

———————

JEFF LOOKS AROUND... he is alone in the empty hangar. He hails Chet: "Hey..." he says uncertainly into his O-P, "we need security at the hangar, but it must be discreet - only our most trusted...."

While he is still speaking, the doors slide open, and Eugenia enters with a team of men dressed in black Special Ops uniforms.

"...Never mind," he says to Chet as he drops the O-P back into his pocket.

"We came as soon as I received word from Bear," she reports. Her eyes are drawn to the bump on Jeff's forehead, and she pauses uncomfortably but avoids mentioning it, introducing her team instead: "These are our best men; they can be trusted," she assures him.

Her Special Ops gear makes her look reassuringly intimidating; Jeff thinks to himself as he nods in thanks. He has to admit that her arrival has eased his fears considerably.

She signals to her men, pointing to positions around the large hangar, and instructs them to split up. Three of them remain with her beside Jeff, while the others take strategic positions around the perimeter.

Moments later, the red light above the hangar door begins to flash as it rotates, and a long, deep-toned buzzer announces that the huge steel door is opening. The dripping-wet Dibjet is conveyed through the opening and soon sits in one of the open bays.

Jeff approaches it, with Eugenia and her contingent close beside and behind him. She positions her shoulder and one leg in front of Jeff protectively as the door opens, her hand securely on her weapon.

Hun Hunahpu emerges first, eliciting a sigh of relief from Jeff and the others as he nods that all is well. Berenger follows close behind, and then EB emerges, giving the nod to Eugenia, instructing her to have Dylen taken into custody. She points to two of her men, who quickly enter the ship to retrieve him, placing handcuffs on the groggy captive and pulling a black hood over his head. They usher him away, following her lead.

"WHERE WILL THEY TAKE HIM?" Jeff asks.

"There is a suitable quarters in the security wing," EB explains, making it clear that he is not headed for a suite at Club Med.

Jeff looks at the laptop bag slung over EB's shoulder. "What is it that you found?"

"Perhaps we'd better debrief in your office," EB suggests, glancing at the others, who nod in agreement. Their expressions seem deadly serious, adding to Jeff's concern.

"Alright," he agrees, noting the concern in his friends' eyes.

"Brandish has gotten a new defensive weapon working," Jeff informs them as they make their way back toward the lab.

The others exchange glances, "That may be impeccable timing," EB notes. Jeff glances at him, getting a hunch about what they might have discovered.

⌘

5

UNCOVERED SECRETS

Jeff is pacing back and forth as EB, Huanhpu, and Berenger gather in his office, fresh from their trip to CNAL. A late afternoon sun is preparing to set in the west, creating a spectacular panorama through the room's expansive windows, but he hardly notices the amazing sight as his mind races. Hunahpu lights the gas fireplace and stands in front of it, briefly warming his hands; the room is cool despite the season — it will be June in one more day.

EB puts his O-P down on the desktop, enlarges it, then opens a collection of documents and drags them around on the screen to reveal their contents.

The documents appear to be scanned images, or possibly photographs, of ancient manuscripts. The handwritten script is mostly Latin, but it is interspersed with quotes in a different language... one that Jeff recognizes. He has seen it in the Cronicis Nirgel.

Jeff and Hunahpu look at each other in surprised concern.

EB and Berenger skip past the writing, focusing instead on an ancient-looking drawing that fills half the page. Its name is written in ornate letters, making it clear to Jeff what it depicts — it reads:

ALBANWR

It is a barren scene with a simple-looking stone structure; Jeff guesses it must be the Vault of Archives. What catches his eye most, however, is the depiction of a domed cavern just beside and below that structure with the Latin inscription:

Promptuarium

"My O-P tells me this is a Latin word for 'Storehouse,'" EB explains. Jeff knows the same Latin word can also be translated as 'Secret Chamber.'

"I'm guessing this is an underground storage vault," EB concludes. Jeff looks at Hunahpu in alarm, but his wizened great-grandfather subtly shakes his head, warning him not to reveal anything.

"It must be a drawing of that island off Greenland where those sons of Maranish were exiled," EB finally surmises. Jeff exhales in relief. It is clear that EB has not made the connection with Loch Harnan.

"Was all of this on Dylen's laptop?" Jeff asks cautiously.

"Aye," EB confirms, "All these were in a hidden file with military-grade encryption. Why do ye suppose they'd be so protective of these old documents?"

Jeff looks to be momentarily at a loss for words... Hunahpu quickly speaks up: "I'm sure that Dylen didn't want to have to explain where he had gotten them," he suggests convincingly. EB and Berenger nod in agreement.

"I'd like to study these," Hunahpu says as he shuffles through the documents on the screen.

"As would I," Jeff agrees.

"Well, the encryption used doesn't allow copying, even when they're open... I'll pass the originals to your O-P," EB says as he forwards the folder. Jeff's O-P chirps as the files arrive, disappearing from EB's screen simultaneously.

"Here's what else we found," he adds as he retrieves another folder from the desktop. He clicks on a CAD[1] file, opening it to reveal a complete floor plan of the castle, including the exact position of its elevators and underground bunkers.

"Looks like we've found the conspirator who assisted in plannin' Azeem's invasion," EB declares. Berengar's face reddens in anger at Dylen.

They open Dylen's secret email inbox. EB taps a message that Dylen had received at three O'Clock this afternoon — just around the time he was boarding their ship for the return to Loch Harnan. Under a subject line that reads: Top Secret, is an alarming message:

AWAITING LATEST INTELLIGENCE REPORT...

"They'll surely become suspicious if Dylen doesn't respond...." Berenger worries.

"I suspect that the lack of his reply will not be good," Hunahpu agrees. "...Can we answer for him?" he asks in suggestion.

"I'll do my best to buy us some time," EB offers as he sits down at Dylen's laptop.

He notices another message that has been received moments earlier:

RESPONSE REQUIRED — WHAT IS YOUR STATUS?

EB looks at the others, then begins to type his response:

NEED MORE TIME, UNABLE TO COLLECT ASSETS. I WAS SENT TO LH UNEXPECTEDLY.

They wait for several minutes, and then a reply arrives:

RETURN AT ONCE.

EB waits for a minute and then replies:

NEGATIVE. DEPARTURE WILL AROUSE SUSPICION. NEED SEVERAL DAYS.

They wait for a reply, growing nervous as the time grows longer. Finally, a response arrives:

THREE DAYS… NO LONGER.

EB types his final response:

UNDERSTOOD.

"WHAT DO you think the odds are that they'll wait?" Jeff asks.

"They want that intelligence… it's valuable enough to wait three days for," Berenger suggests confidently.

"That still doesn't give us much time," EB points out. "We'll need to devote all hands to building those defensive weapons."

"What about the energy shield?" Jeff asks.

Berenger thinks for a minute… "We have a working prototype, but it's only large enough to protect a ship."

"Could it protect a satellite?" Jeff asks.

"Well… yes, if the ship can get close enough, I believe it could," Berenger confirms. "I'll have the mission prepped immediately."

"Not too conspicuously; we don't want to tip our hand," Jeff suggests. The discussion of the energy shield suddenly triggers another idea in his mind. He speaks to the large screen on his office wall: "ABBI… Get me Brandish."

"Yes, sir… calling Brandish."

The haggard-looking Chief Engineer appears on the screen from his lab. After quickly greeting him, Jeff begins probing him with questions:

"How is the full-scale version of the laser weapon coming along?"

"I'm happy to report we're ahead of schedule — it could be ready in a week," he answers proudly.

"That's too late," Jeff says bluntly, "What can you build in two days?"

Brandish looks crestfallen… "T-two days?" He stops and thinks for a minute, "…It won't be easy, but there's a chance…" he begins.

"Whatever it takes," Jeff interrupts, "…our full resources are at your disposal — even if you have to take apart half our Dibjets for parts."

"That won't be necessary… but it gives me an idea," Brandish says, stroking his chin as he considers it.

"Good," Jeff says. "…Next question.…"

Brandish looks nervous again, "…Sir?" he asks cautiously.

"That anti-gravity curtain in your test range — can that be made bigger?" Jeff probes, hinting at where he is going with the question.

A sudden inspiration dawns on Brandish's face as he considers the projected anti-gravity field they are using to simulate the Borgias' anti-gravity weapon. He'd demonstrated it to show Jeff how the beam blocks conventional weapons — even bullets.

"Yes… Yes, it could! We have a great deal of experience with that particular technology."

"Good," Jeff challenges, "How long would it take to create a curtain like that surrounding the castle?"

"T-The …castle?" Brandish stammers. "…Something tells me we have just two days for that as well…" he guesses anxiously.

Jeff nods in confirmation. "One more thing," he adds, "…both of these efforts are top secret. Essential personnel only."

Brandish gulps, "…Of course, they are, sir."

EB LEANS BACK from the laptop; he looks troubled. "We'll need to keep up with Dylen's email… to avoid suspicion," he warns.

"That could be tricky," Berenger notes, "a stumble with the wrong remark could give us away. There's no way of knowing all the matters that Dylen is involved with, let alone responding appropriately to every thread… not without reading months of his email history."

Jeff pulls his O-P from his pocket… "Chet… we need you to impersonate an engineer…."

HOURS LATER, the four of them are standing in Brandish's lab, which has been turned into a makeshift command center for their defensive preparations. Every available engineer has been marshaled to work on components of the required systems, including the best minds at CNAL and RCP—Hunahpu's Research Center in Peru, who are conferenced in remotely.

It is long past dinnertime when Jeff and Hunahpu eventually call it a day, leaving EB and Berenger behind to continue their work. Jeff and his great-grandfather stand silently in the elevator as it smoothly races back to the surface.

"Your assistance with the energy wave equation should help tremendously," Hunahpu says to Jeff, breaking the silence.

"They would have solved it themselves soon enough," Jeff admits.

"I suppose there's nothing more we can do now but wait. "Do you think we should talk to Dylen?" he adds, seeking the wisdom of his great-grandfather's deep experience.

"To interrogate him? ...No, Eugenia and her team will do well enough at that. If we must confront him, we will do it when the time comes, ...when the time is right."

Jeff looks at Hunahpu, expecting a further explanation, but none emerges. "How will we know when the time is right?" he finally asks curiously.

Hunahpu glances at him calmly; "The heart will tell when."

Jeff wrinkles his brow and sighs; that is the second time today that the old man has said those words. It occurs to him that all of his new friends seem to love drama... the memory of Eugenia's overhead leap in flowing robes comes to mind as another prime example of that. The thought suddenly makes him smile.

As the elevator stops and its doors open, Jeff instinctively braces himself for a blinding flood of bright sunlight, only to catch himself self-consciously when he remembers it is night. He hears a familiar voice greeting them and looks up to see General Zobrist shaking Hunahpu's hand.

"I came as soon as I received Eugenia's report," he explains. "Where is the filthy traitor!?"

"I'm afraid there's an even more pressing matter," Hunahpu confides. "We'll brief you upstairs."

Jeff accepts Zo's outstretched hand as he agrees with Hunahpu. "Perhaps we can talk over dinner," Jeff suggests, "I don't know about you, but I'm starving."

"Excellent idea, I'd be delighted," Zo agrees.

Jeff glances at the time on his phone; it is already past nine o'clock in the evening. He dials Isabel's number, surprised that she hasn't already contacted him to ask where he's been.

"Dinner will be ready in 15 minutes; I've set places for the five of you," she announces as soon as she answers.

"The five...?" Jeff begins in surprise. While he is speaking, the elevator's doors open, and EB and Berenger step out. "...Right," Jeff says, impressed as usual, "we'll be up momentarily."

"Aye," EB admits, "I took the liberty of invitin' all of us to dinner. Hope you don't mind."

"I'm beginning to wonder how I ever survived until now without all this help," Jeff says with a sly smile.

⌘

6

GATHERING THREATS

A short while later, the five of them have gathered in Jeff's Media room; EB brings Zo up to speed on the day's events and the imminent threat of a Borgia attack.

"How much do we know about what they're planning?" Zo begins to ask with the focus of a practiced military tactician.

"Very little, I'm afraid," EB admits. Jeff sits thinking as he listens to Zo's questioning. Then gets up and moves to the room's large screen.

"Chet, can you give us a briefing on what Dylen's email contained?"

Chet's familiar face appears on the large screen as he says hello.

Jeff quickly realizes that Zo and Berenger are staring open-mouthed at the sight of a perfect Barrymore look-alike on the screen.

"Oh… sorry," Jeff apologizes. "This is a computer simulation… my uncle's avatar. I take it that he never shared it with you. The resemblance is quite uncanny, isn't it?"

A chorus of agreement rumbles through the room as they study the screen intently. Chet has already begun to answer...

"Dylen's company email account contained 61,376 messages -- 6,042 were received in the past six months. All were regarding official business.

"I also discovered three personal email accounts on his computer and two hidden accounts."

"What can you tell us about the contents of the hidden accounts?" Jeff probes. "How far back do they go?"

"The oldest entries are from three years ago," Chet explains.

The men look at each other with increased concern.

"That's nearly half as long as he's been with us," Berenger notes sadly. "How could I have been so blind!?"

"Don't blame yourself," EB says as he places a hand on his friend's shoulder, "...he had us all fooled, ...the bloody devil."

"We need to know what they're planning!" Zo exclaims, even more earnestly than before.

Chet brings a series of email messages to the screen and begins describing their contents, showing underlined passages as he speaks about them:

"This was received a few months ago... their testing of the anti-gravity weapon was advancing:"

...THE GLACIAL FIELD TESTS HAVE DEMONSTRATED EXCELLENT RESULTS. YOUR ASSISTANCE HAS BEEN MOST HELPFUL; THE AGREED SUM HAS BEEN TRANSFERRED TO YOUR BELGIAN ACCOUNTS.

"I was able to trace the related deposits," Chet continues as a list of transactions fills the screen, totaling twenty million Euros. "It would appear that the weaponization technology was developed with Dylen's help.

"This was received just over a month ago," Chet continues as a new message flashes to the screen, "...the evidence would suggest that it was regarding Jeffrey...."

Jeff feels a sudden pang in the pit of his stomach as Chet's words hit him; the look on his face reveals his swelling sorrow. Hunahpu places a hand on his Great-grandson's back supportively as EB nods in a gesture that lets him know he has no cause for guilt.

The message reads:

A HIGH-VALUE TARGET HAS BEEN DISCOVERED, AND ALL GLOBAL RESOURCES HAVE BEEN MOBILIZED. STAND BY FOR FURTHER INSTRUCTIONS.

The next message arrived about thirty minutes later...

INTERCEPT FORCE IS EN ROUTE. AWAIT INSTRUCTIONS FOR MISSION OMEGA.

About an hour later, another message to Dylen appeared:

TARGET ALPHA IS DESTROYED... REQUESTING INTERNAL CONFIRMATION. THE TEAM IS EN ROUTE TO TARGET BETA.

There is a sullen silence in the room as the highlighted message remains on the screen.

"How did you know that they'd learned about me?" Jeff quietly asks, realizing that they have never discussed the details of that night.

"We were monitoring their communications," EB explains. "The airwaves lit up that night; we knew immediately that it was you they'd found."

THE NEXT MESSAGE, received several hours later, confirmed that Jeff's house had been destroyed. Then, a short time later was a celebratory message:

...MISSION ACCOMPLISHED! TARGET BETA HAS BEEN DESTROYED.

The message includes details of the air pursuit and missile explosion as they plunged into the ocean.

PERHAPS THE MOST alarming message was the one they saw next; it was from Dylen, sent the morning after Jeff arrived in Loch Harnan.

...TARGET BETA WAS NOT DESTROYED - HE IS IN LOCH HARNAN.

This was followed quickly by a reply.

...IS THIS VISUALLY CONFIRMED?
   ...YES, CONFIRMED.

"WAS Dylen in Loch Harnan that weekend?" EB asks Berenger in surprise.

"No, he was with my team at CNAL - we were on high alert... he was required to report to duty with everyone else at 0500 hours."

The five of them pause as they consider his answer.

"Was my introduction to the staff simulcast?" Jeff asks, exploring an obvious possibility.

"No, it was not," EB confirms, "...besides, that was at nine o'clock on Monday morning... this message was sent the previous evening... as soon as we arrived."

Jeff replays their arrival in his mind... the life-changing events of that day are still seared into his consciousness — they are vivid memories. "We didn't meet anyone when we arrived," he confirms, "I still remember how deserted the castle seemed."

EB calls for ABBI: "Bring up the castle security footage from Sunday, April 22nd, approximately eight o'clock in the evening."

The screen is quickly filled with a few dozen video images from various parts of the castle.

"That one," EB instructs, pointing to the lobby camera... "Scan forward... Stop... play from here."

They watch the recording of Jeff emerging from the elevator into the castle lobby; EB notes the time stamp.

"ABBI: Who was at the surveillance console when these frames were recorded... how many security staff were on duty?"

"All of the security staff were on duty — the castle was on high alert," ABBI answers, "they were outside, patrolling the grounds. Only one guard was at the console, Seamus Gill."

"I'll ask Eugenia to question Mr. Gill," EB says as he dials his phone. "Until we know better, Dylen's detention must be kept strictly confidential, including the security team." Eugenia agrees to take a small contingent and discreetly bring Seamus in for questioning.

"I'll accompany her," Zo offers, "she can brief me on what she has learned from our traitorous guest."

"I'd like to come with you... If you don't mind?" Berenger requests. Zo nods his approval and slaps his friend's back; "Of course, Bear, of course!"

"If you don't mind me saying so, I think it may be best if she retrieves him without the two of you," Jeff suggests, "Too large a group could arouse suspicions or send a warning to any others who may be involved. Besides...," Jeff adds, looking toward Isabel standing in the doorway, "I believe our dinner is ready."

As they take their seats at the dining room table, the men continue to discuss plans for the castle's defense. Jeff explains to Zo what Brandish is working on... "It may be a long shot, but it's the best hope we have at the moment," Jeff explains.

"What about sending a ship underwater to breach their antigravity wave?" Zo proposes.

"Too risky," Berenger argues, "there's no telling how deep beneath the surface the wave goes or what the conditions would be like inside it."

"I must agree with Bear on that," EB concurs.

"Well," Zo adds, "I'd feel better at least having a few jets in the air."

"I'll have CNAL launch a few patrols," Berenger offers. "They can keep an eye on the perimeter."

The men agree on the plan and return to focusing on Isabel's dinner. Several courses later, they push back from the table, thoroughly satisfied.

EB's phone chimes, alerting him to a text.

"It's from Genie," he announces as he opens it; "She says that Seamus Gill has gone missing — it would appear that he hasn't reported to duty since April 26th."

"That was the day of the anti-gravity attack," Jeff notes.

"I think it's time I had that talk with our detainee," Zo says as he stands. The others all stand with him.

"Yes - I'll join you," Berenger confirms, "...that is, if there are no objections?" he adds carefully.

Zo quickly agrees, as EB and Hunahpu nod acceptingly, and Jeff motions with his hand to say: " *Be my guest.*

As Zo and Berenger leave the room, EB lays his O-P on the dining room table and spreads it larger, quickly becoming engrossed in CHET's exploration of Dylen's secret email accounts.

Hunahpu places a hand on Jeff's shoulder and calls him aside. "Time is of the essence, my son. You must be quick with your quest... it is more dire than you know."

Jeff looks into his great-grandfather's face, reading the grave concern in his eyes. He shakes his head slightly to signal that he doesn't fully understand; "What is it? ...what don't I know?"

Hunahpu searches Jeff's eyes carefully, gauging how much to share. "Some rather powerful objects may be at risk of falling into our enemies' hands," he begins with caution.

"The Ring and Scepter?" Jeff exclaims in alarm.

EB and Hunahpu both look at him in surprise.

"I know about them, yes," Jeff quickly explains, "...What sort of risk are they in?"

The older men look at each other to decide what to say. Hunahpu continues, "...Dylen knew where the Ring and Scepter are hidden. He knows the security that protects them better than anyone; he installed it."

Jeff's face grows more concerned; a determined look fills his eyes: "We have to check on them... make sure they're secured! They need to be destroyed!"

EB and Hunahpu share glances again, echoing Jeff's concern. "Do you know how t'destroy them?" EB asks hopefully.

"Well, no, I'm afraid not," Jeff admits, "but I have some ideas."

Jeff leans forward, ready to explain his theory when Hunahpu stops him. "I think it would be best if the details are not shared... the less you reveal regarding your quest, the better."

"Well... okay," Jeff reluctantly agrees, "...but at the very least, we need to check that they're still there."

Hunahpu and EB look at each other uncomfortably; "That's the problem, you see...." EB confesses, "their whereabouts were known only to Barrymore."

"As well as Dylen," Hunahpu adds ominously.

"Do you think he knows *what* they are... what they can do?" Jeff asks.

"There's no telling," Hunahpu answers, deep in thought, "it had been nearly two decades since Katkeruus' death by the time he helped with their security."

"He knew something about them," EB notes, "...remember how he commented about them in his office?"

"Yes..." Hunahpu recalls, stroking his beard as he appears deep in thought. "And if the sons of Maranish have been working with him, they would have surely revealed the objects' value.

"I'm afraid we're at terrible risk," he adds, "...terrible, terrible risk."

"But Katkeruus had them once... she was able to be defeated," Jeff suggests, trying to add perspective.

"She was a novice," Hunahpu replies, "...she cared only for her personal vendetta. Even with only that, she caused terrible harm — imagine what the evil sons of Maranish could do with such power!"

"Then we have to find them before our enemies do," Jeff says with resolve. "See what you can learn from Dylen... I'll explore my uncle's ...archives."

The others nod, understanding that Jeff is likely referring to whatever cache of information his uncle had left him for his quest. They sincerely hope that it is enough.

.   .   .

JEFF FEELS his great-grandfather's hand grip his shoulder; when he turns his head, he is surprised to see the kind old man standing with his eyes closed and head bowed. It is then that he hears him pray.

> "Oh God, our Father, the great Ancient of Days. You are Lord of all that is seen and unseen. This great fight that we have waged for so many ages is not our own battle. We do not fight this great evil for selfish ends but for your eternal purpose. We know with reassuring certainty that you stand with us in our fiercest conflicts — indeed, You are our Champion of unassailable might. No enemy can stand when you raise yourself for battle. With this assurance, we call to You for help in this grave hour. As our strong defender, You are our greatest hope."

EB adds an emphatic "Amen."

JEFF IS REMINDED ONCE MORE of the avatar's words: *...spiritual strength...without it, you will surely fail.* A chill runs up his back as the odd stirring within him grows stronger.

⌘

7

THE RING OF DESIRE

CYLCH O AWYDD

(The Ring of Desire)

E B is standing at the door of Jeff's suite, saying goodnight. Jeff offers his older friend a handshake, and in return, EB pats him on the shoulder in encouragement.

"Chin up, my boy. We'll get through this with God's help."

Jeff nods gratefully, although he honestly doesn't share EB's confidence. He turns to his great-grandfather, who stands beside him, and accepts his firm grasp, shaking it heartily. The look in his wizened eyes conveys to Jeff the urgency of his mission. Jeff nods at him in acknowledgment as Hunahpu pats his shoulder and turns to retire for the night.

Deep in thought, Jeff wanders alone down his suite's main hallway, rehashing recent events and the evening's troubling dinner conversation. Hunahpu's words after dinner continue to replay in his mind: *'Time is of the essence, my son. You must be quick with your quest... it is more dire than you know.'*

The open door to his Study catches his eye, and he decides to venture inside. It is a room he has barely used since he arrived in Loch Harnan.

Several lights around the room switch on automatically as he enters, lighting the room's perimeter and a large lamp on the room's impressive desk. It is a comfortable room with elegant appointments and overstuffed leather furniture. He sits down behind the large desk and runs one hand across its rich, glossy surface, then tests the height of the keyboard beside him with his hands — the monitors above it flash to life as soon as he touches it.

It seems as though the terminal is synchronized with the one in the CEO suite, ...he still has trouble calling it *his* office. The screens show an impressive dashboard of stock charts and video feeds that provide a real-time view of the massive company's financial health.

His email account appears on one screen, and Jeff's eye is drawn to a recent message near the top; his pulse quickens as he reads the subject line:

"OUR DEMANDS...,"

Jeff clicks it open and scans its contents.

"YOU HAVE 48 HOURS TO DELIVER TO US — QUOD VIRGAM ET CYLCH O AWYDD."

Jeff recognizes the Latin phrase, referring to 'the Scepter and Ring of Desire.'

Though the message is clearly intended to intimidate him, Jeff feels immediately relieved by the phrase... it means they don't yet possess the dangerous objects after all. He reads further, hoping to catch a clue about where they might be hidden. Scanning through a short diatribe in which the senders argue that they are the objects' rightful owners, Jeff's attention is piqued as he comes to the last paragraph:

"Naught shall remain of Barrymore's secret vault. We cannot be stopped from reclaiming what is ours."

Jeff rereads the words. It seems odd that they would refer only to a vault rather than the whole castle; surely, nothing at all would remain if they were successful in their anti-gravity attack.

'*Barrymore's secret vault,*' he reads the words again... why mention his uncle Barrymore by name? He assumes they are referring to the Secret Chamber, recalling the picture that EB had discovered on Dylen's computer. It unnerves him that their enemies know of the Secret Chamber, but he isn't surprised; after all, the Dyfarniad had been caretakers of the secrets for centuries. It makes sense that they would know about the chamber that contained them.

Then another idea strikes him... the security that Dylen installed for the Ring and Scepter was obviously not for the secret Chamber; it had to be for another vault. The Borgias' impending attack is not targeting the Secret Chamber after all — it is this *other* vault, the one with Barrymore's name ...they are coming for the Ring and Scepter!

Jeff lays his O-P tablet on the desktop and stretches it larger. "Chet, show me the files that EB retrieved from Dylen's computer. Those ancient manuscripts."

The secret encrypted files open, spreading their documents across the screen; he guesses that there are a few dozen, at least. Directly on top is the drawing that EB had shown them earlier. It is filled with notations in a combination of languages: mostly Latin, with some short phrases in ancient Greek. However, the majority are in the ancient script that Jeff recognized from the Cronicis Nirgel.

Written in ornate lettering above the picture's lone stone structure is the name *Vault Degli Archivi*. Beside it is written: *secure ergastulo huius monumentum* '...fast make the prison of this tomb.'

Studying the image, Jeff notices a depiction of stairs leading downward from beneath the Vault to an underground space labeled "Crypt". The underground space is much larger than Jeff had imagined, appearing nearly as large as the structure above. At its center is a large stone sarcophagus — its top is covered with what appear to be stones heaped atop the lid.

Jeff scans the rest of the drawing, focusing on its depiction of the Secret Chamber. It doesn't include any hint of the large spiral staircase or evidence of the secret elevator's shaft. It looks like the means of access was through a different opening… a sloping tunnel shown leading back to the Vault of Archives. He zooms the image larger for a closer look …the ancient tunnel's entry point wasn't inside the Vault — it was just outside, near the Vault's door. Jeff compares the drawing with his memory of the Vault's foyer and estimates that the entry point must be near the foot of the sunlit staircase — beneath Cornelius' suite.

Another nearby underground passage is labeled: *Ascensus Spelunca*, 'Cave of Ascent,' Jeff whispers to himself as he translates it. "That must be where Arubija and his family emerged after the flood." The drawing stops at the opening, but Jeff has a pretty good idea of what existed beneath it — today, it contains their secret underground complex.

Nothing in the drawing hints of another vault anywhere; whatever it is, it must have been built after this drawing was made — probably at the time of the castle's construction.

Jeff turns his attention to the writings. "Chet, can you interpret this script?"

"You don't need me for that," Chet replies, "your O-P is capable of translating 6,909 living languages, plus dozens of ancient texts, on its own. I can enable it if you wish."

"Yes, have it translate all these pages to English," Jeff answers, forcing himself to resist saying please and thank you."

He watches as the handwritten lettering is transformed into nearly identical strokes — this time in English. Notes surrounding the drawings explain what the images depict.

.   .   .

BESIDE THE HEADING: **ALBANWR**

....a note reads: *Born of God's fury - the secret abode of wondrous powers. In this mountain are hidden the mysteries of the Ancient Ones.*

Next to this description is another note in different handwriting: *Herein lies your destiny, my sons.*

THE ANCIENT STONE structure is labeled: **Vault Degli Archivi**

...with the note: *Heed my warnings! Venture not into the crypt of Leanan Sidhe ~ for all who venture there return not to dwell among the living.*

BESIDE A DRAWING of an underground chamber is written: **Promptuarium**

... *Herein lie the mysteries of power. Seek entry to the south-facing Graig Caer, where first light makes its arrow mark. There you will find cerrig mynediad.*

"Chet, why aren't these words translated?" Jeff asks curiously.

"They are names," Chet explains, "...with rough translations, their meanings are:

"Seek entry ...to the south-facing Fortress Rock (Graig C*aer*), where first light makes its arrow mark. There you will find the Entry Stone *(Cerrig Mynediad)*.

BENEATH ALL OF the artfully drawn notations is a handwritten note...

My Sons
This lone page is all that we possess of the great Library of Mysteries,
of which our people were once masters.
In these pages, I have recounted secrets of Arubija that I studied for

six hundred years; guard them well. You are the last of our bastion. It is my dying hope that you will soon return to your rightful place as masters of the Mysterious Powers. It is your destiny to rule all... for time without end.

JEFF FEELS a chill run up his spine as he reads those terrifying words. He already knew that the cost of failing in his quest would be great, but this makes it clear that there is even more at stake than he has realized ...the cost of failure will be paid by far more than just himself — undoubtedly even affecting all mankind!

He taps the document to flip the page forward... taking note of its heading:

FOIRMLEAN DÌOMHAIR MARANISH

(Secret Formulas of Maranish)

The pages are filled with strange recipes, some of which look familiar, such as a formula that combines sulfur, charcoal, and saltpeter...

"...potassium nitrate," Jeff notes to himself, recognizing the formula for gunpowder.

Many of the formulas seem to be for various incapacitating drugs. He continues to scan the pages until he reaches a page about halfway through, where he suddenly stops and feels his heart race as he reads the heading:

QUOD VIRGAM ET Cylch o Awydd

Jeff reads the account that follows it with great interest.

These fantastic implements were conceived by Semjaza's mighty will in the age when our lords ruled the earth ~ before the terrible flood. Called forth from the scroll of the gods, they draw their power from

unseen realms. They were forged in the furnaces of Tir Lai, infused
with powers to enslave and destroy. Semjaza's scepter and ring bring
unassailable dominion and might to the one who wields them.

The account goes on to describe the objects' additional powers.
Jeff has already heard about their ability to turn people to dust and
subjugate a subject's will. The manuscript also describes other
extraordinary powers: teleportation, the ability to render the bearer
invisible, the power to implant hypnotic suggestions, and the ability
to inflict great pain or pleasure.

"No wonder they called him a god," Jeff observes as he reads the
descriptions of what Semjaza's objects could do. Maranish's description leaves out the critical fact of the ring's enslaving and corrupting
influence on its wearer. Jeff scans further, desperately seeking any
clues that could help to destroy them.

He ponders Maranish's reference to the *Scroll of the gods…* recalling
the scroll's mention in the Cronicis Nirgel. Arubija wrote that
Semjaza used that scroll to call forth the giant serpent. The words *'call*
forth' strike him as he considers them, and he thinks of what the
avatar said about the origin of the ring and scepter -- that they
appeared to be from another dimension. The inference was that they
hadn't been created here or *conjured* into existence… rather, they were
imported.

"Chet, what do we know about the other dimension where the
Ring and Scepter came from?"

A small window appears in the center of the O-P screen with
CHET's face…

"You will need to seek that answer — it is the key to your
quest."

Chet's answer surprises him. Although it hasn't supplied the
answer he sought, it wasn't evasive — in fact, it was the most direct
Chet has ever been regarding his Quest. What did he mean by it being
the key?

"Are you suggesting that it's part of a test... like a puzzle for me to solve? ...or is it still a mystery that has never been solved?" he probes.

"It was known once, most certainly," Chet replies, "but your uncle could not discover it. If he had, then he might have succeeded in destroying them."

Jeff runs his hands through his hair as he leans back in frustration; it feels hopeless. How can he possibly solve in mere weeks something that his expert uncle couldn't solve in six hundred years? He has to remind himself that his family hadn't become aware of the ring's power before Katkeruus became corrupted by it. Still... that gave his uncle at least forty years to seek an answer. Given how quickly things are moving, Jeff realizes he may have only a few days!

Based on Maranish's writings, however, it is evident that the Dyfarniad knew of the objects' powers long before then. Jeff suddenly stops as a realization comes to him — one thing that his uncle Barry never had was the thing sitting right in front of him: the secret papers of Maranish.

He begins poring over the ancient text again in earnest, this time looking for any clues that could help him destroy them — in particular, he needs to know more about the laws that control them.

⌘

8

INTERROGATION

"Let's have it again... from the top," Eugenia demands as she leans toward Dylen menacingly.

"I already told you — I swear I don't know what you're talking about! H-how could I be a spy?"

Eugenia stands staring coldly at him with her arms crossed, thinking of how he had contributed to the deaths of both Barrymore and Angus — it is all she can do to keep herself from breaking his nose. She is suddenly saved from the temptation by the door behind her opening; Berenger and Zo enter.

"At ease, Major," Zo orders as he nods to Eugenia approvingly, using her former rank to get her attention. It works, even though she is technically now in civilian life; she takes a deep breath and steps backward, waving toward Dylen,

"Be my guest," she approves.

"Mister Bern, Sir!" Dylen pleads as he stands from his chair, "You have to believe me — I have no idea what they're talking about!"

"Stop the pretenses," Berenger advises sternly. He holds up the thumb drive containing plans for the energy shield... Dylen immediately looks down at his jacket pocket with a terrible realization.

"I-I can explain that... I was just keeping it with me to work on!"

"And I suppose you also just happened to be working on the formula for hampering an anti-gravity feedback loop as well," Berenger says with a hint of anger in his voice.

Dylen becomes quiet, realizing that they have broken his file's encryption. He sits down again with a fearful look on his face.

"We've had a look at your laptop and found its secret email accounts and hidden files as well — we know all about your eight secret bank accounts and the millions in deposited sums. You won't be getting an opportunity to spend any of that, I'm afraid."

Dylen looks stunned, then his face turns deep red as he fills with rage.

"You don't know what's coming," he snarls with a dramatic shift in his demeanor, "You can't beat them... your time is almost up — you'll be dead soon... all of you!"

Berenger pulls out a chair across from Dylen and quickly sits down; he leans forward just as aggressively as Dylen, gritting his teeth to hold back the anger building inside.

"I trusted you like a son! This is the thanks I get... treachery?"

Dylen stares at him coldly. "I'm not your son..." he spits ruthlessly.

Zo puts a hand on Berenger's shoulder to help steady him, sensing that his long-time friend is ready to explode. Berenger looks down and takes a deep breath, collecting his wits, then folds his hands together on the table in front of him and looks Dylen in the eyes.

"Your... contacts... emailed you — they were very unhappy when they heard you'd decided to visit Loch Harnan. It seems the timing is quite inconvenient."

Concern flashes across Dylen's face: "Y-you told them I was here?"

"Yes, but don't worry, they don't suspect anything yet." He reads Dylen's reaction carefully, detecting his growing unease. "We... that is... *You replied to them,* saying that you needed a few days. They graciously agreed to delay their attack, although I'll admit they didn't seem well pleased about it."

"So, you bought yourself some time... a few days — so what? You're still going to die!" Dylen dismisses cynically.

"If we die here, so do you — doesn't that concern you?" Berenger presses.

"I'm ready to die for the cause!" Dylen insists stoically.

"And what cause is that, exactly?"

"You don't understand, do you... None of you understands!" Dylen says with disdain. "Their time has come... the change is already happening — you can't stop it!"

"Whose time, exactly, ...the Eljo?" Berenger asks derisively.

"NO, YOU FOOL ...THE CONFEDERACY!"

BERENGER SLOWLY PULLS BACK from the table and stands, catching Zo's eye. The two of them stand with Eugenia, quietly conferring together. Dylen watches them carefully, but he can't make out what they are saying; the look of hatred in his eyes seems to grow more pronounced each moment.

As the three of them finish their private conversation, Berenger and Eugenia nod to Zo in agreement, then stand back as Zo approaches Dylen.

"You're in quite a precarious position," Zo says to him in dramatic understatement.

Dylen shrugs and practically laughs at the absurdity of the remark.

"We have full access to your secret email accounts... we can impersonate you to tell them anything we'd like." Zo stands staring down at Dylen with his massive arms folded in front of him. "What do you think they'll do when we tell them that you've betrayed them and decided to help us?"

Dylen's face suddenly turns grey, and he shakes his head: "That's not true — they'd never believe you!"

"Oh, it won't be us telling them - it will be you... or at least it will be your email account. Knowing your friends, the Maranish brothers won't spend much time questioning its authenticity... I'm sure they'd be quite happy to make an example of you at the slightest provocation. It would be a perfect opportunity for them to make sure no one else gets disloyal ideas, after all."

"You-you're bluffing! What do you have to gain from lying about me? It won't change anything!"

"I suppose they could take it out on someone else... a colleague, maybe?" Zo says, ignoring Dylen's comment. "I'd bet they'll be quite public about it... They'll want it to be a spectacle, no doubt. I wonder how your friends will feel about you when they have to pay the price for your disloyalty?"

There are small beads of sweat on Dylen's brow as he tries to remain unflinching.

"On the other hand, since you don't seem to mind, we could continue impersonating you. I'm sure there are many things we can learn. That will make your final betrayal even more infuriating to them, no doubt."

Whatever it is that Dylen is frightened of, it seems to be getting worse the longer Zo talks. He becomes more red-faced and agitated.

"You people..." he explodes, his voice dripping with disdain, "... with all of your power and wealth and control — you think you can keep it all to yourselves. Well, your time is over... the new age has arrived!"

"Well, whether that be true or not, it looks as though you, unfortunately, will not be able to avail yourself of either world," Zo reminds him. He turns his back to Dylen and speaks to Eugenia: "There's nothing more we can learn here — take him away."

"WAIT!" Dylen suddenly pleads, "What are you going to do... what will you tell them?"

The three of them glance at one another, then Zo turns back toward him.

"We're going to make it very clear that you have assisted us in every way possible." He pauses and thinks for a second... "The ancient manuscripts that you handed over to us have been especially helpful."

When Dylen hears him mention the manuscripts, his eyes widen, and his hands shake noticeably, eliciting the reaction Zo hoped for.

"Y-you accessed it? That encryption was supposed to be impenetrable — it was for his eyes only..." he suddenly catches himself, realizing that he has said too much.

"For whose eyes only?" Zo asks, leaning his hands on the table.

"It doesn't matter now...." Dylen says despondently, his eyes becoming glassy. "Even if you know now, he can't be stopped."

"Who can't be stopped?"

"Koletis[1]," he answers, "That's not his real name, of course; that's just what he's called." Dylen leans back with a mix of dueling emotions on his face; there is still the stoic loyalty and a clear disdain for all that Hastleworth stands for, but he also looks like a man who has just lost his house in a fire — everything he had is gone, along with all hope. He seems wholly broken and despondent as he looks up at Zo and the others with a sincere expression for the first time...

"Look, I know I can't stop you from saying whatever you want to them about me..." he sighs deeply and then leans forward, his face revealing that something greatly troubles him.

"I have a fiancée," he confesses, "...she was the one who recruited me." He looks at them pleadingly: "They'll kill her... or worse! Please don't make her think I turned my back on her!"

"If you cooperate, then we'll ensure that they know you weren't disloyal," Zo offers quickly.

"How? What do you want?"

Eugenia steps forward: "Who else is involved — where is Seamus Gill?"

Dylen hangs his head; "He was the only one I knew about... we haven't heard from him since the last anti-gravity attack — he was sent to retrieve the objects; I told them it was a suicide mission."

Eugenia glances at Zo and Beringer, then looks back at Dylen with an angry expression: "Give us the location of the secret vault and its security!"

"It won't do you any good — Lord Hastleworth changed the access codes. You'll only be killed if you try."

"Killed?" she challenges.

"Barrymore insisted — the security measures are lethal," Dylen explains.

Eugenia glances at the others and then looks Dylen in the eyes: "TELL US," she orders.

⌘

9

THALIARD

J eff has been studying the Maranish manuscript for hours, carefully reading every historical note and each formula's description for hints about what gave the objects their powers. He keeps seeing references to a 'Realm of the gods' that seemed to have been clearly visible to Semjaza and the other Dark Lords. It appears, however, that even though they could apparently see and even communicate with it, this realm couldn't be reached on a physical level, even by them. Except, that is, through the use of that Scroll... the Scroll of the Gods.

In his writings, Maranish bemoaned that the Scroll had not survived the great flood. He speculated that it had been lost, along with the Scepter, in the destruction of Semjaza's palace.

Jeff realizes that Thaliard only had the Ring... the Scepter wasn't found and retrieved by Barrymore until hundreds of years after Maranish died. Yet he is amazed to read what Maranish wrote of the night that the Scepter was lost — the night of the flood. His account is written in shadowy imagery, as if from the Ring's perspective. It tells of the approaching storm and rising waters. Semjaza is said to have been on the balcony of his palace's highest tower, using the Scepter to shield the golden city from the raging floods, when suddenly someone appeared before him — described as a God 'Most High' — more powerful than Semjaza or the Ring's creator. He was dressed in robes of many colors and held in His hand a gnarled wooden shepherd's staff. Semjaza knew him — he tried to use the scepter's power against him, but was immediately overwhelmed by the powerful visitor's fierce rage. In his attack, Semjaza himself was turned to dust by his own blast, and the Scepter plummeted from the tower's heights. The Ring flew toward the victor's wooden staff and became embedded in its gnarly head as the watery cataclysm that followed obliterated the golden city.

More than a year later, after Arubija emerged from the mountain, the great staff was miraculously washed ashore on the rocks of Albinwr, where Arubija found it.

It occurs to Jeff that Arubija could not have known anything about what happened to Semjaza or the city of Atlan. No account of that was ever recorded in the Cronicis Nirgel. Maranish's writings provide an answer to the mystery — describing how Thaliard, a leader of the Nirgel from the tribe of Dyfarniad, learned of a way to release the Ring from the safety of the Staff. Once it had been released, Thaliard was corrupted by its influence. He experienced visions of the recorded events through the Ring itself. With the Ring's help, he grew strong in his knowledge of the Mysteries and eventually led the great rebellion that began the thousand-year war.

Maranish wrote of this with pride, calling the rebellion a great achievement and regaling the Ring's 'liberator' as the Nirgel's greatest leader. Jeff soon understands why, as Maranish finally reveals that Thaliard had been his father.

THE STORY SEEMS INCREDIBLE — Jeff would have considered it nothing more than unbelievable folklore if not for the facts of his recent experiences. It again points to the Shepherd's Staff as the key to destroying the Ring and Scepter, or at least rendering them powerless. The vivid memory of the Staff flying into his hand and bursting into flower fills his mind, somehow confirming to him that all he has read is true.

His mind drifts to the Shepherd's Staff — the question that he had asked the avatar still haunts him: how *did* the Shepherd's Staff know that his uncle had died? The word *know* is not really accurate, of course; he doesn't honestly think that the Staff has a consciousness; it's rather more the way a computer *knows* a fact. He postulates that it must have some kind of innate memory and an advanced means of sensing.

Jeff then considers what he has just read, realizing that if the ancient Nirgel leader *learned* how to release the ring from the Staff, then the secret had to have been found here... in the Secret Chamber. If the means of releasing it were recorded, there is hope that the means of destroying it are also given!

HE GLANCES AT HIS WATCH; it is nearly midnight. *Perhaps just an hour in the Secret Chamber...* he tells himself. Quickly shrinking the O-P, he tucks it into his jacket pocket and starts for the door. The expansive domed rotunda is empty and silent as he pulls his suite's doors closed, trying to minimize the echo created as it clicks shut. He scans the vast space for any sign of people, taking the opportunity to note the locations of each security camera. He can't be too careful, given their recent discovery of spies, even among the security staff.

Arriving at the office suite, he speaks quietly into the access panel before using it: "ABBI, disable voice response."

A light on the access panel flashes, acknowledging the command, then he places his hand on the palm scanner, hearing the door latch quietly click open. After slipping inside, he makes a complete pass through the suite, assuring himself that he is alone, and then enters the library and latches the doors behind him. He decides to use the elevator that Hunahpu had shown him; it is definitely a faster means of access than the long spiral staircase he'd discovered earlier.

He can't help thinking of Maranish's ancient drawing. As far as he can tell, the elevator's shaft must be very close to the ancient tunnel it depicted, possibly even intersecting it.

THE LIGHTS of the narrow hallway interrupt his thoughts as the elevator comes to a stop. He repeats the sequence that Hunahpu showed him to open the hidden door and sees the lights in the Secret Chamber brighten as he enters, causing him to stop and admire the scene. He still hasn't gotten used to the brilliant sight of the amazing Chamber's plush furnishings and shining bookcases.

Walking to the golden bookstand, he retrieves Neuvel's watch from his pocket and holds it in front of him, remembering how Hun Hunaphu had shown him how to use it. *"Lego Cylch o awydd,"* he says aloud before placing the golden timepiece into the bookstand's pedestal.

Nothing happens. Jeff waits for a full minute as the bookstand remains still. He is about to try a different command when it suddenly whirs to life and begins moving slowly along its track in front of the bookcases. Jeff is excited to notice a series of books springing from their places, each sticking out an inch or two and waiting to be retrieved. By the time the bookstand stops, it has left a trail of selected volumes halfway around the room. Jeff's heart sinks as he sees the number of volumes — this will not be as easy a search as he hoped.

With some trepidation, he makes his way to the bookstand and reaches for the first volume just above it. He waits until the huge book has been lowered to the pedestal and the mechanized arm has retreated before running his hand over its gleaming cover. It is engraved with the words *Gwrthryfel Mawr,* and beneath them is a series of ancient markings that he can't make out.

He pulls out his O-P, instructs it to translate, and then lays it over the engravings.

Great Rebellion, it reads in English, followed by dates: *Anno Domini 200 ~ 1103.* Jeff understands it to be a history of the Thousand-Year

War. He knows from Maranish's manuscript that the Ring had something to do with the start of that conflict.

The golden book is not sealed the way that the Cronicis had been. He carefully lifts the heavy cover and examines the first page inside. It has no title page, beginning instead with a commentary that sounds more like a novel than a history book, as he places the O-P on it to translate…

> *Herein is recounted the terrible and tragic war spawned by Thaliard's treachery. In the fourth month of the year 200 AD, on the twentieth day, Thaliard betrayed his brothers and slew in that day more than one hundred thousand souls.*

The account describes how a force of Dyfarniad Scribes then methodically hunted down influential leaders and noblemen from the Gryf and Huawdl lines and executed them with their families.

The surviving Gryf desperately regrouped and formed a strong resistance, securing a defended border where they and the Huawdl could be protected. The Gryf and Huawdl fought side by side — for a century or more, Jeff estimated, before the Huawdl fled from Albanwr.

Jeff scans the book urgently, looking for references to the Ring or Scepter, finding only scattered mentions of Thaliard's Ring, with references to the strange powers it conveyed upon him for spying on his enemies and giving him enhanced physical strength. It gave him great power to command his fellow scribes and captives — some sort of mind control, as far as Jeff could gather.

Jeff is surprised to read a passing comment that the Ring's power could not compel '…one *who God protects.*' He stops and rereads the claim, wondering why such a religious reference would be included in what appears to be a strictly secular historical account. It is written as a simple fact without further explanation.

His remaining scan of the book finds nothing else of significance beyond a painful history of the long, bloody war. As Hun Hunaphu had shared, the Dyfarniad forces were eventually decimated from within by bitter rivalries and jealousies, until those who remained were weakened to the point where they could no longer defend their stronghold.

It was Maranish himself who wore the ring then, having inherited the Leader's mantle from his father; it was unclear, though, whether the Shepherds' Staff ever actually selected him. He was already an old man at the war's close; the final Gryf attack caught him sleeping, allowing the victors to capture and secure the Ring.

Surely Cornelius had never read this account, or he would never have given the ring to Katkeruus.

On the other hand, the image it painted of Maranish was of a weak and inept man... obviously not the fearsome character that his father Thaliard had been... nor as fierce as his own sons, for that matter. It became clearer why the decision was made to banish him rather than execute or imprison him; he was not seen as a serious threat. However, Jeff could also see how his cancerous bitterness had poisoned his sons.

Jeff closes the book's golden cover and steps back as the bookshelf retrieves it, pulling it into its storage position with a click as it latches into place. The pedestal immediately moves to the left, stopping at the next waiting volume as it is retrieved and lowered onto the bookstand.

JEFF EXAMINES the new book's gilded cover, inlaid with gems and adorned with exquisite engraving; it appears much older than the first book and far more elaborate. Its inscription reads *Liberatricem Commemorans*, apparently celebrating the "Liberation" of the Dyfarniad from the other tribes.

The title page repeats the words on the cover:

Liberatricem Commemorans

As the O-P translates the page, Jeff sees that it includes a declaration of the book's authorship: *Inscribed by the hand of Thaliard ~ Prince of Eljo and Lord of the Nirgel.*

Jeff recognizes the name Eljo with a foreboding acknowledgment. Turning the page, he waits for the O-P to translate and begins reading.

> *I, Thaliard, writing with my own hand, record here the glories of our great victory and the secrets of the Ring that have aided our crusade.*
>
> *The Ring... infused with the presence of our lord Semjaza... the Ring is to be praised. Through its power, the dark lord makes himself known to any who wear it - revealing hidden secrets and terrible wonders. It is by the aid of its dark power that we have prevailed over our enemies.*

JEFF STOPS reading and steps back from the book. There is something deeply unsettling in its writing... not just the words that Thaliard had written, but the book itself. He pages forward uncomfortably, noticing what appear to be strange incantations and accounts of gruesome experiments performed on their prisoners, complete with horrendous anatomical drawings.

He slams the book shut and pushes himself away, feeling suddenly nauseous.

⌘

10

SANCTUS VIRGAM

(Holy Staff)

U nbeknownst to Jeff, Hunahpu is dropping to his knees at that exact moment with an urgent burden to pray, lifting his hands as he begins calling out to God on Jeff's behalf. He feels as if he is pushing against something... a dark power that is seeking to overwhelm him. It seems as if its evil presence is pressing in around the entire castle.

JEFF HAS STAGGERED backward and is bent over, feeling increasingly dizzy and disoriented. He turns to find a seat but manages only to place his hands against the nearest bench as he collapses to his knees. As he tries to get up, he feels like something is pressing down heavily on his shoulders, forcing him to the floor. It tightens around his throat and chest, making breathing harder and harder.

HUNAHPU RAISES his arms urgently and prays aloud, combating the darkness and forcing it back. He wrestles against the onslaught as he begins to call on powers that are even more ancient and immense — Heavenly powers.

IF NOT FOR the dark of night, anyone looking would see the swirling darkness now encroaching on the castle from outside, encircling it in a vortex of black smoke that tightens as it gathers, constricting and growing thicker as its choking evil closes in.

EB IS SOON AWAKENED by the unsettling presence as well. He sits up in his bed as he senses the raging battle ensuing around him. Rising, he begins to pace in his room as he prays — somehow knowing that Jeff is in danger.

IN ANOTHER PART of the castle, Eugenia awakes, makes her way to the kitchen of her suite, and sits at the table, trying to make sense of the profound turmoil in her spirit. She finally lowers her head into her arms as tears fill her eyes and begins to pray for Jeff. Her urgent intercessory cries flow spontaneously under a sudden unction of the Spirit.

THE SMALL FORCE of prayer warriors continues to grow as Morna Baird and her daughter, Bridget, meet unexpectedly in their living room with an unexplainable shared burden to pray together. They drop to their knees with desperate tears in their eyes.

THE KIND-HEARTED MISSIONARY, Eusebios Christos, is quietly meditating with his open Bible when the call for intercession seizes him like a fever. Like Hunahpu, he steels himself against the growing tempest, responding with a forceful rebuke against the evil essence that seems to be closing in around them.

IN EACH OF THEIR ROOMS, Berenger Bern and General Zobrist are also stirred by the growing urgency of the Spirit's moving. Each of them begins praying with great unction as they sense the danger closing in. More lights start to come on throughout the castle and up and down the rows of cottages as members of the staff and grounds crews join in the urgent call.

JEFF CAN BARELY BREATHE; he kneels, gasping as he struggles with all his strength against the malevolent presence that seems to hover above him, crushing his soul as it drives the breath from his lungs. Words from the avatar fill his mind as he remembers them...

> it will demand spiritual strength and no small measure of
>   God's help...

Jeff knows that that is his only hope, but he doesn't know what to do to get it — if he could only understand what it means!

A VOICE suddenly breaks the silence around him, echoing in the cavernous chamber — it sounds silken-tongued and sinister as it whispers just above his head, sending a terrifying chill up his spine.

"*You are weak...*" it taunts, "*...What power have you to challenge me?*"

Jeff feels the pressure on his throat ease, giving him a chance to draw in a desperate gulp of air. The voice draws closer — just beside his ear....

"Surrender to me… Serve me as your forefather Thaliard
did, and I will make you strong!"

Jeff can't speak — he still can barely breathe — but he shakes his
head in refusal, defying the evil force that is holding him. He knows
now what it is… who it is….

"I WILL NOT SERVE YOU, SEMJAZA!" he objects adamantly
through gritted teeth.

"Such a pity, weak one… choosing death so needlessly…
and so soon in your young life. What good was your
uncle's brave sacrifice… You failed before you began."

The evil presence gloats as it savors its victory.

"Such a worthless protector you were… proof that the
great prophecy of the Tenth Mantle Bearer was but a
lie. See how far the once mighty Niergel have fallen.
When I've finished destroying you, I'll make an end
of all of them… nothing stands in my way now — the
world is again mine!"

THE PRESSURE on Jeff's throat tightens as he feels his life being choked
out of him. A desperate plea fills his heart — he hardly recognizes
what it is as it pours from his soul… unencumbered by humanistic
challenges or vain arguments… born entirely of desperate defiance…
a will to live… it is a plea for deliverance… a plea for mercy… it is, in
fact, **a *prayer***.

Its answer is needed urgently and comes instantly — words
suddenly fill his thoughts… so clearly that it feels as if they are
shouted at him. He can't speak or even utter a sound, yet the words fill
his consciousness with such force that it is as if he is shouting them
aloud….

. . .

"...VENI SANCTUS VIRGAM!" he hears himself cry out in a silent scream. As those words echo through his mind, he feels a desperate urgency to stretch one of his arms into the air, using his last remaining surge of strength.

IN THE SAME INSTANT, something like a cannon blast immediately explodes behind him, and shattered glass rains down from high above, as **the Shepherd's Staff flies into the air**. When it reaches his hand, its touch instantly releases a **massive shock wave** emanating from the center of his chest, blasting outward in all directions like an expanding sphere of light!

THE DARK FORCE that holds him is instantly obliterated as the sphere of light fills the chamber, purging its evil presence completely! An instant later, the thick, smoky mist around the castle is vaporized by the expanding shock wave, as if it had been blown away by a giant explosion, scattering its remnants on the wind. The castle is left untouched — a peaceful calm settles over all of Loch Harnan as the glowing moon and bright stars once again break through the black darkness.

JEFF COLLAPSES with his head against the bench, gasping in gulps of air as he catches his breath and rubs the soreness in his throat and chest. As his head clears, he looks over at the Shepherd's staff in his right hand, feeling the strength of its smooth wood surface against his palm and fingers. He uses it to help himself stand, feeling shaken and still not grasping what has happened. As he turns, he sees the floor in front of him covered with leaves and bits of broken glass; he examines the ancient staff in his hand, now smooth and bare, as strong as freshly cut wood.

He looks upward at the place where the staff had been stored and is instantly frozen in rapt attention by what he sees... the Staff's case has been shattered; he expected that, but just beneath the place where it was stored, Jeff sees a message written. It is etched into the golden wall of volumes in lettering that still glows like a hot flame — stretching across the golden bindings of countless books as if hand-written by a giant. The script is beautiful, unlike any font he has ever seen... It's in English:

Behold... My strength is made perfect in weakness.

Jeff's already weak knees give out beneath him — he staggers backward onto the bench, sitting on it with a stunned expression as he leans to stare at the incredible sight. His attention returns to the Staff in his hands, and he lifts it, resting it horizontally across his open palms as he stares at it in disbelief.

"*Veni Sanctus Virgam...*" he repeats in a whisper, then translates the Latin phrase with a sound of awestruck wonder in his voice: "Come ...Holy Staff." At that moment, he understands how the Staff had known of his uncle's death — indeed, he can somehow sense as he holds it that it *knows* a great deal about his family... and about *him*.

As he looks back at the message written above him, however, he is at a loss as to what it could mean. "Strength is made perfect..." he reads again, "...in weakness ...perfect in weakness," he repeats, still unable to make sense of the odd message. How could such a display of virtually limitless power have anything to do with weakness?

After pondering the astonishing events for a long while, he finds himself no closer to understanding the mysterious message. With his heart returning to a normal rhythm, he feels himself nodding off. He looks at his watch, realizing the early morning hour, and puts a hand to his head as he remembers his jujitsu class in just a few hours. He briefly considers calling out sick — something he has never done before in his life, but he soon drops the idea and stands to head up to bed.

After several steps, he pauses and looks back at the book still lying on the bookstand… the scolding that Hunahpu had given him about leaving the Cronicis unsecured still rings fresh in his mind — and this is undoubtedly a more dangerous book than that. Gripping the Shepherd's Staff tightly, he leans down and grabs his timepiece from the pedestal as quickly as he can, then watches as the library's mechanical storage system collects the ominous volume and tucks it safely away while all the other unread volumes retract as well.

A final whirring sound draws his attention, and he turns to see the Staff's shattered case lowering down to him; it waits for him to deposit the lifesaving object. Jeff runs his hand over its smooth wood surface one more time in admiration before carefully sliding it inside; then, he watches as the case is returned to its place high above.

⌘

11

BARRYMORE'S SECRET VAULT

E ugenia seems to go easy on Jeff during their morning training; it is almost as though she knows what he went through overnight, though he doesn't dare talk about it. Or, maybe she has just noticed how exhausted he looks.

It occurs to him that she doesn't seem to be her usual buoyant self either; she seems concerned — the look is something that he has never seen from her before.

As they are walking out, Jeff asks how the interrogation with Dylen is going. She looks at the floor uncertainly….

"As well as expected," she answers.

"Did he give us the vault's location?" he probes further.

Eugenia is wrestling with instructions from Zo and Berenger, as well as from her grandfather, not to tell Jeff where the vault is located.

"He did… sort of," she answers a little evasively. Jeff looks at her, waiting for her to continue. "He said it's protected with booby traps," she explains further.

"Do you trust him?" Jeff probes.

"On that point, I think I do; I can't see a reason for him to lie about that."

"Unless he's buying time," Jeff postulates.

Eugenia gives that idea some thought; Jeff can see the wheels turning and guesses that she is running it through several scenarios. "You have a point," she finally responds, "we should keep a close watch on it until we know more."

"EB told you to keep the location from me, didn't he?" Jeff says insightfully. "I'm not surprised; he and Hunahpu are in cahoots." Eugenia doesn't answer but admits he is right with a quick lift of her eyebrows.

THERE IS an awkward pause in the conversation as they walk silently down the empty hallway; Eugenia breaks the silence with a cautiously worded declaration...

"I sensed somethin' last night... it was somethin' I've never felt here before — it seemed very dark and foreboding." She looks over at him, catching his eye... "It woke me up. I just wanted you to know... I prayed for you."

Jeff is taken aback by the comment; he isn't sure how to respond. He knows immediately what the dark feeling must have been, but he has no way of knowing what she knows about the Secret Chamber, and he can't risk revealing it to her. More than that, he can't remember a time when anyone else had admitted praying for him, aside from maybe his mother or grandmother when he was very young. For lack of a better idea, he decides to play dumb.

"What do you mean — what kind of foreboding feeling?"

Eugenia cuts through his attempt with laser precision: "You may not realize it yet, or even believe it's possible, but you're important to Him... to God, I mean."

Jeff shrugs, an uncomfortable expression revealing genuine humility... "Yeah, I know the job is really important...."

She cuts him off: "I don't mean that — I'm not talkin' about Hastleworth Enterprises or even the Niergel — I mean you... God cares about *you* more than you realize... more than you can even imagine." She seems to catch herself, not wanting it to sound like she is preaching; "Look..." she says carefully, "...I'm not tryin' t'make you believe anythin' you don't want to. I just know that's a fact...you're really special to Him."

Jeff looks at her speechlessly, thinking to himself that she couldn't offend him if she walloped him with a pole — which, come to think of it, she had already done.

The truth is that he still hasn't been able to shake the uncomfortable feeling from last night's events. The experience has been unexplainable on so many levels... the possibility that God is real seems like the easiest part of the picture to accept. Whether he realizes it or not, last night's events have been a turning point for him — there is no way he can recall what happened without accepting that God had intervened... it gives him goosebumps thinking about it. Now, hearing Eugenia say what she just said has amplified his unease tenfold. It isn't just her words — it is the way they seem to reverberate inside him like a million butterfly wings, sending a chill up his back and making it suddenly difficult to breathe.

The silence between them is palpable as he processes it all; Eugenia begins to feel nervous about his reaction. Then Jeff finally speaks:

"...You take after your grandfather," he manages to say as he clears his throat enough to regain his voice, "...EB and God are old friends, I think."

"I think you're right about that," she agrees with a broad smile, feeling a sigh of relief, "but he's not the only one."

Jeff doesn't doubt what she is saying for an instant, although he feels like he is an outsider looking in at it with more than a little amazement... maybe even a little envy, he realizes.

THEY WALK a little further before Eugenia comes to the hallway that leads to her suite. She points over her shoulder as she says goodbye: "I have to go that way," she explains. She smiles at him warmly, "I'm glad we talked."

"Me too," he answers sincerely. He pauses for a second, rubbing a hand across the top of his head... "Do you have plans for dinner? I mean... I'd like to talk some more... to finish the conversation if you want."

She tilts her head to one side slightly as she grins in a sly smile, "We're in danger of imminent attack, and you're thinkin' o' dinner..." she quips, "...I knew there was somethin' I liked about you."

Jeff acknowledges she is right; it is pretty crazy — "It's settled then, provided we're not defending the ramparts, let's plan for six o'clock at my place," he invites, "Isabel makes a phenomenal soufflé."

Genie nods and agrees, "I'd be delighted."

Jeff is watching her walk away when she glances back over her shoulder and catches his eye, responding with a friendly smile. He raises his hand as if he intends to wave, but then thinks better of it and self-consciously rubs his head instead. She grins, nods goodbye, and continues.

———

ENTERING HIS SUITE, he greets Hunahpu and EB, who are conversing in his sitting room; they stop short as he enters, giving him the impression they don't want him to hear what they are discussing.

"How was your trainin' this mornin'?" EB asks.

"Fine, thanks... I think Eugenia decided to have mercy on me today," Jeff confides. "She'll be joining us for dinner tonight, by the way."

Without missing a beat, EB and Hunahpu look at each other... "Dinner? Here... tonight.... We'll be busy this evenin', I'm afraid." EB glances at Hunahpu with a coaxing expression.

"Yes, that's right," Hunahpu agrees, "we're... ah... going to give Brandish a hand with the defensive preparations."

"That's true," EB confirms, "...and Bear is launchin' the energy shield mission to that satellite — we'll need to be monitorin' it carefully."

"Oh, ...well, maybe we should join you and help with all that," Jeff suggests, feeling embarrassed about his misplaced priorities.

"Nonsense!" both of them say at once. "You've been workin' hard enough as it is," EB continues, "...and I'm sure the two o' you have a great deal t'discuss... in her official capacity as head of Intelligence, that is."

Jeff stops and looks at both of them for a moment as their intentions dawn on him. "For a couple of former secret agents, the two of you are terrible liars," he admonishes. Despite the transparency of their motives, Jeff decides not to challenge them further; honestly, he secretly appreciates their attempts. He shakes his head and looks down, realizing that he is still in his workout clothes, then excuses himself to head upstairs and get ready for the day.

JEFF MEETS Corporal Tanner in the simulator. Although they have already graduated to live flight training, the simulator is still the safest for teaching complex maneuvers.

"Welcome back, Sir. It's good to see you again."

"It's good to be back," Jeff agrees as he shakes Tanner's hand and climbs aboard, settling into the pilot's seat.

The Corporal describes the session's mission — having become accustomed to Jeff's style, he no longer bothers with scripted flight plans, opting for simple objectives.

"We're going to focus on water-air transitions," he explains, "while not especially complex, it's easier to practice those here — seeing planes nosedive into the ocean in real life tends to unnerve people who may be watching."

"Fair enough," Jeff agrees with a smile.

By now, Jeff knows how to power up the simulator on his own — he quickly loads the default location and soon is navigating the undersea passage.

"A new record!" Tanner notes with a smile, looking at his watch as they blast out of the mountain shaft. As long as it is only in the simulator, he has resigned himself to Jeff's daredevil antics — he is starting to enjoy them, to be honest.

They work through various maneuvers: ascending to the surface, lifting off from a stationary float, blasting out of the water at high speed, nosediving back into it, and landing on the surface. Jeff is soon inventing his own maneuvers — sinking wing-first, tail first, landing upside-down, spinning into the water like a corkscrew — even rolling the ship across the water's surface wing-over-wing.

Tanner is glad he has been wearing a helmet for all of Jeff's simulator sessions.

Attempting one more maneuver, Jeff blasts into the air and flies high into the simulated clouds. He is planning to try replicating the precarious evasive dive that EB pulled off on the night they first met. Suddenly, Loch Harnan's castle catches his eye, and he notices something from high overhead that he hasn't seen before.

He immediately veers off from his intended flight path and begins to circle the simulator's perfect rendering of the castle below. As he circles it, he can't help comparing the sight with the ancient drawing from Maranish's file.

It occurs to him that there is a pattern in the way the castle has been built; from what he can see and recall, the vault of archives is located near the castle's center, in the wing that contains his grandfather's suite. He flies low overhead to confirm the location of the huge skylight above its grand staircase. Judging from the position of the castle's central dome, he can also estimate that the secret chamber is diagonally across the rotunda from there, directly under the wing of the castle that contains the offices. That leaves the third of the castle's three cloverleaf wings without a hidden chamber of its own. As Jeff considers this, he can't help but feel it violates the amazing symmetry of the place, the perfect balance infused in every detail. This is even more interesting when he considers what the third wing contains... his own suite... and his uncle's.

Naught shall remain of Barrymore's secret vault...

Those words from the threatening email he received last night flash suddenly to mind as he ponders the puzzle. He quickly concludes that it is due time for him to pay a visit to his uncle's suite.

Still, in mid-air, Jeff immediately hits the red panic button on the center console, ending the simulation and returning them instantly to the training room.

"Wh-what… w-hy'd you do tha…." Tanner questions, taken by surprise.

"Just remembered something that I need to do — it's kind of urgent," Jeff half-explains as he unhooks his seat belts and hits the switches to open the simulator's hatch. He is out the door before Tanner can question him any further, leaving the poor corporal baffled but not surprised.

IT IS Jeff who is surprised to find Hunahpu waiting for him upon entering his uncle Barry's suite. From the look of things, a search of the place has already been conducted. EB's voice from down the hall reveals that he is there, too. Jeff watches his older friend emerge into the main room… Eugenia follows closely. The two of them stop talking abruptly when they notice him.

"I should have guessed I'd find you all here," Jeff says with a sigh of resignation. "Are you any closer to finding the access codes for Uncle Barry's secret vault?"

EB and Hun Hanahpu look at each other in surprise, then EB turns to Eugenia… "Perhaps we'd better go and check on Brandish," he suggests to her, "…We'll leave the two o' you t'discuss this alone."

HUNAHPU NODS to him with a serious expression, waiting silently until they are out the door, then looks at Jeff.

"You're not ready," he begins, breaking his silence. "How did you know to seek it here?"

"It seemed like the likeliest place," Jeff answers. "What makes you say I'm not ready — not that I'm disagreeing with you."

"Have you found the means to destroy them?" Hunahpu challenges.

"Well, no... not yet, but we can't leave them here — we can't risk letting the Eljo get them!" he argues emphatically.

"It's too risky," Hunahpu insists, "we can't take the chance of you or anyone else being influenced by their powers."

"You mean, by Semjaza's powers," Jeff clarifies.

Hunahpu's eyes narrow, and he waits silently for Jeff to continue.

"Eugenia told me that something woke her last night... an oppressive darkness," Jeff explains, looking at his great-grandfather intently to gauge his reaction. "I suspect that you felt it too." Hunahpu continues to listen, not answering. "I'm certain that Semjaza was the source of that darkness — I met him... without a doubt, it was him... in the Secret Chamber."

Hunahpu rears up in his chair and grips both armrests in surprise. "Why didn't you tell me this sooner?"

"What was I going to do, blurt it out in front of EB? I still don't know what he knows about all this."

Hunahpu grows quiet again, "...I suppose you did well not to mention it to him," he commends. "Can you describe what happened?"

"Every detail!" Jeff assures him, "I'll never forget it! He nearly killed me."

Jeff describes his discoveries in the manuscript from Maranish and then recounts his experience with the book written by Thaliard... he doesn't dare even to repeat the book's name, saying only that it seemed to record dark incantations and horrific accounts of torture. Then he describes his encounter with the dark, misty figure and his near demise.

"How did you escape?" Hunahpu asks anxiously.

"I was rescued... that's the only explanation," Jeff confesses, still struggling with the fantastic truth. "I was on my knees and barely able to breathe — it felt like I was being crushed; in another moment, I would have been unconscious.

"That's when words suddenly flooded my mind. I know they weren't memories — I've never heard them before ...VENI SANCTUS VIRGAM!"

"Come, Holy Staff," Hunahpu interprets as he studies Jeff's face.

"That's right. It was like they were spoken into my mind — I heard them as clearly as if they'd been spoken, yet without a sound. What happened after that is really incredible...."

Jeff is staring into the distance as he relives the extraordinary experience. "I heard something shatter — it was glass breaking. There was the strongest urge to reach out for something, and just as I did, it flew into my hand — it was the Staff — the Shepherd's Staff!

"The next thing I remember is a blinding light. It lit up the whole chamber as bright as daylight."

Hearing himself repeat the account aloud shocks and challenges him — he doesn't dare believe it, yet it is all undeniably true!

"After the flash of light, I could tell Semjaza was gone — his dark presence was ...gone. But I wasn't alone — I felt a different presence in the room, one that was the exact opposite... it felt like life itself; peaceful but also troubling and unnerving ...I felt out of place ... afraid, but for a different reason... like I didn't deserve to be in the same room."

HUNAHPU LISTENS WITH RAPT ATTENTION, studying Jeff's eyes intently as he speaks. "What have you concluded that it was?"

Jeff holds a hand against his head as he shakes it slightly in a gesture that admits he can't deny the obvious conclusion... "It was... well, it was God. I've searched for another explanation, but nothing else fits."

"Just because the Great Staff flew to you? Perhaps there's some natural explanation," Hunahpu challenges, trying to gauge whether Jeff truly believes what he is claiming.

Jeff looks at him uncomfortably... "There's something else — you need to see it yourself."

⌘

12

THE TIME OF MY FAVOR

"In the time of my favor, I heard you,
and in the day of salvation, I helped you."
~ 2 Corinthians 6:2

J eff is shivering with nervous anticipation as the two of them make their way to the office suite and then down to the Secret Chamber. The sight of broken glass is immediately evident as they enter — the room's lights reflect off each crystalline shard, making them appear as if they are a thousand sparkling lights.

Far more marvelous than that, though, is the sight of the beautifully scripted lettering emblazoned across the golden bindings high above the floor. It still glows miraculously, as if it were just written in molten gold.

HUNAHPU GASPS aloud as he looks up and beholds the mysterious writing. He immediately drops to his knees and lifts his hands in awestruck praise. His eyes are closed tightly, and he silently raises his face toward heaven as if basking in warm sunshine. A look of amazed gratitude fills his countenance, and Jeff notices a tear escape his great-grandfather's eye and run down his cheek.

HUNAHPU'S unpretentious act of worship makes Jeff feel like he is eavesdropping on a deeply personal moment. He looks at the floor uncomfortably and happens to notice one of the leaves from the Shepherd's Staff lying at his feet — it is shriveled, dry, and brown... but at the end of its attached stem, Jeff notices that a few seeds have appeared. They are no larger than a pea but unmistakably seeds. As he scans the floor, he sees that all the other leaves have small clusters of seeds too.

He drops to one knee and carefully picks one up; when he does, the remnants of its leaf and stem instantly turn to dust, but the seeds drop into the palm of his hand unharmed. Curious, he picks up another, and the same thing happens, then several more, soon collecting a handful of the mysterious seeds.

He sits down on the bench, distractedly letting the pile of seeds fall from one hand to the other. A shudder runs through him as his mind replays the previous night's events, recalling one of Semjaza's comments in particular — something about a *'prophecy of the Tenth Mantle Bearer....'*

HUNAHPU'S VOICE suddenly breaks the room's solemn silence. His words send a chill through Jeff....

> *"Dear God of our fathers,"* he prays, *"we are humbled in your presence and by this evidence of your great love for us. In this chamber, You, O God, have heard our voice, and seen our affliction, our toil, and our oppression ...and brought us out of it with a mighty hand, and with an outstretched*

arm, and with marvelous power, and with signs, and with
wonders.

"*It is by this act of your own hand that we know you will not*
forsake us. You alone have been our hope and our salva-
tion. Even if the mountains shake and the seas roar, we
will not be afraid because you are God over the wind and
sea, whose voice they obey.

"*Give us endurance and wisdom in this fight, that we may*
prevail. For the sake of your kingdom and the glory of
your name."

After he has finished praying, he kneels a while longer, staring in wonder at the magnificent script emblazoned across the golden books. Finally, he holds out a hand toward Jeff: *"Tsarëkamë" (help me up)*, he requests.

Jeff stands and offers his hand, steadying himself as his great-grandfather lifts himself to his feet. Hunahpu straightens and walks steadily, belying his advanced age, and finally takes a seat on the bench. Jeff sits down beside him.

"Forgive my distraction," he apologizes, "it is a moving sight ...a very great wonder," he looks upward, pointing his open hands toward the writing. "This verse has special meaning for me — I remember when Barry taught it to me ...centuries ago."

"Verse?" Jeff asks.

Hunahpu reaches into his pocket and pulls out a small Bible, thumbing through it. "Here it is," he points out, "in Second Corinthians, chapter twelve — look at verse nine."

Jeff takes the Bible from him, finds the place, and reads it silently. As he does, Hunahpu quotes its words from memory:

"*He said to me, My grace is sufficient for you: for my power is*
made perfect in weakness. Most gladly therefore will I
rather glory in my weaknesses, that the power of Christ
may rest upon me."

Another chill runs up Jeff's spine as he hears his great-grandfather's voice and reads the words. The experience from last night flashes through his mind so vividly that it is as if he is reliving it, making him shudder.

"There were many times when those words comforted us and gave us strength to go on," Hunahpu recalls. In great loss, we learned that our weakest times delivered to us our strongest faith — when hope was at its end, then Christ's power surged the most strongly."

A thought strikes Jeff as he considers Hunahpu's words: "The flash that I told you about... the presence... is that what it was — the power of Christ?" There is a hint of fear in his voice. "It was real... it was so tangible — so powerful!" He looks at Hunahpu with a sincerely awestruck expression, "Was that Him ...was that Christ?" His voice sounds hopeful ...searching.

Hunahpu doesn't answer him directly; instead, he begins to share a story.

"I have to confess that I saw a number of unexplainable things in the jungles of Yucatán and Peru... supernatural things. Unlike what you described, none of those could have been attributed to Christ. They were dark manifestations of darker powers."

Jeff thinks about his meeting with Semjaza and shudders slightly.

"It was Barry who first introduced me to the truth," Hunahpu continues, "— he showed me what it truly meant for someone to have life... to know the author of life."

He straightens in his seat and folds his hands, thinking about those early days. "When I first met Barry, the thing that set him apart the most was the way he cared for others. He didn't hide his convictions, but he didn't pressure anyone into sharing them. It wasn't just a matter of following religious principles for him — he cared genuinely. I suppose it was his heart that got me thinking more than anything else at first. Barry showed me what it meant to be a Christian ...what it truly meant. Not that I was an easy convert, I must say; it took decades for God to get through to me.

"What finally convinced you …what was the tipping point?" Jeff asks — there is a noticeable anxiety in his voice.

Hunahpu slowly rubs his hands together and considers the question — his brow furrows slightly as feelings from long ago resurface in his mind. "It was nothing like the revelation that you have received… nothing as incredible as this," he says as his hands open expressively. "But God's work in my life was no less real.

"When I first arrived in Loch Harnan, I knew little about faith… all I knew of Christian faith was what I had witnessed among the Conquistadors. Believe me, they were a rather poor example of it, for the most part.

"I saw in them outward signs of religion; these are easily professed and were most frequently hypocritical, but I was yet to learn that true repentance is far more difficult and far less common. Men will more readily attend to the most multiplied and minute ceremonial regulations — such things are pleasing to their egos — but true religion is too humbling, too heart-searching, too thorough for the tastes of most men; they prefer something more ostentatious, superficial, and worldly.

"Outward observances are temporarily comfortable, you see; the eye and the ear are pleased; self-conceit is fed, and self-righteousness is puffed up, but they are ultimately delusive and good for nothing. I have been with many men in their hour of death and have seen how the soul needs something more firm than ceremonies and rituals to lean upon in that hour. In the day of our judgment, we will require more to defend us than self-justifying vanities." He looks at Jeff with a great fire of conviction in his eyes…

"…Indeed, apart from vital godliness itself, all religion is utterly vain; when offered without a sincere heart, every form of worship is a solemn sham and an impudent mockery of the majesty of heaven!"

Jeff is surprised by how strong and emphatic his indictment is. His great-grandfather pauses for a few moments and looks again at his hands, then continues in a quieter voice…

"…Yet what man is capable of godliness?" he admits, looking Jeff in the eye.

. . .

THE QUESTION CATCHES Jeff off guard — if any man seemed worthy of claiming the mantle of 'godly,' it is the kind-hearted old man sitting beside him. Yet his question has cut Jeff to the quick; a pang of remorse welling up inside.

Hunahpu leans forward again and clasps his hands together, deep in thought. "Alas, it hangs beyond our grasp, like a life-sustaining feast before a starving man and just out of his reach. Man is incapable of earning it or aspiring to it." He looks at Jeff with a kind expression and adds, "— but he can receive it."

"How?" Jeff asks quietly. His eyes have become glassy with tears for reasons he can't understand.

"Ahh, that is the right question," Hunahpu replies reassuringly. His elbows rest on his knees again as he clasps his hands together in deep thought, looking upward at the miraculous writing. "The purity of a godly heart comes from the only source of purity. It cannot be created from within us any more than black tar can be used to wash us. No... a heart's cleansing is a Divine act.

"Yet, before the heart can be cleansed, it must be opened," he glances reassuringly at Jeff for a moment, then continues his thought, "...an unyielded heart is often like a prison with no door -- it must, at times, be torn open. This heart-rending is divinely wrought and solemnly felt. The Savior's knocking upon a heart yields a secret grief that is personally experienced, not subtly in a way that can be missed, but as a deep, soul-moving work of the Holy Spirit upon the inmost conscience. It is not a matter to be merely talked of and believed in, but is keenly and sensitively felt in every living child of this living and vibrant God. It is powerfully humiliating and completely sin-purging, but it sweetly prepares us for the gracious consolations that proud and un-humbled spirits can never receive."

ALTHOUGH QUESTIONS FLOOD Jeff's mind, he isn't able to ask them; his chest seems heavy, and his eyes are too clouded to see clearly... tears have begun to leave streaks down the sides of his cheeks, and he struggles to regain composure, feeling hopelessly conflicted over his inability to fight off the feelings he is experiencing.

Oddly, the barrage of doubt-filled arguments and counter-points that would typically have flooded his mind has all at once begun to seem meaningless — even absurd. The weight of his soul's guilt is crushing all of his futile arguments like so many paper bulwarks. He finds himself kicking them aside as if they are worthless annoyances, scattered like obstacles in the way of an infinitely more urgent goal. He is the starving man that his Great Grandfather had just talked about... the thing that he starves for is what astonishes him the most. For the first time in his life, he understands the deep unspoken need in the center of his soul — it is a yearning for God's favor, yet every sinew of his being is wounded by the realization that he will never be good enough to earn it!

Heaped on top of all this turmoil is the overwhelming weight of his new responsibilities — and the impending battle for which he knows he is utterly unprepared.

HUNAHPU PRAYS SILENTLY as he watches the struggle seizing his young heir. Jeff drops his head into his hands as the unfamiliar feelings wash over him — he feels wave after wave of guilt and inadequacy, but even more profound is an inexplicable sense of separation; a feeling that he is cut off from the thing that overwhelmingly matters most — his soul's only hope.

"ULLPUKUY NOQAWAN WAWÁY (*Kneel with me, my son*)," Hunahpu offers as he turns and drops to his knees beside the bench. Jeff joins him with urgency, dropping his head into his arms as he collapses against the seat. The moment he does, it is as if floodgates open — he begins to weep bitterly.

His great-grandfather waits as the flood of Jeff's pent-up sorrow and remorse finds its release; Jeff weeps uncontrollably for several minutes, then looks up, apologizing as he wipes his drenched eyes.

"What you are feeling is God's hand," Hunahpu counsels. "When He touches us, we can't help but sense how far we are from His perfection. It was Barry who knelt beside me the night I first felt it. He said something to me that I have never forgotten: '*Godly sorrow is the bridge upon which God's mercy travels...*' he called it '*the thoroughfare of Grace.*'

"I began to see that all men's attempts at religion have one thing in common, they are only man's attempt to reach out to God. This is why Christ's coming was so profound, you see; the way that Jesus showed was completely unexpected by men — it was God reaching out to man — in an act of humility greater than any that the world had ever known."

THERE IS a long pause as Hunahpu kneels quietly in silent prayer while Jeff continues to shake with small sobs. He places his hand on Jeff's shoulder as he speaks again.

"There is an ancient Hebrew word that means 'one who saves from destruction' — more precisely, it meant 'one who saves from sin.' In English, that word is translated as 'Savior' — in Hebrew, the word is also a name: 'Yeshua' ... 'Jesus'.

"The Bible explains that godly sorrow is the tool he uses to bring repentance. People often confuse repentance with penitence — but they are nothing alike. Penitence is something a man chooses to do; it's a human act. Repentance is a gift from God's own hand — it comes when *He* chooses, when we are drawn by His spirit — it is the rending of a heart, so that he can open it ...so that he can cleanse it."

Jeff is listening intently to his great-grandfather's words as the tears continue to rain from his soul.

"What you are feeling, my son, is a great gift. The key is to accept it — that is where the choice comes in. God does His part with the drawing, the repentance, and the rending of heart — it is up to us to accept His grace …His forgiveness. The starving man must take and eat the feast that he is offered in order for it to save him.

"Barry led me in a prayer that night… I still remember every word. It was a simple prayer of acceptance, acknowledging that I was a sinner …that was easy, I knew I could never merit God's favor. It was a prayer accepting His gift of forgiveness; a gift that was only possible because Jesus had already taken my punishment for me, on His cross."

Hunahpu looks at him with a kind expression: "If you're ready to accept an invitation of friendship from the God of the universe — to let Christ alone be the master of your life — then it would be my life's greatest joy and honor to pray that same prayer with you."

Jeff can't find his voice to speak, but he answers with an anxious nod of his head.

"In the New Testament Book of Romans, we're told that it is with his heart that a man gains righteousness by believing and with his mouth that his confession of this belief is made, leading to salvation. It is a simple and straightforward promise: if we confess with our mouth that Jesus is Lord, and believe in our heart that God raised Him from the dead, we will be saved." Coaxing Jeff to join him in praying the words aloud, he asks: "Are you ready to do that?"

Jeff doesn't hesitate, he is desperate for his Great Grandfather's leading and quickly nods yes. He anxiously repeats each phrase as Hunahpu says them…

"Dear God… You gave your Word… that if I confess to you my sin… You are faithful in your promise to forgive me… and to cleanse me completely… I believe that Jesus paid the penalty for all of my sin… and that his victory was proved when He rose again from the dead. Jesus, I am accepting you now as my personal Lord and Savior… to live for you and serve you… for the rest of my life. Thank you for forgiving me, …saving me, …and giving me eternal life in your family! Thank you for breaking the bars that have held me as a captive… and for leading me out into your freedom… with joy unspeakable in the presence of Your glory! … Amen!"

AS JEFF FINISHES PRAYING, he feels a mix of confusing emotions swirling through him. He is feeling guilty and undeserving, but also strangely accepted and comforted, as if he is being welcomed in a way that transcends any experience of love he's ever known before.

He soon realizes that the turmoil and anxiety he was feeling have somehow been replaced by a deep-seated peace — he can sense that something is different, something is tangibly different! Unbelievably, the fear and guilt that weighed so heavily on him just moments ago have somehow been replaced with feelings of unconditional acceptance. He hasn't felt this free and joyful since he was a little kid!

"I-I feel… different…" Jeff admits, a smile curling the edges of his mouth involuntarily. He forces himself to frown as he wipes his wet eyes; "I sh-shouldn't be so happy… I have no right to be," he complains stubbornly, but loses control of his frown and feels a larger smile take its place in spite of himself. He looks at his great-grandfather with an awestruck expression….

"He's here now, isn't He? I c-can feel Him," he says as he bows his head humbly; he is afraid to look up.

"Ari, jutan yaya, *(Yes, grandson.)* You feel the trembling joy of *first grace* — it bids you to draw nearer to Him, but also makes you dearly conscious of your soul's guilt. It is a conflict, wonderful and glorious — to sense the grandeur of God's presence, with His power to create life or to destroy. It inspires in any gracious man a solemn awe… a holy fear… yet it is a fear with the terror taken out of it. His presence now carries no charge of judgment… only the love of a father, newly reunited with his child.

"Indeed," he adds, placing his hand on Jeff's shoulder, "it is the blessed joy of newly redeemed souls, when they first meet their Lord, to find that His unfathomable love is so great that it obscures even His infinite majesty."

Jeff looks at Hunahpu with an amazed expression — his great-grandfather's words exactly describe the confusing mix of emotions raging within him; a tear escapes his eye yet again, but this time it is a tear of astonishing joy.

⌘

13

REJOICING

When EB arrives, Jeff is sitting by the fireplace, deeply engrossed in his reading. Hunahpu greets him at the door, privately whispering the news of Jeff's new birth, naturally leaving out the details about the Secret Chamber. EB seems stunned that their young friend's conversion has come so quickly.

"Are you certain of it?"

"As certain as I am of my own," Hunahpu assures him.

EB follows his friend into the sitting room and notices Jeff immersed in his uncle's worn-looking Bible.

"He's been reading like that for hours," Hunahpu explains in a hushed voice.

"You don't have to whisper," Jeff declares, looking up with a subtly amused expression, "it's as amazing to me as it must seem to both of you."

He looks back down at the Bible in his hands: "I honestly had no idea that this book is so incredibly profound," he admits, waving at the pages, "So far, I've only just read the Gospels and the book called Acts, and now I'm into..." he pauses to check his place "...the Letter to the Romans. This man, Paul — how did he write like this? I mean, it's as if he could see inside men's hearts... not to mention his logic in the way he expounds on his points — it's irrefutable!"

"Yes, well... I suppose that's why it's called Gospel," EB replies with a ring of the wit that Jeff has come to expect from him. He clears his throat as if to signal that his next comment will be meant more seriously; "Genie asked me to remind you that she'll be over around six o'clock."

Jeff glances at his watch, noticing it is after five o'clock, then snaps his Bible closed and climbs from the chair. "Wow... It's that late already?" He suddenly looks shaken. "I should go get ready... Are you sure you won't join us for dinner?" The question is almost an afterthought.

EB and Hunahpu look at each other with their best poker faces; "No, regretfully not - we really must be seeing how the defensive preparations are going... helping out in the weapons lab and all that," EB explains.

"And monitoring the energy shield mission...." Jeff reminds him skeptically.

"Yes! Right! That too!" EB agrees. Not waiting to become entangled in any further questioning, the two of them quickly excuse themselves and say goodbye.

Jeff watches them leave with an amused shake of his head, then finds himself smiling as he recalls his hallway conversation with Eugenia that morning; he can hardly wait to tell her about his life-changing afternoon.

⸻

AFTER SHOWERING and changing into a suit, Jeff is preparing to exit his room when his eye falls on the small seed on his nightstand. He placed the mysterious curiosity there when he emptied his pockets earlier. Picking it up, he rolls it gently between his fingers, recalling the scene that it elicits in his mind. He smiles as he thinks of the amazing experience with Hunahpu in the Secret Chamber and gratefully squeezes the cherished seed in his closed hand. With hardly a thought, he drops it into his jacket pocket and pats it appreciatively.

Isabel seems to be smiling more than usual as she busily prepares the night's meal; Jeff can hear her singing and humming as he makes his way downstairs. Before he can step toward the kitchen, he hears his doorbell ring, and ABBI announces Genie's arrival. He quickly reaches the front door and pulls it open to greet his dinner guest.

THE SIGHT that meets him stops him in his tracks. Genie stands looking at him with a demure smile; her long hair is elegantly arranged in an impressive style that looks as if it might have taken half the afternoon to prepare. It beautifully frames a pair of large pearl earrings. She is dressed in a formal black evening dress with a tastefully dipping neckline, accentuating a stunning matching pearl necklace. The dress is a little shorter than Jeff has seen her wear and clings tightly to her impeccably toned thighs. A pair of chic high heels finishes off the look.

Jeff is speechless, staring at her face, looking a little stunned. He finally comes to his senses and steps aside to welcome her in. She seems radiant, obviously flattered by his reaction.

"I hope you don't mind that I dressed up a bit," she comments nervously, "I couldn't have y' thinkin' that I just but beat people up all day."

A joke crosses Jeff's mind about not minding being beaten up by her, but he wisely keeps it to himself.

Entering the sitting room, Eugenia takes a seat in one of the overstuffed armchairs by the fireplace, crossing her legs. Jeff feels his chest flutter in a mild heart arrhythmia and does his best to hide his blushing as he offers to get her something from the room's small bar.

"Sparklin' water would be wonderful," she answers with a smile.

He opens a freshly chilled bottle, fills both their glasses, and then hands one to her as he sits opposite the fire.

"So," he begins with genuine interest, "what made someone as... that is, who looks... I mean, ...a woman — person! ...a person like you — what made *you* want to become an undercover agent?"

It is Eugenia's turn to blush slightly as she excuses his fumbling, "I don't remember, honestly," she answers, considering the question as if it has never been asked of her before. "I suppose I just always wanted it, from my youngest memories. I'm sure it had somethin' t'do with *Shan'er*... my gran'da. Hearin' his stories of adventures with Barry and all that. Of course, my Nanna's self-defense trainin' lessons helped a great deal."

"Your Nanna... you mean EB's wife Gretchen?" Jeff clarifies carefully.

"Aye, she was an enormous inspiration to me. She made it a point to be sure I could handle m'self."

"She obviously did a wonderful job," Jeff compliments.

"Oh, you have no idea! I owe m'life to her lessons — they have saved me countless times."

Jeff watches her take a sip, finding it easy to imagine how she must have handled herself in those situations - her unsuspecting opponents probably never even saw it coming. He is enjoying the chance to get to know her better.

"EB hasn't spoken about your parents. Do they live near here?" he asks curiously.

She lowers her glass and looks briefly at the fire before answering, "I guess I can see why it hasn't come up," she says, looking suddenly more serious, "...he has a hard time talkin' about it. My folks died when I was young... I was ten years old."

"I'm sorry...." Jeff says sincerely. Thoughts of his own childhood rush suddenly through his mind.

"It's alright; I like talkin' about them," she answers reassuringly. "They were on a business trip together, that's what they told me at the time — I learned the truth years later that they were on a mission in Estonia; their plane crashed. Sabotage was suspected but never proven. I suppose at first it was vengeance that motivated me to become an agent, but Nanna helped me past that — she helped me see that forgiveness is a far better healer than vengeance is."

"That must have been hard for her...." Jeff supposes.

"It didn't seem t'be. I guess you would need to have known her to understand that... she was quick to forgive; she said that bitterness only infects our own soul and poisons us — we only hurt ourselves by it. It's probably been my life's most valuable lesson."

She smiles as she thinks about her childhood, staring into the fire as she recounts it; "Dadda used to take us on simple trips... campin' mostly. He taught me t'fly-fish and how t'cook over a campfire. We even went fishin' and campin' in America once — in Montana."

She looks up at Jeff, drawing him into her story as she speaks; "They both loved languages..." she continues, "they spoke nearly a dozen tongues between them. I guess that's where I got my love for foreign languages. They would play a game... at least it was a game to me... where each day we would speak in a different language — all day long." She appears to relish the memory as if it were from just yesterday.

"Mara Escutia...," Jeff thinks aloud; that was your dad's name. EB is your mother's father?" Jeff notes after a short silence.

"Aye, ma's father."

"Her loss must have been difficult for him... fathers are protective of their daughters," Jeff sympathizes.

"I suppose you're right about that," she agrees, "he took it pretty hard. I sometimes wonder how he would have gotten through it without Nanna."

"Something tells me that you were a big help to him as well," Jeff observes.

She nods gratefully as she stares into the fire, deep in thought.

"You miss your grandmother, don't you?"

Genie nods quickly and forces a smile as she wipes a tear from her cheek.

"It must be comforting, though, knowing that they were Christians... knowing that you'll see them again," Jeff adds, suddenly remembering some of what he had learned in his afternoon's reading.

"That's what Jesus said, right? That he was going to prepare a place for us."

Eugenia looks up at him with a surprised expression. Before she can question him, he offers a timid confession.

"I-I wanted to tell you as soon as you walked in, but wasn't sure how to say it... Something incredible happened to me today, something amazing. I never thought I'd say this, but... today I met Him... I committed my life to Him... to Christ!"

Genie looks stunned as an astonished smile comes over her face.

"My great..." he starts to say, catching himself, "...Hunahpu helped me; he showed me how... I never expected it to be so —real!"

"I can hardly believe it.... What caused your change of heart?" she nearly stammers. "...I-I'm so happy for you!"

"All I can say is that you were right this morning about that dark feeling last night. I can't explain more except to say that you were right. I think your prayers had something to do with it... with all of it... with last night, with today... with everything."

"I wasn't the only one," she quickly explains, "...we all did — we all felt the same thing last night — we all prayed."

Jeff's eyes flash with excitement — "Genie, I met Him... I mean, I really met Him... it was Jesus!" He leans forward in his chair, looking as excited as if he were cheering on his favorite team's best play. "There's so much I want to tell you, but I can't right now... so much more!"

GENIE LOOKS as though she is stunned, surprised, and thrilled on so many levels that she doesn't know how to react. She immediately jumps from her chair, reaches out her arms, waves for him to stand, then hugs him tightly as she rocks him from side to side and bounces slightly up and down. Jeff has never seen her so thrilled... in fact, he has never seen anyone so genuinely happy!

While they are hugging, Isabel walks in to announce their dinner. Genie looks at her and nearly shouts: "Jeff has been Saved! He's Born Again!"

"Oui! Je sais!¹ Isn't it wonderful!" Isabel answers with a broad smile as she lifts her hands high — "Praises be... merci Jésus!²"

Jeff can't help laughing aloud; it is a laugh of unbridled joy — a joy like he has never felt before. Genie waves anxiously for Isabel to join them, and Jeff soon finds himself in a three-way hug as Isabel shouts praises while Genie squeals in celebration, and Jeff laughs in joy.

The three of them have tears on their cheeks as they finally end their embrace and slowly recover, wiping their eyes.

"The angels are rejoicing!" Isabel says joyously. "Your name has been written in the Book of Life — forever, you will be safe in His arms." She places both her hands on the sides of his face and kisses him on both cheeks; "I'm so happy! It's like it's my own son!"

⌘

14

CANDLELIT DINNER

When Jeff and Genie finally make it to the dining room, he notices that the lights are dimmed, and Isabel has positioned lit candelabras along the large table. He looks at Eugenia, a little embarrassed, and then at Isabel: "Wow, candlelight," he says nervously. Looking back to Eugenia, he adds: "If you'd rather, we can have the lights…."

Genie reassuringly places a hand on his arm, smiling at his nervousness, "I think it's lovely… let's keep them."

He nods acceptingly, then interrupts a moment of awkward silence by drawing out her chair for her and pushing her in as she sits down.

"I seem to recall that the last time I offered you a chair, you politely refused," he jokes as he takes his seat.

"You weren't offerin' me a candlelight dinner then," she answers with a smile. "Besides, I was keepin' an eye on Blandus and his goons." She nods toward the giant mirror behind where Jeff had been sitting; he remembers that Blandus' bodyguards had been standing just inside the double doors, directly across from that mirror and a short distance from where she had seated herself.

"Wow... thank you for that," Jeff says in realization, "It's a relief to know that it wasn't because you didn't like me."

"Well, I didn't say that exactly," she says with a sly grin, touching his hand to show that she is joking.

Isabel places a pair of beautifully arranged salads in front of each of them, then offers a choice of wines.

"None for me, thank you," Genie says gratefully. She looks at Jeff and explains, "We're technically on high alert; I'd like to keep a clear head."

Jeff nods to Isabel that he will pass on the wine as well.

As Isabel leaves the room, Genie sits with her hands folded in her lap expectantly. It suddenly occurs to Jeff that they should say grace for the meal.

"Forgive me," he says, taking his hand off his fork, "I'm a little new at this... I suppose we should pray first."

"I can say it if you'd like," Genie offers.

"It's alright; please allow me," Jeff says sincerely. He closes his eyes and bows his head forward, sitting silently for a moment, then begins to offer an impromptu prayer.

"Father..."

Jeff feels a slight shudder of emotion as he grasps the true meaning of his new heavenly relationship for the first time.

> *"...I know I can call you Father now...*
> *"Thank you for opening these blinded eyes... and tearing my*
> *heart open so that you could wash it. I never knew how*
> *much joy a heart could feel! I know I don't deserve the gift*
> *you've given me and can never repay my debt to you."*

He pauses, remembering that he is saying Grace;

"We're thankful for this food — and for all of the amazing
things you have provided. Please bless this meal to
strengthen us and use the resources you've given to
advance the work you want us to do for you. Jesus, I know
that the work is Yours and that you will defend us with
Your power — just as you have defended us already. Please
give strength, inspiration, and protection to all of our
friends working in this cause — we are truly grateful for
such an assembly of selfless people; it's enormously
humbling to lead them.

"...Finally," he adds, choking back the tightness in his
throat after a short silence, *"...we ask you to honor the*
sacrifices of so many who have given everything in this
fight... even their lives... and ask you to comfort those who
have loved them and remain behind. Thank you for the
hope of rejoining them one day — and of seeing You face to
face ...Amen."

There are tears on Genie's cheeks when Jeff looks up. He offers her
his still-folded napkin, but she politely refuses it and picks up her
own, using it to carefully dry her eyes.

"I'm usually much more stoic than this," she apologizes.

"Yes, I've noticed that," Jeff says, making a playful jab at her usually
steely demeanor.

She taps his hand in a mock slap: "Stop it!" she exclaims with an
acknowledging smile.

She looks at him for a moment, finding it hard to believe the
change she sees in him. "What, exactly happened t'you today? It's
amazin' how different you are."

Jeff thinks for a moment about how to answer her; "It wasn't just
today... It was everything leading up to it since I've been here."

He wants desperately to tell her everything — to describe the
Challenge and the Secret Chamber with its golden books and the
Tower Lab and the fossil evidence and the mysteries of his family's

history — and most of all, his encounter with Semjaza and the power of the Shepherd's Staff!

"There's a lot I can't tell you right now that I want to — I really want to, but I just can't. All I can say is that it just all hit me today when Hunahpu was talking to me. He told me about his own experience of meeting Christ. Did you know that my uncle Barry led him to the Lord?"

"Oh, no, I didn't know that," she answers in amazement, "that's so cool."

Jeff describes to her the way he was feeling when Hunahpu spoke, and the Spirit began working in his heart: "While he was telling it, I felt unsettled inside, really deeply — like I was feeling a gnawing somewhere deep inside me. Hunahpu explained what I was feeling; he said that *an unyielded heart is a prison with no door -- it has to be torn open* — he said it was a gift when God does it; it's the way he cleanses us.

"One of the things that really hit me was something that he said my uncle shared with him: *'Godly sorrow is the bridge on which God's mercy travels...'* he called it *'the thoroughfare of Grace.'*

Genie studies Jeff's eyes as he describes the experience, sensing the authenticity in his words and feeling a deep stirring in her own soul as he speaks.

"Hunahpu led me in a prayer." Jeff leans forward and stares into the distance as he recalls it, then looks intently into her eyes...

"Genie... when we prayed together, something happened inside me... it was something real, something powerful — I can't describe it, but it changed me... it really changed me! I could feel His presence — Jesus was right there, right beside us! It made me feel thrilled and ashamed at the same time — I felt so much joy and yet knew that I was so unworthy of it!

"Hunahpu just looked at me and seemed to know exactly what I was feeling — he described it perfectly, calling it the *trembling joy of first grace.* He explained how the grace I was feeling bid me draw nearer to God, but also made me more conscious of my soul's guilt. It's like a father embracing his prodigal son who has returned — the son feels guilty, but the father only feels love. I loved the way he put it; he said that,

> 'it is the blessed joy of a redeemed soul, when he first meets the Lord, to find that His unfathomable love is so great that it obscures even His infinite majesty.'"

"That's so beautiful," Eugenia comments quietly with a look of wonder, still searching his face.

"Yeah… it is," Jeff answers in a half-whisper, scanning her face and looking intently into her eyes.

They silently search each other's eyes for a long moment, then each looks down at their plates shyly. They both wonder whether there is more to what they feel than can be explained by the candle-light and intimate conversation alone.

Jeff nervously decides to change the subject, shifting to their current threat.

"How is the interrogation going?" he asks, clearing his throat. "What have we learned from Dylen?"

Genie looks momentarily startled as the subject changes, straightening in her chair.

"Oh… It's gone well… as well as expected. He kept goin' on about somethin' called the Confederacy."

Jeff's attention is piqued as he recalls Blandus mentioning that, too. "What did he say about it, exactly?"

"Just that they can't be stopped, and we're all goin' to die… the usual hysterics. He did say somethin' interestin' about that hidden encrypted file on his laptop — the one containin' the ancient manuscript. He said it was intended for *Koletis*. That's some kind of code word, apparently."

"Koletis," Jeff repeats, quickly searching for where he has heard that word before. "If I'm right, that's an Estonian word; it means something like *the Monster* or *The Beast*. He thinks for a minute, "You said your parents' mission was in Estonia; did you ever hear why they were there?"

"No, I... wait... do you speak Estonian?" she asks in surprise.

"Only a little," he admits. "I stayed in Helsinki one summer, back in college, and met a friend there who was from Estonia; it's right on the Gulf of Finland, across from there," he explains, acting as if there was nothing the slightest bit unusual about it.

Genie shakes her head, deciding not to ask what he was doing in Finland or how he learned Estonian in one summer — that would be an interesting conversation for another time. "Do you think there's a connection?" she asks instead.

"It's certainly an interesting coincidence," Jeff notes.

"That mission was part of an old campaign," she recounts. "It went dark after the entire mission team was killed; all of 'em died in supposed accidents, as I recall — it was long before my time with the company, of course. I've always wanted to reopen that case — looks like it's time."

THEY HAVE BARELY TOUCHED their salads when Isabel arrives with the main course; she lifts the silver covers from their dishes to show them her remarkably prepared Double Chateaubriand with potato and spinach soufflés.

"These will be right here when you're ready for them," she says, unperturbed. "Can I get you anything... more water?" She refills their glasses as both of them nod gratefully and begin with their salads in earnest.

Their conversation is more casual as they shift focus to the amazing meal. Jeff shares some pointers of his own on gourmet cooking, and Genie explains the finer points of rendering an opponent unconscious with a well-placed karate chop. They are smiling and laughing, having pretty nearly the best meal of their lives, and, of course, the food is also delicious.

They have just tasted Isabel's chocolate mousse when Jeff's O-P chimes; he lays it on the table between them and answers the call from EB.

"Hello, my dear," EB says to Genie as he sees her, "I trust the two o' you've had a good meal?"

"Isabel prepared the most fantastic Chateaubriand, and I've never had a potato and spinach soufflé before… it was amazin'!" she raves, looking at Jeff with a smile as he agrees.

"It sounds extraordinary!" EB acknowledges. "Is that the flicker o'candlelight I'm detectin'?" he teases with a twinkle in his eye.

"Ah *Shan'er,* quit bein' such'a wee wean," she scolds him with an embarrassed blush.

EB lets out a hearty laugh, then recovers his focus and grows more serious. "I think the two o' you had better come t'the office right away; there's somethin' you'll want t'see."

⌘

15

A NEW POWER

"Terribly sorry to interrupt your dinner," EB apologizes, greeting Eugenia and Jeff as they enter the office dressed in their dinner clothes.

"We were just finished," both of them respond simultaneously, nodding to each other in agreement.

"What is it you wanted us to see?" Jeff looks back and forth between EB and Hunahpu, searching their faces.

The men glance at each other briefly, then EB points to the large display screen on the wall just behind him as Hunahpu taps a few keys. The screen fills with a camera feed from a point in Earth's orbit, showing a clear image of a satellite with its spread solar array.

"This footage was taken fifteen minutes ago from the ship that Bear launched this mornin' carrying the energy shield," EB explains.

In the distance, a sudden flash of light catches their eye, drawing their attention to the translucent outline of an Eljo ship as it fires a missile. They watch the missile's fiery tail speed closer to the satellite until it suddenly explodes in a bright flash, about 100 meters short of its target.

"Looks like the shield worked," Jeff observes gratefully. "Did we sustain any damage?"

"None at all," EB confirms. "That's the beauty of Bear's design; it absorbs the energy thrown at it and recycles it into the shield. The more that's thrown at it, the stronger it gets."

As he speaks, they watch two more missiles being rebuffed the same way. Then, in a blinding barrage, they watch the ship unleash what appears to be its entire payload, leaving a massive debris field of shrapnel recoiling outward from the satellite.

"Well, that seems to be good news," Jeff notes. The video feed cuts back to a live image, and Jeff considers the scene for a moment — the enemy ship still hasn't moved. "Do you think we should order our crew to destroy the Eljo ship?"

"We were considering the same thing," EB explains, looking at Hunahpu, "but there's no way to be sure they've truly depleted their armaments."

"It could be a pretense to get us to lower the shield," Hunahpu observes.

"That's right; why else would they maintain position?" EB adds.

Jeff studies the enemy ship quietly for a moment. "They could be bluffing," he postulates, "...they must know that they'd be blasted the moment they turn to run."

———

As they debate the question, Eugenia stands watching the screen; she suddenly raises her arm, pointing at it with a perplexed expression. "Look!" she exclaims.

The others turn their attention to the live video feed as the cloaked enemy ship begins to draw closer, approaching until it has reached the very edge of the protective energy sphere. At that range, they can clearly see the pilots' helmets, which appear to stare at the Hastleworth crew behind their mirrored visors.

Jeff suddenly has an uneasy feeling. He recalls the first time he looked into an Eljo pilot's helmet — that had been an eerie feeling, but this is worse. This feels disturbingly similar to his encounter in the Secret Chamber... it's a feeling of foreboding darkness. The others have sensed it too.

"Father in Heaven, protect us..." he hears Hunahpu pray quietly.

What occurs next makes this even more ominous and unsettling. As they watch, the enemy pilots fall limp, dropping back against their headrests as if they have been rendered unconscious. A mysterious gray mist begins filling the enemy ship's cabin — Jeff is sure that the mist emanates from inside the pilots' spacesuits. He studies the scene with trepidation as the mist re-forms into separate and distinct clouds.

No sooner have the strange clouds formed than they morph again, this time oozing from the ship itself and re-forming in the vacuum of space. Swirling like a menacing storm, they soon breach the energy shield — passing through it as if it isn't there. Jeff and the others watch incredulously as the threatening clouds move past the satellite and approach the Hastleworth ship.

Hunahpu hits the comm button and speaks urgently to the crew: "Abandon your position! Do not allow those clouds to approach your ship! I repeat: abandon your position — pull back immediately!"

The radio crackles as the ship's captain responds; his voice sounds confused. "Please repeat... What clouds, Sir? The satellite is secure; there's nothing in front of us. I repeat, we don't see anything — instruments detect no activity."

As Hunahpu repeats his warning, Jeff suddenly feels something in his jacket. He guesses at first that his cell phone is vibrating, but as he is checking it, he feels the strange buzzing again... it isn't the phone... it is coming from his jacket's side pocket. He carefully reaches into it, expecting to find it empty, but instead pulls out the pea-sized object, marveling at it as it vibrates in his hand. He barely remembers dropping it there, but he recognizes it — it is one of the seeds from the Shepherd's Staff.

Now Berenger's voice can also be heard on the radio from CNAL

Mission Control — he is ordering the crew to pull back, but the ship has gone silent.

Jeff stares at the seed in the palm of his hand, which is now vibrating even more rapidly as the evil clouds draw nearer. He feels a growing dread but anxiously recalls how the Staff had saved him from a swirling mist just like this one — he begins to pray under his breath for God's help.

Oddly enough, what comes to mind in answer to his prayer are his uncle's test results — he is reminded of how the Shepherd's Staff reacted when the Ring or Scepter was in proximity — it had vibrated! He whispers the avatar's words to himself as their meaning suddenly strikes him: *any line of sight is all that's needed....*

Looking at the small seed in his hand, he struggles to understand. This is just a seed — could it really possess the power of the Staff it came from?

There is crackling from the radio, and they hear a desperate plea from the ship — the pilot is choking as he gasps... "C-Can't b-br-brea-eath!"

Something comes over Jeff suddenly — without another thought, he runs past the others, grasping the seed as he drives his fist into the screen and fixes his eyes on the ominous swirling clouds.

"PER... IMPERIUM CHRISTI, SANCTUS VIRGAM! (...In the power of Christ, through the Holy Staff!)," He shouts desperately....

The **blinding flash** that erupts from his fist surprises him, filling the room and then instantaneously blasting through the orbiting ship. Jeff watches the screen as the menacing clouds are shattered in an intense flash of light, leaving only a momentary trace of wispy fragments as they fade out of sight.

JEFF FEELS dizzy and collapses to his knees; he is physically and emotionally spent. If his eyes were open, he would have witnessed Hunahpu dropping to his knees and lifting his aged hands in grateful worship. Eugenia stands with her mouth agape, a wave of emotion and wonder flooding her — the stirring in her spirit immediately brings tears to her eyes, clouding her vision as they stream down her face. She staggers to the desk chair and half-collapses into it.

Jeff feels EB's hand on his shoulder as his older friend kneels behind him in grateful wonder.

They hear the recovering pilot's raspy voice on the radio moments later: "Wh-What just happened?! What w-was that?" There is a short pause, and then he continues, "...Whatever you did... it saved our lives... I thought we were done for... Dear God! Thank You... it saved us..!"

A cheer comes over the radio from Mission Control, and then Berenger's noticeably shaken voice is heard requesting a series of instrument checks and health reports from the crew. "Get a gravity beam on that Eljo ship," he instructs, "I want it dismantled for a full analysis."

GENIE WIPES her eyes and looks around the room at the other three, all kneeling on the floor. She is shaking slightly as she sits at the desk, but manages to bring up a series of telemetry feeds on the computer, scanning for any trace of suspicious energy signatures; every reading appears to indicate that the threat has been eliminated. No signs of life or activity can be detected in the Eljo ship.

She accesses the satellite next, using its sensors to scan the horizon — no other ships can be seen within range of its sensors, but they have seen Eljo jets cloak themselves from radar before.

She then examines the satellite's view of the Earth, looking for any sign of a cloaked attack. She is still studying it intently as EB helps Hunahpu to his feet.

"Scan for extra-spectral distortion," EB suggests, making his way to the desk to gaze over her shoulder. A wide sweep of most of the hemisphere detects nothing.

While they are busy scanning, two ships that Berenger had ordered into orbit the moment the Eljo attack began are just arriving.

One immediately sets about securing the Eljo ship while the other fighter docks with the energy shield's cruiser to check on its crew.

Hunahpu approaches Jeff, who is staring distractedly at the monitor screen.

"It's not wise to look them in the eyes...." Jeff suddenly repeats to himself mysteriously.

"I beg your pardon?" Hunahpu asks, not following Jeff's comment.

"That was what EB said the night he came for me," Jeff explains. He turns and looks at the three of them; "You knew what they were... You all knew — didn't you?" His words are not a question.

"We suspected," Hunahpu confesses. "We couldn't be sure without actually meeting one of them, which we had managed to avoid until now."

"That black mist...." Jeff says, glancing at EB and Eugenia uncertainly before looking back to Hunahpu. His great-grandfather's eyes warn him not to speak freely about his experience in the Secret Chamber. Jeff turns toward the monitor again and adds quietly, speaking in Quechua: "*Chaytaj tukuy ima Sumjazaqa pampa suyu (...that was the form that Semjaza had.)*"

Hunahpu brushes the beard on his chin thoughtfully between his thumb and forefinger, moving to a chair to sit down. It looks like he is not surprised by Jeff's information.

"What are they?" Jeff asks, turning to face everyone.

Genie sits quietly; she has no intention of answering. EB looks at Hunahpu with a slight nod, yielding the task to his much older friend.

"They are Eljo," Hunahpu answers.

"Yes, I know, but... *what* are they?" Jeff tries to clarify.

"The Eljo are an old enemy... very old indeed. They were once called the Elouid race — offspring of Giants, known as the Nephilim."

Jeff immediately recalls Arubija's account, and the hair on his arms and neck stands straight as he remembers them; *Nephilim giants* — they were the children of the dark lords. The Cronicis' description of Semjaza replays in Jeff's mind ...*chief among the lords!* He listens intently as Hunahpu continues.

"The book of Genesis records that these Nephilim were the spawn of fallen angels — they were giants who were half supernatural creature and half man."

Fallen angels... Jeff ponders, understanding that these are the *sons of god* that Arubija wrote about *...the dark lords ...Semjaza himself* was one of them!

"Their offspring, the Elouid," Hunahpu continues, "were supernatural beings themselves, but with human bodies. Various ancient writings credit them with enormous psychic abilities, allowing them to perform levitation, mind control, remote sight, and telekinesis."

Jeff can't help making the connection between these traits and those ascribed to the Ring and Scepter, not to mention his recent encounter with Semjaza himself. He rubs his throat distractedly at that memory and takes a deep breath.

"But how?" he questions, "how could they become ...what we saw tonight? Weren't they destroyed in the Flood?"

"Their bodies were, certainly," Hunahpu explains, "but it would appear that their supernatural half remains."

"As best we can determine," EB chimes in, "the Sons of Maranish must have learned a way of summoning them from whatever dark place they existed. They built those pressurized suits for them, like some kind of hideous army."

"Why didn't you tell me this before?" Jeff challenges.

"Would you have believed us?" Hunahpu wisely answers.

"SPEAKING OF UNBELIEVABLE," Genie says, suddenly interrupting as she taps a few keys and then points to the large monitor. "I skipped this back a few seconds. This was just recorded," she explains as she lets the others watch the delayed video stream without further elaboration.

The replay shows their boarding team onboard the Eljo ship, standing beside the motionless space suits of its Eljo crew. They have placed restraints on the captured crew members as a precaution, and the scene begins with them cautiously unlatching the pilot's helmet and slowly lifting it off. The team immediately gags and rushes to close their face shields as a horrible stench fills the enemy ship. The suit is neither empty nor automated, as they had supposed; looking down at the exposed pilot's face, they see a rotting corpse instead.

The crew bravely continues their examination, steeling themselves against the overwhelming instinct to flee the scene as quickly as possible. Eugenia and the others watch the results of bio-scans of the corpse on screen, listening as a member of the medical team in CNAL interprets the analysis.

"The subject is male," she reports, "bone structure indicates an adult, approximately mid-twenties." She pauses as she examines the telemetry more closely; "this is odd," she says, stopping to be sure she sees the data correctly, "the body is missing several vital organs… liver …pancreas …its heart is missing."

Jeff and Hunahpu exchange a glance; Jeff feels his stomach turn as he remembers the stories of the Maranish brothers' cruelty.

"How long ago did he die?" EB asks over the comm channel.

"It's hard to say without a full autopsy, Sir …those suits have been preserving them somewhat. From the degree of dehydration and decomposition, though, I'd say that this man has been dead for several years."

As she is speaking, one of the boarding crewmen suddenly collapses. The doctor immediately checks readings from the fallen crewman's biosensors: "Ensign Shawns has only fainted; he appears alright — it would be best to get him to fresh air as soon as possible."

The crew commander signals for two crewmen to take the Ensign back to their ship. "What should we do with the bodies?" he asks Mission Control.

There is a short pause as Berenger confers with the medical team and others, then issues orders.

"Leave the bodies where they are; we'll do a full evaluation on base. Meanwhile, the doctor would like a bio-scanner positioned overhead for ongoing analysis. Power down all the ship's systems and ensure that its engines and weapons are fully disabled."

"We're on it," the Captain confirms, signaling his team to search the ship for the central system overrides.

Berenger pauses and then adds... "We still don't know what reanimated those things ...make certain their restraints are secure."

JEFF STANDS LISTENING, then turns to look at the others; he signals Eugenia to mute the line. "Who else knows the truth about the Eljo? I take it Berenger doesn't?"

"It was felt that the fewer who knew, the better," EB explains, "... the lack of hard evidence before now has made it seem rather incredible, to say the least. Aside from Barry, ...and, of course, Gretchen, their true form has been known only to those in this room," he explains.

"I have a feeling that even with the hard evidence, it will still seem incredible," Jeff says candidly. He turns back to the monitor again, quietly thinking. "Do you think they're gone — those two?"

"What does your heart tell you?" Hunahpu asks in a tone that sounds more like a coach's suggestion than a question.

Jeff looks down silently into his open hand at where the seed had been — the seed that had transformed into that flash of light and vanished. "They won't be back," he quietly confirms, echoing the mysterious confirmation he feels deep inside.

⌘

16

WATERY GRAVE

Jeff silences his alarm, quickly deciding to skip breakfast for a few more minutes of sleep.

"ABBI, wake me in thirty minutes," he requests, half asleep.

It seems like no time has passed when ABBI's voice greets him again.

"Your training in the gym begins in fifteen minutes."

Jeff stumbles from bed to splash water on his face, plunging his whole head under the faucet of cold running water. Five minutes later, he is running downstairs in his gym clothes. He pauses at the kitchen counter to accept Isabel's thermos of coffee. Hunahpu and EB are seated at the table discussing the previous night.

"Running late," Jeff explains with a thumb pointed over his shoulder. He grabs a steaming muffin from the counter and heads out the door.

GENIE IS MOVING a little slower than usual herself, although that just means she has opted for traditional push-ups rather than the handstand version. She seems willing to overlook Jeff's being a few minutes late. She is all business, however, when it comes to the day's training.

She tosses Jeff a Dragon Pole. "You remember th' *luk dim boon Gwan*," she says, naming it as she lifts her's above her head and spins it like a propeller blade.

Jeff rubs the bruise on his forehead as he nods, wincing slightly as he touches it. Genie tosses him a padded sparring helmet as she puts one on herself.

"We'll take it a bit slower this time…" she begins, making sure he is carefully following along.

By the end of the hour, Jeff has nearly mastered several blocking and ducking maneuvers, but has a long way to go in mastering anything like Genie's airborne helicopter attack. He accidentally jabs her hard in the ribs with one of his awkward attempts, knocking her across the mat.

This time it is Genie who is wounded.

"I guess we're even now," she winces painfully as they end their workout. Jeff thinks of all the bruising he's received over the past month-and-a-half and is inclined to disagree with her about that — they're definitely not even. He keeps the thought to himself as he rushes to help her up.

She is still wincing and holding her side as he walks her back to her suite, where a nurse from the Infirmary is waiting to look at her injury. Despite her obvious discomfort, Genie smiles as she says goodbye to him at her apartment door, giving his hand a gentle squeeze.

CORPORAL TANNER IS in the launch hangar with a ship already prepped and waiting when Jeff arrives for the day's pilot training.

"I thought I'd save time on the preflight check by doing it ahead of time," Tanner explains. "It seems we're always running out of time."

Jeff sees the hangar doors already opening and nods to him with a smile as the ship begins to nudge toward it. Moments later, they are dropped into the water, and Jeff submerges, heading for the underwater exit.

"We all heard about what happened last night. " I just wanted to say thanks for what you did," Tanner says sincerely, "... stopping the attack, I mean." Everybody's still talking about it — the whole thing was so amazing! What *were* those things?"

Jeff flinches, uncomfortable, unsure how to respond.

"I guess word travels fast around here. It's God who deserves the thanks for that," he confesses humbly. "I can't claim any of the credit."

"Well, whether you claim it or not, it's the third time you've done something to save our necks since you got here, the way we count it," Tanner emphasizes. "The troops are all behind you; all of us are counting it a privilege to serve under you, Sir."

Jeff accepts Tanner's comment with a thankful nod, but inside, he feels deeply conflicted. He doesn't feel he deserves any credit for the outcomes of the recent attacks, much less anyone's loyalty. Eugenia, EB, Berenger, and Brandish deserved the real credit, not to mention Hunahpu's invaluable guidance.

"It's been a pretty wild ride since I got here, that's for sure," he finally concedes. "There are a lot of others who deserve the credit more than I do — God most especially."

"Yes, Sir," Tanner accepts.

"So where are we off to?" Jeff asks, hoping to change the subject. They have just emerged from the undersea access tunnel, and Jeff levels off, bringing the ship to a stop in the open ocean.

"Thought we'd do some underwater maneuvers today," Tanner explains. "We'll start with a bottom landing; just take her down slowly."

"How deep is the bottom here?" Jeff asks as he directs the ship downward.

"The terrain here levels off at around three hundred meters,"

Tanner explains, "there's a ledge out a bit further that drops off to a thousand meters or so."

Jeff recalls that the excavation site where his uncle discovered the T-Rex skulls was on the ledge not far away. He directs the ship toward the general direction he remembers from his earlier visit to the site and, almost purely by chance, comes across one of the stone markers.

As their ship's lights illuminate the nearby seafloor, Jeff's eye falls on a sight that startles him. There in the silt just beyond the excavation marker are the shattered remains of several Borgia super suits. A few of the suits' limbs are missing, and the helmets are smashed, but Jeff can see that the remains of the suit's occupants are still inside.

Jeff can immediately rule out any Eljo presence in the area, a skill that surprises him. He somehow knows with unquestionable certainty that this discovery poses no threat; at least, not a supernatural one, anyway.

"These must be the pilots from last month's anti-gravity attack. Can we record this and transmit the location?" he asks Tanner.

"Yes, sir," Tanner acknowledges. He flicks a few switches, causing the scene to appear on one of the ship's screens, then zooms in on the remains and snaps several shots, tagging each of them with the ship's exact coordinates.

"Send it to Brandish," Jeff instructs, "we'll need to send down a cleanup crew."

Tanner agrees and quickly sends off the images via an encrypted transmission.

The discovery gives Jeff a sudden idea.

"The ledge is not far from here?" he asks.

"Just a few hundred meters ahead," Tanner confirms. Jeff accelerates forward, watching the sea floor carefully as the ship's lights illuminate it.

"There!" he says as he points out the sight of a wing section lying in the silt, not far from the edge of the ledge. He studies its image on screen; it appears to be from the enemy bomber. Jeff continues past the edge with redoubled determination, seeing the deep expanse grow black beneath them as they enter the deeper water. He swings the ship around, shining its lights on the undersea cliff's edge, then dives downward, following the rock wall into the depths.

The lower they dive, the darker it becomes. Huge piles of boulders and rocky debris litter the steep slopes as they follow them deeper until the terrain begins to level off. They can see only what is within the range of their lights, which reach only a dozen meters in each direction.

"How do we increase the scan range?" he asks, recalling that the ships are equipped with long-range scanners.

Tanner flicks a few switches, and an image is projected across the inside of the ship's windshield, providing a computer-enhanced view of the terrain in front of them. Jeff stares in stunned silence as he takes in the sight — it's breathtaking.

Although essentially colorless, the scene extends far into the distance, revealing every rock and feature of the mysterious depths. The computer suddenly highlights several odd shapes on the distant sea floor, tagging them with labels.

"Bingo," Jeff says as he sits looking at the wreckage from the large aircraft. It appears to be part of the bomber's underside. Its wrecked landing gear is visible as it sits upside down on the sandy bottom; parts of its uni-wing structure remain, though its tail section and most of the fuselage are missing — apparently blown off by the explosions that destroyed it. Of greatest interest to Jeff, however, is the dome-shaped appendage attached to its underside.

"The anti-gravity weapon…." Jeff concludes aloud as he realizes what he is looking at. "It looks intact!"

Jeff hits his radio uplink, speaking into his headset…

"…ABBI, get me Brandish, it's urgent."

A moment later, Brandish appears on the ship's dashboard monitor.

"Is everything alright?" he asks with concern as he sees Jeff's face on his screen.

"Yes, we're fine," Jeff assures him. "We've located the missing bomber — it looks like its anti-gravity weapon array is intact. You should have a look at it."

Brandish studies his computer screen, reviewing the video feed and telemetry streaming from Jeff's ship.

"The flight recorder from that plane was recovered close to shore in the tail section," Brandish explains. "It looks like these sections are in much deeper water — that explains why we couldn't locate them. We'll dispatch a salvage crew immediately!

"Nice work, gentlemen."

⌘

17

URGENT SEARCH

ack at his suite a little over an hour later, Jeff brings Hunahpu and EB up to speed on his discovery. A diving team has already begun collecting the wreckage.

"What's the latest from Dylen's email?" Jeff asks with serious interest.

"CHET has managed to hide Dylen's absence quite well. They don't appear to suspect it just yet," EB shares. "They seem to be distracted by last night's events. There is quite an uproar over the loss of their spacecraft. They are not aware of the fate of their Eljo pilots, as best we can tell."

"Do you think they'll accelerate their attack plans?" Jeff worries.

"I expect just the opposite," Hunahpu posits. "Until they can understand what happened to their ship, they will call off the attack."

"Aye. It's bought us some time. Let's hope it's enough," EB agrees. "They're expectin' a report from Dylen as soon as possible. I've instructed CHET to invent somethin' that'll throw 'em off track a bit."

EB is scanning his O-P while he speaks, to see what CHET has come up with. He brings it up on the large screen.

HASTLEWORTH TOP-SECRET TELEMETRY REPORT:

AN ATTACK ON ONE OF OUR SATELLITES WAS REPELLED AT 2100 HOURS. THE UNIDENTIFIED SPACECRAFT IS ASSUMED TO BE OF BORGIA ORIGIN. THE ENEMY SHIP EXPERIENCED A WEAPONS MALFUNCTION....

The rest of the report is filled with detailed technical analysis and telemetry data showing that the ship suffered a *catastrophic depressurization.* In other words, it exploded.

"Well, that should give 'em somethin' t' look into," EB says approvingly.

AFTER LUNCH, Jeff excuses himself, intending to head to the office suite. As worrisome as the Borgia's impending attack may be, his mind is even more distracted with thoughts of his Quest, struggling with how he'll ever fulfill it by destroying the Ring and Scepter if he can't even locate them!

Just as he walks past the front door of his uncle Barry's empty suite, he suddenly stops and stares at it. Somewhere inside that suite is the hidden entrance to his uncle's secret vault... he feels sure of it. Hunahpu had practically admitted as much when Jeff found him inside it with EB and Eugenia just after Dylen's interrogation.

On a whim, Jeff stops and places his hand on the door's access panel.

"Welcome, Mr. Sutherland," ABBI announces as the computer welcomes him, causing the door to click open.

He slowly makes his way down the main hall as the lights switch on, finally coming to his uncle's private office.

"Now, where would I hide an access code if I were you...." he whispers under his breath as he begins to search the room.

He starts with the desk, carefully searching each well-organized drawer. His uncle had certainly been meticulous — whatever disorder might be evident, Jeff assumes it is due to EB and Eugenia's searching. Like them, however, he isn't able to locate anything that appears to hint at the secret vault's location or access code.

He boots the computer and tries searching that one as well, soon finding that it appears to be synchronized with the computers in the main office suite and his own home office, making the folders and documents familiar. He concludes that the answer does not lie there either.

"CHET..." he says, pulling the O-P from his pocket, "did Uncle Barrymore leave any other hidden files or messages for me anywhere?"

"Can you be more specific?" CHET answers a bit evasively.

His answer makes Jeff suspicious, as if hinting that there could be any number of hidden messages from his uncle that he hasn't yet discovered.

Jeff decides to be direct with CHET, admitting to the avatar what he was looking for: "I'm trying to find the access code for my uncle's secret vault."

"I am unable to assist you with that, I'm afraid."

CHET's answer leaves Jeff guessing whether the avatar is unaware of the answer or has been instructed not to reveal it.

Jeff thinks for a minute and poses the question differently: "Did Uncle Barry have a place where he kept sensitive documents or valuables anywhere in his suite? A place where he kept things for protection?"

"Ah," CHET intones, "The means for conveying such secrets has already been shown to you."

Jeff's brow wrinkles... "Do you mean in Lab Turrim — and ...my suite?"

"Your uncle spent many years preparing for your arrival. Each message he meant for you was left where you will most likely find it."

CHET's words seem striking. It stands to reason that the suite his uncle built for him would be the most likely place to find such a message; he has to agree. But what if Barry didn't know how the Shepherd's Staff would react to him? The unusual growth of leaves and the Staff's recent demonstrations of power were surprises even to Hunahpu. Barry wanted to keep Jeff from finding the Ring and Scepter to protect him from them; maybe that's no longer a valid concern.

Jeff gets up from the desk chair and closes the O-P, dropping it back into his pocket as he restlessly walks to the open doorway at the back of the large office. The adjacent room contains his uncle's collection of rare fossils, painstakingly organized into sections that denote their scientific groupings. He remembers how God used his uncle's exhaustive research to help open his eyes to truths that he could never have been convinced of otherwise. He breathes a prayer of thanks as he considers it, sighing as he gives the room of fossil specimens a last look for the time being before turning to leave.

As he turns toward his uncle's office again, its amazing symmetry comes into focus. He notes that, like the library, it is circular, with sections of bookcases arranged most of the way around, wrapping around the office entry and spanning the entire wall in front of the large desk. At one end of the large room, the bookcases encircle a sitting area with a leather couch and armchairs that invite a visit with a good book for a long, comfortable day of reading. He wishes that he had that luxury right now. He then notices that each bookcase section has a small brass plate attached to it, engraved with a name.

Daniel, Isaiah, Ezekiel, Amos, Joel, Hosea, and several others.

Jeff recognizes the names from his Bible, understanding that they are all Old Testament prophets. A cursory scan of the shelves reveals an impressive collection of study texts and commentaries, all organized according to each prophetic book. It doesn't surprise Jeff that his uncle's books are meticulously organized.

He looks back to the large desk and imagines his uncle sitting at it, writing a letter or studying one of his fossil specimens. He so wishes that he could have met the amazing man in person just once. After staring for a long moment, he finally stirs himself, then quickly walks out, switching off the lights.

THE CLUES SEEM to keep leading him back to his own suite and the Tower Lab, frustrating him; he is feeling increasingly that he needs to study the Ring and Scepter himself if he is ever going to destroy them.

Lost in thought for the rest of the day, he barely talks during dinner. His silence draws the notice of Hunahpu and EB as they sit together.

"Your discovery of those weapon arrays was excellent work," EB congratulates him, trying to engage Jeff in conversation.

Jeff simply nods. It is evident that he is barely listening.

EB and Hunahpu look at each other, sharing the conclusion that their young protégé is wrestling with a considerable problem that has consumed his full attention. They don't have to ask what it is, assuming immediately that it involves his Challenge.

MEANWHILE, Jeff is replaying a conversation with the Tower's avatar from a few days earlier… it was in their discussion about the Ring and Scepter…

"…why is it impossible to destroy them?" Jeff remembers asking.

"It would appear that their origin is not of this earth," the avatar had answered mysteriously.

"Not of this earth?" Jeff recalls repeating, *"...you mean, they're alien — from another planet?"*

"Not another planet... another dimension," the avatar corrected.

Jeff remembers studying the results of his uncle's analysis of the objects. Heat, cold, radiation, wavelengths of light and sound, all known gases... even blunt impacts had no effect whatsoever ...no chemical agent could produce any effect at all.

"It's like they weren't even there," Jeff mumbles to himself.

"I beg your pardon?" EB asks, but Jeff offers no response, apparently unaware of the question or even that he has been heard mumbling.

Jeff is thoroughly preoccupied, reliving the feeling of despair that had come over him as he reviewed the Lab's extraordinary analysis. The conclusion that he had reached at the time silently reverberates again in his mind: *Even a hydrogen bomb couldn't touch these things!*

Jeff's thoughts finally come to the avatar's comment that the Shepherd's Staff could share the same mysterious origin. More importantly, that origin may have something to do with the Staff's connection with his family:

" *It's like the Staff has been keyed to recognize our family,"* he recalls observing.

"More precisely, a specific member," the avatar replied... *"There can be only one."*

⌘

18

SAFEGUARDED

For the next several days, Jeff splits his afternoons between working in the office and visiting the Secret Chamber. It takes him a day to clean up the broken glass and remnants of the Staff's amazing seeds. Once they are safely retrieved, he begins using the time to look for information on the Ring and Scepter — searching the golden volumes endlessly. He works his way through all of the books that the incredible Chamber offers to him, but is disappointed at how little is written about the ancient artifacts. He recalls that they are mentioned in Thaliard's *Liberatricem*, but still refuses to open that book again. It makes him shudder to remember the encounter with Semjaza that he experienced the last time he opened it.

It bothers him that in all his studies, he is still unable to reconstruct an account of Arubija's dealings with the Ring. Jeff can't help sensing that it had been the Ring's spell that initially held Arubija captive to Semjaza's will. Why else, Jeff reasons, would he have spent all those years in the dark lord's service? However, he hasn't found any indication that Arubija understood this or realized the ring's power. If that was true, then it begged the question of how he was able to break free of it. It seems increasingly certain that something freed him from Semjaza's control; it must have happened years before the flood.

Jeff suddenly remembers something the avatar said when introducing the objects: *Arubija was able to resist their power at least once....*

As he considers that, words from the book of *Gwrthryfel Mawr* — '*the Great Rebellion,*' come to mind; he remembers wondering about them at the time. It said the Ring's power could not compel '...one *who God protects.'* He wonders if that had been how Arubija escaped the Ring's spell.

SEVEN WEEKS HAVE PASSED since his Challenge began, and his search still seems fruitless; this is beginning to look like a mystery that he will never be able to solve. Glancing at the clock, he realizes the late hour — he is feeling exhausted from the stress of the impending deadline for his quest and finally decides to head upstairs to his room.

As he passes Hunahpu's partially open door, he sees the light on and knocks.

"Allin tuta awkiy ...*good evening, Grandfather,*" he says as he accepts an invitation to enter. The old man has been reading; he stops and waits for Jeff to speak, sensing that something is troubling him.

"How many of the Chamber's books have you studied?" Jeff asks him, wondering whether the wise old man can help him with his latest problem.

Hunahpu removes his reading glasses and lays them on the table. "Not all, but a great many," he answers curiously.

"The Shepherd that Arubija met... was that Christ?"

Hunahpu thinks for a moment. "The Bible mentions a number of events in ancient times where Christ is believed to have appeared to men long before his incarnation in Bethlehem... scholars call them *Theophanies.* Abraham is thought to have met him, as well as Jacob and Moses; Joshua met him at Jericho, and three Israelites encountered

Him in a fiery furnace in Babylon." He looks at Jeff as he considers it, "It would stand to reason that Noah may have been visited by Him as well... then why not Arubija?"

"Could Arubija have first encountered Him earlier — before the flood... I mean, like years before?"

Hunahpu considers the question... "What makes you ask?"

"Well, it's just that Semjaza's power over him — the Ring's spell — was apparently broken. That must be how he left the dark lord's employ and moved to Atlan Plaen," Jeff explains.

"I see," Hunahpu accepts thoughtfully, "you feel the Ring kept him in Semjaza's service. What makes you think Semjaza didn't simply allow him to go?"

"Does that sound like Semjaza to you?" Jeff challenges.

Hunahpu considers the question, rubbing his chin thoughtfully. "It is a compelling theory, I must admit... but the Cronicis makes no mention of another meeting," Hunahpu points out.

"I know..." Jeff admits, "I was hoping you might have come across something in one of the other books."

"I'm sorry, no," Hunahpu says sadly.

Jeff thinks for a minute... "Our version of The Cronicis says it was translated in 331 AD; who would the translators have been at that time?"

Hunahpu looks at him as the realization dawns; "It would have been the Dyfarniad Scribes — Thaliard's scribes. You may have a point, my son," he says in admission. "Perhaps we had better consult the earlier scrolls."

"Do they still exist... what condition are they in?" Jeff asks in surprise.

"There is only one way to find out," Hunahpu answers. He stands and wraps his robe around his pajamas; "come," he says as he heads through the door.

TEN MINUTES LATER, they are standing in the Secret Chamber, staring again at the golden volumes and the amazing message that has been etched across them by God's own hand.

"The question is: where to begin," Hunahpu says thoughtfully.

"It would have happened around the time that he met *Eirian*...his wife," Jeff offers, "something must have happened — whatever it was changed the whole story."

"Yes, you're right," Hunahpu agrees as he accepts the golden time-piece from Jeff's hand. He looks upward to the row of sealed glass cases at the top of the bookcase, then speaks softly to the timepiece: "Diarium Arubija."

The bookstand moves to the center as the mechanized bookcase selects and gently lowers one of the sealed glass cases containing an extremely ancient scroll and slowly lays it down.

"The case contains inert argon gas and a precise degree of humidi-ty," Hunahpu explains, "It should be in exactly the condition it was in when it was sealed... however, that was only two hundred years ago. I can't speak for its care before that."

HUNAHPU CAREFULLY LIFTS the large sealed tube and carries it to the other side of the room, approaching a long table with a glass-covered surface that is slanted upward; it is at least twenty feet long. He posi-tions the scroll's tube just above a similarly sized tube attached to one end of the tabletop, connecting it there.

As soon as it is locked in place, the adjoining ends of the tubes open with a swish of equalizing pressure, and the scroll slides down to the table, still protected from the room's air. Once in position, one end of the scroll is gently pulled across the table, unrolling it beneath its glass top. It unfurls slowly, taking a long time before it finally reveals the entirety of the ancient scroll's contents underneath the glass.

It is written in an unrecognizable, densely packed script. Jeff pulls his card-sized O-P from his pocket, requests text translation, and then lays it on the glass table. They watch as it expands taller until it has covered the scroll's full height. Using the O-P's tall-thin form as a scanner, Jeff draws it across the entire length of the unfurled scroll, capturing its contents.

Once it has been fully captured, Jeff reverts the O-P screen to its normal size. They can see that the text has already been translated — it is densely packed but easily readable.

"Find 'Eirian,'" Jeff instructs.

The O-P instantly searches the text and then jumps to a point about a third of the way through, stopping to highlight Eirian's name. Jeff leans closer and examines the writing; even in the O-P's English facsimile, he can make out differences in the stroke and thickness of the letters that allow him to locate the start of Arubija's entry there in his diary. It begins a few lines before Eirian's name.

> *Semjaza's cruelty and oppression weary me. For twenty-eight years, I have labored in his service, and though I have earned wealth at his hand, it is with a terrible vexation of my soul. Today I met the fairest flower of beauty I have ever seen — Eirian was her name. In her meeting, I was made to know the error of my service and am determined on the morrow to resign from Samjaza's work.*

The following entry is written with heavy strokes, as if in anger; it appears to be several days later.

> *My intent to resign has unleashed in Semjaza a greater fury than I have known. His evil ring glowed more brightly when he raised his scepter, but he became enraged when it failed to coerce or slay me. He spoke of Eirian with threats to give her as a wife to Garbhach, his cruel Nephilim son, if I*

*would not continue to serve him. I would surely rather die
than continue in his service, but fear greatly for Eirian's fate.*

Jeff and Hunahpu look at each other curiously, wondering what caused Arubija's apparent sudden immunity to the Ring's control. The difference in his next entry is distinct; the handwriting appears calm, with confident strokes.

*The next morn, I departed early to warn Eirian of
Semjaza's threat. There, I met her father, Aiwyn, a man well
advanced in years. Upon hearing the news, he rent his robe
and fell upon his knees as he prayed to Yahway. His prayer
stirred within me the remembrance of my father and
Methuselah with their worship, causing me to bow with him
as tears filled my eyes.*

*He led me to an altar of stone, where he sacrificed a lamb
from his small flock, one without blemish. We humbly cried out
for Yahway's help and mercy, continuing there all day.*

*"We must trust in Yahway for deliverance!" Aiwyn encour-
aged as I arose to depart.*

*The hour was already late, and the road was dark. When
I had walked a great distance under the moon's light, I was
joined suddenly by a stranger who walked alongside me on the
way. He was a large man and strong — I could see in the
moonlight that he held a large staff in his hand and wore no
sandals on his feet. He spoke kindly to me, yet his words were
astonishing, and my heart burned within me as we walked
together.*

*"Yahway has heard your prayer," he said to me as we
walked together. "He has looked kindly upon your distress. Be*

assured, you will see deliverance from Semjaza's hand on this very night."

After a while, we came to a split in the road, and he began to depart from me.

"What is your name?" I implored him.

"One who is," he replied, bowing his head with a friendly nod as he departed.

Upon my return to the city, I saw a great commotion and asked those who stood nearby what was the cause of it.

"Garbhach has been slain in battle. Semjaza's fury is greatly kindled... he is sending a full legion of warriors to avenge his son's life."

I watched the dark lord's troops assemble in a vast company as they prepared to depart for battle. Then Sardaar, Semjaza's trusted Regent, saw me arrive and summoned me.

"Your skills are required at once," he insisted, "Samjaza seeks a powerful new weapon to crush his enemies."

He motioned to a battalion of fearsome Nephilim soldiers, calling them near. "Clear a way for the Tinker! He must go to the palace at once!"

The formidable squad immediately surrounded me and began to push their way through the dense crowd, ruthlessly striking down or tossing aside everyone in their way until they had deposited me at the door of Semjaza's palace. I looked up toward the palace ramparts to see Semjaza staring down at me with an angry scowl.

As I walked the great hall toward my workshop, Semjaza himself stood before me. His face appeared cold and hard; he *spoke in a low voice so as not to be overheard. The disdain in his heart was unconcealed.*

"His hand is upon you — I fail to see what value He finds in you; nonetheless, I cannot compel or harm you when under His protection. Therefore, I will make you a pledge — construct this final munition for me, and I'll release you to go where you will."

"What about Eirian and her father?" I challenged.

"They will not be harmed," he said with bitterness. "Betray me, and they will surely feel my wrath!"

Jeff looks up at Hunahpu as they both realize what protected Arubija. "It was an act of God," Jeff says in dismay, "how do you replicate that?"

Hunahpu grows silent and steps backward to take a seat; he thinks of Lydia's fate and the fates of Jeff's parents, who had not been spared, as he quietly answers: "He is sovereign... we cannot compel Him." Then a thought occurs to him, and he looks at the message written across the golden books' volumes.

Behold... My strength is made perfect in weakness....

"It would appear..." he says as he stares at it, "...that He has already made His choice."

Jeff understands his great-grandfather's meaning — he is the one who God has chosen to protect; he can still recall the jolt of the Staff's power as it flowed through him, now on two separate occasions. *"His strength..."* he repeats to himself, *"...His protection."*

⌘

19

ELUSIVE QUEST

J eff groans at the sound of ABBI's wake-up call. He and Hunahpu hadn't arrived home from the Secret Chamber until nearly two o'clock in the morning. He swings his feet to the floor and rubs his tired eyes with a wide yawn, staggering to the bathroom to splash some water onto his face. It takes every ounce of his willpower to begin getting ready, finally finding a spark of motivation as he remembers his morning workout with Genie.

As usual, Hunahpu is waiting at the table when Jeff reaches the kitchen; he wonders briefly whether the old man ever actually sleeps. Jeff lifts his coffee mug endearingly with both hands and breathes in its aroma, then takes a long sip, savoring the rich, dark flavor. Isabel is standing beside him with the coffee pot to refill his cup the moment he puts it down.

"I can see you were up late last night again," she observes, sounding for a moment like a disapproving mother. "It's certainly none of my business, I know," she quickly adds, "but you can't continue burning both ends of the candle — it will catch up with you soon enough."

"The coffee is excellent this morning," he compliments, winking in an admission that she's right as usual. Isabel smiles as she shakes her head dismissively and turns to retrieve their breakfast.

Once Isabel is out of earshot, Jeff lowers his voice and leans closer to Hunahpu. "About last night… I was thinking about it, and it makes sense — God's protection, I mean."

He pauses for a moment as he looks at his great-grandfather, tempted to reveal to him the mission of his Quest; he wants to confide in him that he *…has to…* destroy the Ring and Scepter. It isn't just a concern for keeping them out of enemy hands — it is his Quest!

While he considers it, however, the memory of the avatar's caution rushes to mind: *"these facts … must never be revealed beyond these walls."* He sits back in his chair again, struggling with his inner conflict.

"God will protect as He ordains," Hunahpu suggests, reading Jeff's face. "We must not presume upon His grace; He is a sovereign God — we must never forget this truth."

Jeff lowers his gaze as he humbly agrees. He looks up again a moment later as another thought strikes him.

"We're also supposed to trust Him, aren't we? I mean… if He asks us to do something… then we should trust that He'll help us do it, right?"

Hunahpu nods encouragingly. "He is, indeed, trustworthy," he agrees. "If the entire world should betray us, or we Him, He will remain faithful. His is a reckless mercy, given without our merit or deserving."

The poignancy of Hunahpu's answer resonates in Jeff's spirit — the words *"reckless mercy"* convey such a profound picture of **unconditional love** … it seems the perfect description of God's heart as Jeff has begun to understand it.

Isabel arrives with their plates, overhearing the last comment. "I can surely say Amen to that, praise the dear Lord's name!"

Jeff nods in agreement and takes a bite, complimenting her cooking with a satisfied moan of approval.

"I'm glad you like it," she says with a flattered smile as she walks away.

Jeff sits eating for a few minutes, then looks at Hunahpu again and lays down his fork. "Given all that's happened, I think it's time that you told me how to find Uncle Barry's secret vault."

His comment seems like a sudden change of subject to Hunahpu, who is caught off guard by it.

"What makes you believe that I know where it is?"

"I know that Dylen revealed its location to Eugenia, Zo, and Berenger during his interrogation," Jeff reveals. "I'm guessing they must have shared it with you and EB."

Hunahpu does not deny the claim but avoids confirming it either.

"When we have learned how to destroy them, then we will be ready to face their power," Hunahpu says quietly. "Nevertheless, the access code is still unknown. The vault's location is meaningless without it."

Jeff has to admit that his great-grandfather is right, yet there has to be a way — his Quest depends on it!

GENIE IS DOING her morning warm-ups when Jeff arrives at the gym. She is using one of the stationary cycles as he enters, making the speed of its spinning wheel resemble an airplane's turboprop. Jeff is pretty sure that if it were a propeller, she'd be airborne.

She slows to a more reasonable pace as she notices him, switching the bike's workout computer to cool-down mode. Jeff tosses her a towel, which she uses to wipe her face as she slows her pace for another thirty seconds. Climbing off, she immediately starts a set of deep knee bends and then sits on the mat doing extended leg stretches. Finally standing again, she begins running in place. She points to his feet and waves for him to follow, insisting that he join her; then she takes off running along the track painted onto the floor, around the perimeter of the large gym.

He can easily keep pace with her steady jog.

"How's your rib feeling today?" Jeff asks as he comes alongside her.

"Not too bad — it only hurts when I breathe," she jokes, making light of the fact that the comment is actually true. "It's gettin' better."

She stops after one lap and places her hands on her knees, gently rubbing her bruised rib.

"To be honest, the thing I miss th' most is bein' able t' punch." She nods her head toward the punching bags beside them.

"Funny," Jeff chimes in, "I was just thinking that's something that I don't miss at all."

A split second later, he feels a jab in his ribcage as she lands a lightning strike punch. When he shoots a glance at her, she is innocently standing with her hands on her knees as if nothing has happened; the expression on her face is playful but signals that he'd better watch it. She smiles as he winces and rubs his side.

"I feel better now," she jokes.

Jeff can't be angry with her... or hit her back, as much as he considers it. He just shakes his head and smiles at the joke.

She dries off with her towel as she walks with him to the weapons rack and tosses him a fencing foil. Its thin, flexible blade and rounded tip seem much safer than the Dragon Poll.

Her lesson progresses quickly from simple footwork and parrying to more complex counter-parry and contra-parry maneuvers.

Jeff soon assumes the stance she has taught him and points his sword toward her: "En Garde," he challenges authoritatively.

The next thing he knows, his sword is flying out of his hand, leaving him rubbing his smacked wrist.

"This is th' *prise de fer* ("taking of the blade") usin' a circular contra-parry," she explains. "The key is in th' speed and precision o' th' strike."

After an hour of repeated sword retrievals, Jeff feels like he is just beginning to get the hang of it.

THEY WALK TOGETHER in the hall afterward, catching up on small talk.

"I've been thinking about the secret vault," Jeff reveals, raising the topic carefully. "What did Dylen say about its security, exactly?"

Genie looks at him with a deadly serious expression: "I still can't tell you where i'tis, if that's what you're askin'," she insists forcefully.

"I know... I get it," he assures her, "I'm just trying to understand if he gave us any clues about the security. Did he say if there's just one code or several, for instance?"

"Only that the security measures are lethal. It was an interrogation; he wasn't exactly bein' cooperative at the time. He only said that Barry had changed the access code, and he didn't know what it was."

She stops walking and turns toward Jeff. "You can't be thinkin' o' tryin' t'crack the code," she warns emphatically. "Your uncle was never one for idle threats — if he warned that the security is lethal, then it certainly is!"

Jeff briefly studies the fire in her eyes and gradually accepts her point. Trying to guess the code would be futile and stupid, he admits. Yet he knows there has to be some way to gain access — his Quest depends on it!

⌘

HANGAR 7

ABBI announces EB's arrival as Jeff and Hunahpu sit at breakfast on Saturday morning. Jeff has been up since before dawn, now more anxious than ever to solve his challenge. *Could the Ring and Scepter be defeated in the same way as those Eljo pilots and Samjaza's ghostly apparition?* He is deep in thought as he sits at the kitchen table, pondering the idea. He is still distracted when EB enters.

"We leave fer CNAL in twenty minutes if you'd still like t'come along," EB says, noticing Jeff's hesitancy.

Jeff struggles for a moment with whether he should spare the time away from his search, then decides that the change of scenery might do him some good.

"Sure, that sounds great," he agrees. He is just about to offer EB a cup of tea when he sees Isabel hand his friend a steaming cup and saucer, beating him to it.

She places a dish of muffins on the table and sets a plate in front of EB. Jeff grabs one from the stack and cracks it open, releasing a wisp of steam that confirms they are fresh from the oven. The expression on his face reveals his delight as he takes a bite.

"Since you've put it that way, I don't mind if I do," EB says as he follows Jeff's lead and takes one for his own plate, copying Jeff's proven method. "You should try one of these!" he says to Hunahpu as he takes a bite and raises it toward Jeff as if he is toasting him with it. Jeff smiles and tips his muffin back at his older friend in solidarity.

"Well, since you both insist...." Hunahpu accepts, repeating their technique.

Isabel touches her cheek as she watches the men exaggerate their approval. Then waves at them dismissively with a wide smile before turning to leave, clearly flattered.

HUNAHPU HADN'T INITIALLY INTENDED to accompany Jeff and EB on their visit to CNAL, but agrees to come along after Jeff's coaxing. EB lets Jeff do the piloting as they move silently beneath the waves, giving Hunahpu a chance to see firsthand how his great-grandson is doing in his training. Jeff's natural talent is plainly obvious; in fact, Huanhpu smiles as he recognizes where he has seen such skill and enthusiasm before — in Lydia, Jeff's grandmother.

As their ship approaches CNAL's hidden underwater entrance, Jeff turns the controls back to EB, watching in amazement as he sees the vast cliff face of solid rock in front of them split open and the steel doors behind it part.

Berenger is waiting at the docking port to greet them as they exit the ship several minutes later.

"I'm sorry it's taken so long to arrange your first visit here," Berenger apologizes as he welcomes Jeff and the others.

"It's good to see you, Bear. I'm the one who should apologize," Jeff insists, "I should have made the trip sooner."

"Well, it's not as though you've had nothing better to do," Berenger points out. "The past six weeks have certainly been harrowing, if nothing else."

"Something tells me we're not out of the woods yet," Jeff shares.

"I must agree with you, unfortunately," Berenger concedes.

"Speakin' o'which, what have you learned from the captured ship?" EB asks, getting directly to the purpose of their visit.

"Right!" Berenger agrees. "Follow me; the analysis is being done in one of the hangar bays nearer the surface."

He leads them to the main concourse level and then boards an elevator to the Topside Hangars. They exit the elevator nearer the surface, where Berenger leads them to the end of a long corridor. He swipes his card on the security pad beside a set of double doors with a large number 7 painted on them and pushes it open. Holding it, he waves for the others to follow him in.

Jeff straightens in surprise at the sight that meets them. The ship's size is what surprises him most — it is enormous, filling much of the large bay. Teams of engineers in white garb are everywhere, studying the ship inside and out.

"We're still looking at environmental samples to see if we can determine where it was built," Berenger explains as he offers white environment suits to each of them. "These are to avoid contaminating any potential evidence."

Stepping into the suits and zipping them up, the men pull covers over their shoes and hair and don rubber gloves, looking like a team of surgeons as they board the ship.

Berenger lifts his face mask to cover his nose and mouth, signaling that the others should do the same, then leads the way to the ship's flight deck. Jeff can smell the offensive odor left by the Eljo crewmen's corpses even with his mask on.

"Any luck determining the identities of the crew?" Jeff asks.

"I'm afraid not," Berenger admits. "It's as if they never existed, the poor devils." He stares at the empty pilots' seats, which are still in their reclined positions. "Autopsies revealed that they were barely nineteen when they died."

Jeff has to struggle to move past the topic, willing himself to shake off its horror.

"Where are the bodies now?" Jeff queries. "I'd like DNA samples from them if that's possible."

"They're in our morgue. We already ran their DNA against all the national databases, but I'll arrange for samples to be brought over."

"Did the ship's flight records indicate where it launched from?" he asks, changing the subject as he takes several deliberate steps toward the ship's front windows.

"The mission appears to have originated in the western Mediterranean... a group of small islands west of the Riviera," Berenger explains. "We're focusing satellite recon on the area."

"Could they have been launched from underwater?" Jeff queries.

"It doesn't look like the ship is capable of undersea travel," Berenger says. "At least, none of its instrumentation appears to support it."

"We think that it's a replica of our design?" EB asks to confirm the initial report.

"Yes," Berenger acknowledges. "Its hull, propulsion, and computer systems are a perfect match. But it would appear that they weren't able to get their hands on the undersea designs."

"Or they simply decided not to build that capability into this particular ship," Hunahpu suggests. The others nod silently as they consider the idea.

"He's right," EB acknowledges. "We need to find where their ships are being built if we want any chance of stopping them."

"If this ship can't tell us, perhaps the destroyed bomber contains a clue," Jeff suggests. "Brandish said that the anti-gravity weapon array we discovered was made with Borgia designs, not copies of ours; those could be a good place to start."

"It's worth a look," EB agrees, pulling out his phone to call Brandish. He quickly finds that there is no cell signal in the underground hangar.

"How's the wifi here?" Jeff asks, pulling his O-P from his pocket.

"The hangar has excellent network coverage," Berenger confirms. Jeff expected that to be the case, judging by the amount of tech gear the engineering team was using.

Jeff expands his O-P to tablet size and raises CHET.

"Please see if Brandish is available," he requests.

A MOMENT LATER, Brandish appears, speaking to them from his lab's wall monitor.

"From the way you're dressed, I'd say you're either standing in a clean site or preparing to do surgery," Brandish says as he sees their anti-contamination gear.

"It's the captured Borgia space plane," Jeff explains, aiming the O-P to give him a better view.

"That's a relief," Brandish replies with a dry wit, "I'd hate to think of the poor chap's chances if it were surgery."

The men all agree with him, their smiles concealed behind their surgical masks.

"Have you been able to learn anything from the Borgia weapon array?" Jeff asks, getting to the point of their call.

"The assembly is still being de-constructed," Brandish reports, "but its components appear to be intact."

Jeff looks at EB and Berenger for confirmation that he is posing his next question correctly as he continues.

"Be on the lookout for markings that could reveal where the ship was built. Anything at all that could help trace the source of its components."

"That shouldn't be hard," Brandish offers. "There are only a handful of facilities in the world capable of producing the supercon- ductors required. Their circuit boards all carry electronic signatures — they won't be hard to trace. After that, it's just a matter of tracking where the orders went."

"Do you think the manufacturer will tell us?" Jeff asks skeptically.

"Who said anything about asking?" Brandish answers without batting an eye.

Jeff isn't sure he's comfortable with the idea, but then remembers what is at stake. "Right, it is a matter of life and death, after all," he concedes.

BACK AT LOCH HARNAN, later that evening, EB rises from the dinner table, followed by Hunahpu. Jeff has been quiet throughout dinner once again — clearly preoccupied.

"Given the late hour, I'll be takin' my leave now. I'll be seein' you both in the mornin' for chapel," EB announces.

"Good... that's good...." Jeff says in a distracted voice that reveals that he hadn't actually heard what EB said; his mind is miles away. EB and Hunahpu exchange an acknowledging glance, and EB shakes the old man's hand, saying goodnight.

Knowing that something is weighing heavily on his great-grand-son's mind, Hunahpu walks with him into the sitting room and takes a seat beside him. After a brief silence, Jeff speaks.

"Do you think Uncle Barry left us the access code for his secret vault?" he asks, revealing the subject that occupies him. Jeff knows he cannot reveal his Quest's subject directly, but carefully probes at it from around the edges.

He continues without waiting for Hunahpu's answer. "I'm concerned about the Ring and Scepter ...it seems irresponsible for us to leave them unguarded. The longer they remain unmonitored, the greater the danger that someone will find a way to get to them!"

Hunahpu is unwavering: "The means for their destruction must be found before the vault is opened."

"But how can that be determined without the objects themselves?" Jeff asks in exasperation. He runs a hand through his hair as he struggles with the logic. "How can we know unless we try?"

"What is it that you would try?" Hunahpu asks wisely. "Barry was unable to destroy them over the course of many years — what makes you think you can do it?"

Jeff sits silently, exercising tremendous restraint in not revealing the goal of his Quest.

"I honestly don't know," he finally confesses in a resigned tone. "I only know that it must be done; I have to try."

Hunahpu looks at him closely, seeming to detect in Jeff's urgency the unspoken purpose of his struggle. He doesn't reveal his suspicion as he continues, as usual, offering advice that is profound in its simplicity.

"You have searched for the answer within yourself. Perhaps you should seek it from a source outside of yourself," he advises, surprising Jeff.

"Outside? What do you mean — should I be looking somewhere else? Where have I missed?"

"Not where, but who," Hunahpu corrects.

"Who then?" Jeff asks with a hint of frustration.

Hunahpu pauses for a moment before answering...

"...Who do you believe selected you as the Mantle Bearer?"

"Selected me?" Jeff asks, surprised by the question, "...I guess it was the Shepherd's Staff."

"Not *what* selected you ...who?" his great-grandfather clarifies patiently.

Jeff stops to consider it. The answer is obvious, making him wonder why he hadn't answered correctly in the first place.

"It was ...God," he finally admits.

Hunahpu looks away from Jeff, staring thoughtfully into the fire as he continues, "There are times when God gives us tasks to do that we have no means of carrying out; by all practical measures, they are impossible. Those are the times when we trust Him because we must. If a man desires to learn faith, then those times are God's *greatest* gift — they are the times when He is most invested in teaching it to us."

He turns to look his great-grandson in the eyes, placing his hand on Jeff's wrist: "Ask Him."

⌘

21

CHAPEL GUEST

J eff is unusually quiet during breakfast on Sunday morning. Isabel and Hunahpu both notice how introspective he seems and keep their usual small talk to a minimum.

He hasn't been able to shake the words of advice that Hunahpu had given him after dinner, and, for the first time in his life, he has spent much of the night on his knees. Throughout the night, he was acutely aware that his great-grandfather was awake himself; Jeff could hear him from time to time as the old man's impassioned outbursts gave voice to the Spirit's moving in his soul.

ABBI's voice breaks the kitchen's silence, announcing EB's arrival. He lets himself in and joins them in the kitchen, instantly picking up on the subdued mood in the room. He quickly recognizes Jeff's distracted look — it is the same look that had been on the young man's face during dinner the night before. EB gives Hunahpu an inquisitive glance, and the wise old man places his hands on the table, one atop the other, with a momentary close of his eyes — signaling that Jeff has begun seeking God for the answer he needs.

EB seems to understand readily, quietly taking a seat without speaking.

"Who's our speaker for this morning's service?" Hunahpu asks him.

"A gentleman from New York," EB replies, "He's been with us before... an energetic chap, as I recall. He runs a mission for the homeless there."

"Ah, now that's a calling that requires faith," Hunahpu points out, giving Jeff a knowing glance. "Perhaps he can offer a lesson or two on how to approach it."

Hunahpu's comment barely registers with Jeff; barely... but it does register. *A calling that requires faith...* the words seem to hang in the air.

JEFF HAS BEEN LOOKING FORWARD to attending chapel — it is the first chance he's had since his life-changing experience in the Secret Chamber with Hunahpu.

Genie meets the men as they reach the rotunda, joining her grandfather to walk from the castle to the chapel, just as she has on hundreds of Sundays before. She smiles as she greets Jeff and Hunahpu, comfortably taking hold of EB's elbow.

Jeff takes in the full scope of the enormous cathedral as they approach it. 'Chapel' still seems like a remarkable understatement for the impressive structure. He nods to Genie as he holds the door for her, giving her a quick smile.

Genie can't help noticing that while his mouth smiled, his eyes did not. She keeps the observation to herself, but can see that something is weighing on his heart.

When they reach their usual pew, EB slips in first behind Hunahpu, surprising Genie, who has become accustomed to his waiting for her to enter first. She slides in behind him as Jeff enters behind her. EB smiles as they sit.

"I hope you don't mind," he whispers to her as they settle in, "I thought a change o' scenery might be'n order," nodding toward Jeff.

She squeezes her grandfather's arm while dismissing what he implies with a shake of her head. Her expression assures him that she and Jeff are just friends and colleagues, nothing more; the slight blush in her cheeks, however, hints at something else to her grandfather's familiar eye.

As the congregation stands for the first hymn, Genie takes one of the two hymnals in front of her, and EB quickly grabs the second one, leaving her to share hers with Jeff. EB smiles to himself as if he's just been the mastermind of a brilliant plot.

The pair are sitting closer together after being reseated, a fact not lost on EB or Hunahpu but to which Genie and Jeff seem oblivious.

JEFF IS amazed at how different everything seems to him now; it is as though he is hearing every word of every song for the first time — albeit, for many of them, that is actually true. The odd sensation strikes him with a powerful sense of jamais vu[1].

THE CHAPEL'S PASTOR, Colby Abbott, soon introduces their guest speaker for the morning.

"It's our great pleasure to welcome Dr. Konnor Booth to our chapel this morning," he announces in introduction. "Doctor Booth is the founder of the Kelly Street Mission in the South Bronx, New York City.

"Doctor Booth and Lord Hastleworth met one another years ago... on a commercial flight, I believe," he looks over at their guest, who nods in confirmation. "Ever since that first meeting, he has been a dear friend of this chapel, as he was of Barrymore as well...."

Dr. Booth nods with a saddened expression at the mention of Barry's name.

"Barry often shared how impressed he was with the doctor's work in New York, which provides housing and meals for over 1,000 homeless and indigent men per day; but, more importantly, provides hope for these men's souls." Reverend Abbott pauses and extends his arm toward him as he finishes his introduction with a personal note: "Please extend a warm welcome, if you will, to Doctor Konnor Booth."

A shower of sincere applause fills the large Chapel as Konnor makes his way to the pulpit. He begins by thanking Colby for his introduction, pausing to express his sorrow over Barrymore's passing, and then leads the congregation in a short prayer. He says amen upon ending his prayer, but then stands silently for nearly a full minute, his eyes still closed.

Jeff watches him intently — as he stands there, something about the man seems to emanate grace; it pours from his spirit like an aura that washes over Jeff's soul. As Jeff watches him closely, he detects a subtle nod of Konnor's head just before he opens his eyes — as if he is acknowledging an inaudible instruction. As he does, he looks directly at Jeff, making eye contact for a brief moment before looking down at the pulpit to thumb through his Bible.

The congregation is spellbound, silently waiting as if sensing something unusual is taking place; the sense of anticipation in the room is palpable. Konnor walks around the pulpit, standing in front of it with his Bible in one hand — his finger lodged inside, marking the place he has turned to.

"As has occasionally been my habit, I had two sermons prepared for this morning, intending to choose which one to deliver depending upon how the Lord seemed to be leading in today's service." He looks down at his Bible for a moment and then looks up again: "But I won't be preaching either of those messages. Instead, I feel another message has been laid upon my heart." He glances at Jeff again before casting his eyes over the entire auditorium as he continues.

"This morning, if you'll allow me, I'd like to talk about *hearing from God*."

A chill runs up Jeff's spine as Konnor speaks those words.

"What does it mean to hear from God?"

The echo of his words reverberates through the silent auditorium.

"How does God speak?" He pauses for a second and then turns to walk across the platform as he asks a different question: "WHY does God speak?"

The room remains silent; the congregation stares in rapt attention.

"It may shock you to know that if you are a confessed believer in Jesus Christ, YOU have already heard God's voice! You may not have recognized it as such, but you have certainly heard it. The very experience of Salvation requires it.

"...the Spirit says, Today if you will **hear his voice**, harden not your hearts..., Hebrews chapter three, verse seven.

"Behold, I stand at the door and knock: if any man **hears my voice** and opens the door, I will come in to him and will sup with him, and he with me. Revelation chapter three, verse twenty.

"You know that voice. When you were cowering in your shame and guilt, it is the voice that said: 'I love you — I forgive you! — I accept you exactly the way you are in this very moment, including everything that makes you feel ashamed!'

"When you were torn by grief or remorse, it's the voice that said: 'I will never leave you or forsake you!'

"When your heart felt crushed by the world's rejection or your own sense of worthlessness, it's the voice that said: 'Come unto me, you who are laboring and are heavy laden, and I will give you rest. It said: "You have value to me! You are beautiful to me! You were worth giving everything I had — I emptied Heaven for you! I DIED for you!'

"And what's more — I conquered death for you when I rose from the grave! I've prepared a place for you! I'M COMING AGAIN FOR YOU!"

ECHOES OF AGREEMENT turn into gasps of joy and moving expressions of praise as Konnor's words reverberate in hearts all over the chapel. Jeff feels himself reliving the amazing experience of his own conversion, fresh tears welling up in his eyes.

"So the first thing we must learn about hearing from God is that we are continually hearing from God!" Konnor stretches both of his arms wide as he makes the point.

"So why does it sometimes seem so hard to make out what He is saying to us?" He opens his Bible to the place he had marked with his finger and reads aloud:

"Hebrews chapter 12, verse 2 says, "Looking unto Jesus, the author and finisher of our faith, who for the joy that was set before Him endured the cross, despising the shame, and has sat down at the right hand of the throne of God."

"Well, Konnor, you say, I thought you were going to talk about hearing God speak? What does *that* verse have to do with God speaking to us? ...EVERYTHING.

"Let me ask you this... whenever you heard God's voice in the past... all those times when he spoke to you about his love for you and choosing you and accepting you, what was he sharing? He was sharing his HEART. He was sharing what matters most to Him.

"Let me repeat that... he was sharing what matters most to HIM.

"So the next key to hearing from God is understanding WHY He speaks... it is understanding God's HEART.

"This is why Paul wrote in Colossians 3:2, 'Set your minds on what is above, not on what is on the earth.'

"If there's one truth I've learned from life, it's that whenever my thoughts have been fixated on the things and people around me, I inevitably miss what God is doing right in front of me. When I try to accomplish in my own power what God intends to do for me, I rob myself and others of the gifts he freely offers from his heart.

"The great truth is that God doesn't need my permission to be God, and He certainly doesn't need my help. Yet my struggles to take over for Him imply precisely that. Just because He has given me a task doesn't mean I should do it in my own power. When I take it upon myself to fix whatever needs fixing, I'm telling him that I don't trust Him to have my best interest at heart. Setting your mind on things above means totally trusting Him, His direction, His decisions, His Word — and His heart.

"Believe me, I know that it's not easy. The reality of life is that there will be difficult moments. There are times when I have to ask, "When will this ever end?" How can we possibly come out of this victoriously? How can I even come out of it at all? Questions like these can plague our souls at times. These agonizing moments remind us that we are not in control; God is. Unfortunately, too many times, I think I'm in control; those are the times when God's voice invariably falls silent.

"While the issues we each face are different, God's Word remains the same. If we look to Jesus, we will find that the challenging situations in our lives will pass. Why? Because He orchestrates the beginning and directs the ending. He is sitting at the right hand of God's throne, watching us try to come to grips with something that He knew was coming before we were even born. Be reassured that God knows that the lesson is greater than the difficulty.[2] The ultimate victory that He provides is greater than the ultimate challenge!"

JEFF, who has been sitting on the edge of his seat listening to Konnor's words, suddenly settles back against the pew as if something has just hit him right between the eyes.

⌘

22

IMPOSSIBLE

As soon as the service ends, Jeff makes his way to Konnor and introduces himself.

Konnor greets him warmly: "It's great to meet you, Mr. Sutherland. Colby has spoken of you — you're Barry's nephew?"

"It's Jeff. Yes, that's right — The long-lost prodigal," Jeff jokes, although he can't help admitting that the words are entirely true the moment he says them.

Konnor's smiling gaze seems to peer into Jeff's soul as he shakes his hand: "Welcome home."

Jeff senses innately that Konnor isn't referring to his arrival in Loch Harnan; he is talking about his new birth. Something in the way he expressed his welcome thrills Jeff's soul and reverberates inside him until it involuntarily escapes his lips in reply: "Praise God! ...I guess it's better late than never."

"It's never late," Konnor answers without missing a beat. "It's always in His perfect timing," he adds with a friendly smile.

Jeff is stopped momentarily by the comment, which inserts itself into the swirling mix of thoughts racing to assemble themselves in his head - still unable to form a coherent image. He re-fixes his gaze on Konnor; "I'd love to invite you for lunch... that is, if you're free?"

Konnor looks to Colby at his side, "I believe Pastor Abbott has arranged plans...."

Colby places a hand on Konnor's back as he gestures toward Jeff, "Please, by all means!"

"You're both invited — or all of you, if there are others!" Jeff insists.

"That's very kind," Colby says, "But it's quite all right. I have a feeling there are some things the two of you may wish to discuss. I will be quite happy to spend a quiet afternoon with Mrs. Abbott... no offense, Konnor."

"None was taken," Konnor answers with a smile.

Colby excuses himself and turns to greet the long line of parishioners waiting behind him. Konnor nods his head toward the crowd in an uncomfortable admission that he needs to do the same, and Jeff quickly acknowledges that he understands.

"Take your time," Jeff says with a smile. He hands Konnor a card from his pocket; "Call my number when you're ready, and I'll come to the lobby and meet you," he offers.

Konnor agrees gratefully and then turns and joins Pastor Abbott.

ABOUT AN HOUR LATER, they sit together in Jeff's parlor, drinking ice water — Konnor's preference — and discussing some of Jeff's struggles. Hunahpu and EB have been invited to Eugenia's for lunch, agreeing among themselves to give Jeff some time alone with his guest.

As he meets with Konnor, Jeff remembers his conversation with Hunahpu the night before, recalling his great-grandfather's words without mentioning them aloud — they echo in his mind:

> "There are times when God gives us tasks to do which we have
> no means of carrying out...."

"Has there ever been a time when you felt God asked you to do something that was impossible?" Jeff asks Konnor seriously. "I mean, not just difficult, but really not even possible?"

Konnor looks at Jeff, somehow recognizing that it is not just a curious question — he senses that Jeff is struggling with something impossible himself. He leans forward in his chair as he answers with a confirming nod of his head.

"Oh yes, I know exactly what that feels like," he acknowledges as he looks back at Jeff with excitement in his eyes. "It was around the time that I met your uncle; things were looking pretty dismal for us at the Center. Our resources were way past dried up — the Center was deep in debt, and we had lost most of our staff; those who remained hadn't been paid in weeks. I'll never forget that morning when we received an eviction notice from our landlord for being six months behind in rent, and on the same day received a letter from the city exacting fines for health code violations, along with notice of a legal action to shut us down."

Konnor looks at Jeff intently as he describes the bleak circumstances.

"All of that was bad, I won't deny it," he continues, surprisingly, "but that wasn't what had me the most troubled that day. We'd been through financial challenges before, and God had always come through when His timing was right. In fact, the more desperate things became, the more anticipation I felt because I knew His answer would have to be coming soon!"

Jeff studies Konnor's face in amazement as he recognizes that his words are absolutely heartfelt — he senses that Konnor's deep faith has been tested in waters far deeper than anything Jeff has ever faced.

"What was it, then… what was the thing that was impossible?" Jeff asks.

"I'd been working in the Bronx for several years," Konnor explains, "and every day I walked the streets brought more awareness of the problems there. I don't mean just crime and urban decay — there was something much deeper going on than that. It was an insidious evil that seemed to grip the area, feeding off the people's misery and anger. It seemed like everyone there lived under a shroud of hopeless-ness. I knew that just treating a few people's symptoms wouldn't cut it — giving guys a warm bed and three meals a day wouldn't save them from what had infected them. There weren't any treatments that could reform these guys.

"I'd been struggling for weeks with a deep sense that God was asking us… asking me… to do more. I felt He wanted me to change these men's lives — to change the city they lived in. I felt it from every pore in my body, with every breath, every waking moment."

"But how could you ever do that?" Jeff asks, "How could anyone do that?"

"That's the point — it was impossible!" Konnor agrees.

"The more I wrestled with it, the more I poured myself into trying to accomplish it — adding more and more counseling sessions, addic-tion treatments, and outreach programs. I gave it everything I had, filling every available minute of every day until I had become completely exhausted. But nothing seemed to be working — things around us just kept getting worse.

"On that morning when all that bad news arrived, I was totally spent. I remember closing myself in my little eight-by-eight-foot office and thinking how futile it all seemed. I'd poured everything into the Center — everything! It was my whole life's work — and it was all crashing down around me. When I closed my eyes to try to pray that day, I just cried; I was at rock bottom.

"That's when I heard Him. It wasn't an audible voice or anything like that, but it was God's voice, just as sure as I'm talking to you, and what He said *floored* me.

"I still remember it like it just happened. It was the words of Gala-tians 2:20, spoken into my mind in crystal clarity."

> *'I have been crucified with Christ, and it is no longer I that live, but it's Christ living in me….'*

"It stopped me in my tracks. I'd probably read and quoted that verse hundreds of times before, but the sound of it at that moment carried infinitely more meaning than I'd ever understood or even imagined. It was like God had smashed me over the head with it, saying look, you blind fool, this isn't *your* work; it's *Mine!* You're dead! Your own efforts are just dead works — they can't possibly bear living fruit.

"Then I heard Him say as plain as day: 'Give ME a chance — leave it ALL to me!'"

Jeff stares at Konnor in wonder, taking in the depth of emotion on his face; he can feel the extent to which the experience he is describing has changed him, to the very bottom of his soul. Jeff can't help feeling a shiver run up his spine as Konnor's lesson echoes within his own heart as well.

"I have to admit," Konnor continues, "I was so shaken up that I couldn't even remember the rest of the verse — I had to look it up. I turned to it in my Bible and stared at the words, rereading them over and over:

> '...and that life which I now live in the flesh I live in faith, the faith which is in the Son of God, who loved me, and gave himself up for me.'

"Faith! The word washed over me like a tidal wave. All along, I thought I *was* exercising faith — I thought I was trusting the Lord for our needs. I realized at that moment that I wasn't trusting HIM at all — I was trusting in some idea that my own efforts would be a formula for receiving rewards from God. If I did my part, He would do His part — as if He needed my help! I was trusting in myself first and expecting God to honor my effort.

"But I suddenly realized that I was dead! It no longer had anything to do with me — it was one hundred percent the work of Christ, living in me.

"That was it! That was the answer! I had to surrender the work to Christ — to give it all to Him, holding back no fragment of it. Trusting Christ meant trusting that He had our best interest at heart — realizing what was already completely obvious — that He loved the men at the Center way more than I ever could. He cared about the work — it was HIS work! And if the God who spoke the universe into existence wanted that work to happen, then there was nothing on earth or in Heaven and no power in hell that could possibly stop it.

"I had been reading the burden He placed on me all wrong — He wasn't asking *me* to do more. He wanted me to simply let *Him* do the work changing men's lives — He wanted to change the city, with or without my help, and He actually needed me to get out of the way!"

"What did you do?" Jeff asks after a short silence.

"The only thing I could do — I gave up — I surrendered — I turned it all over to Him. I admitted to Him that I had only made a mess of it and dropped the whole mess at His feet. I was willing at that moment to walk away if He wanted me to — or to die serving the work if He wanted me to; it didn't matter which way it went because whatever happened was going to be His work, and I knew it was going to be perfect.

"I guess you stayed," Jeff says with a smile.

"That's where the story gets really amazing," Konnor continues with a sparkle in his eyes. "No sooner had I made that decision than the phone on my desk rang. It was from a National Charity inviting me to speak at their annual convention. The honorarium they offered was almost the exact amount of the city's fines. I sat staring at the City's open letter on my desk as they spoke and couldn't help laughing out loud with joy. They paid my airfare to Phoenix — I could never have gotten there otherwise — and it was on that flight that I met Barry; he was on his way to the same conference.

"The conversation we began on the five-hour flight continued over dinner and then at breakfast the following day. I told him about the Center and shared what I just told you, without mentioning the Center's financial need. As we were getting up from breakfast to head to the convention hall for the conference, he slipped a check into my hand, saying he felt that the Lord had impressed the amount upon him. I nearly fell over when I opened it — it was six months' rent, almost to the penny.

"Well, it just kept getting better and more incredible after that.

Things went well at the conference, and the organization offered to provide a generous commitment of backing for the Center — enough to pay the staff and reinstate those who hadn't been able to stay on. Barry stopped in New York on his way home and visited our facilities. He was so appalled by the conditions he found that he bought the building and the empty lot next door and commissioned the construction of a brand new facility in its place. We moved in a year later.

"Since then, over 20,000 men have come through the Center's programs, and more than half of them have overcome serious drug and alcohol addictions, most finding a genuine relationship with Christ. I honestly believe that none of that would have happened if I hadn't given it all back to God on that desperate morning. If it hadn't been impossible, I might have continued trying to do it all myself and missed the most incredible outpouring of blessing imaginable. I needed to see the truth — that it was His effort that mattered and not anything that I ever could have done.

"I learned the most valuable lesson of my life — not just in my head, but in all of me — in my heart. That with Him *nothing* is impossible."

⌘

23

NO EASY SURRENDER

J eff spends the night pondering what Konnor told him about surrendering his quest to God. His new friend had been adamant that such surrender was the only way to achieve his impossible task.

Nonetheless, Jeff can't help feeling that if he had shared with Konnor what his impossible task is, his advice might have been different. In fact, the more he ponders it, the more doubtful he becomes that Konnor's example even comes close to his own Quest. His mission is to destroy two supernatural objects with infinite power — how can anything else compare with that?

He can relate to one part of Konnor's experience — Jeff is honestly ready to lay down his quest. He wants to walk away from it more than ever; if he could, he would do it in a heartbeat. He would never have chosen such a mission in the first place if he'd had anything to say about it. Unfortunately, there is too much at stake now; their very survival depends on his success... not to mention the fate of the Niergel itself... and maybe even the whole world.

AT THE BREAKFAST TABLE, Hunahpu perceives Jeff's troubled look and breathes a silent prayer for his great-grandson. It is apparent that Jeff's conversation with Konnor did not provide the answers he hoped for. He waits for Jeff to speak first.

"Konnor has had quite a life," Jeff notes with genuine admiration. "His experiences have been pretty amazing."

"More than your own?" Hunahpu challenges with a good-natured prod.

Jeff reflects on all he's encountered since his arrival and has to concede that his experiences have also been pretty amazing. He tips his head with a subtle shrug, admitting that he's made an excellent point.

"Were his experiences instructive for you?" Hunahpu asks, wondering whether they provided any help to Jeff.

"They were, to a degree," Jeff offers with a bit of hesitation. "I'm just not sure they apply in my case."

The rise of Hunahpu's eyebrows signals his surprise. "What is it about seeking God's help that you feel does not apply?"

"Well, it's not that I don't need God's help," Jeff quickly backpedals. "I just don't know if the way Konnor went about it would be the best approach... for me."

Jeff honestly wishes he could explain his quest to Hunahpu. He'd give anything for his wise great-grandfather's advice.

"Ah... it is the surrendering that challenges you," Hunahpu infers surprisingly. He catches Jeff's look of surprise and quickly explains, "I've had my own conversations with Konnor in the past. I know of the experience to which you refer."

Jeff studies Hunahpu's eyes, trying to gauge whether he feels that Konnor is right.

"This form of surrender may not be what you assume it to be," the old man begins to explain. "Our surrender to God is not a 'giving up.' Rather, it is a submission to His lordship. It is the surrender of our plans and desires to accept what He desires."

"Well, if that's what it is, I thought I'd done that already. How does that get me any closer to…, well, doing what I have to do?"

"Your particular challenge is a solitary quest, I must admit. However, that does not mean you must complete it alone. In fact, it can only be completed with help from God Himself."

The avatar's words echo in Jeff's thoughts once again… *'it will demand spiritual strength and no small measure of God's help.'*

JEFF STARES at his great-grandfather as he digests his words, feeling utterly lost on how to achieve them. His voice falters as he confesses to him….

"I…I don't know what that means. I don't know how to do that."

"That, my son, is the true mission of your quest. That is, most of all, what you must learn."

JEFF STILL PONDERS Hunahpu's words as he arrives at the gym for his training session.

Genie seems fully recovered from her bruised rib. At least it doesn't appear to be preventing her from completing a rigorous warmup routine. She silences her watch alarm and waves Jeff toward the weapons rack, handing him a massive-looking broadsword.

"Since y' did so well with yer fencin' lesson, I think it's time ye learned to handle a real sword. No one's likely t' be attackin' ye with a fencin' foil."

Jeff holds the heavy sword in his hand, wondering how likely it is that he'll be attacked by anyone with one of these, either. He keeps the thought to himself; he's more worried about getting through this session alive.

"Shouldn't I be wearing a coat of armor or something?" He says, only half-joking.

"Don't be worried; I'll take it slow, for starters. It's fairly intuitive, really—ye'll see."

She takes a stance, holding the hilt of her sword with both hands as she raises it above her shoulder.

"Remember all we've learned until now, bein' mobile, keepin' yer balance, blockin' the strike. For today, we'll just focus on control — gettin' used to the swing. Learnin' the weight of it." She spins her sword by the handle as if it's a cheerleader's baton and then raises it again.

"Do I need to do that?"

"Not yet, but you will," she says with a sly smile. She lowers her sword toward him in slow motion, waiting for him to block it. Jeff raises his with a clang as they make contact.

Genie immediately lifts and strikes again, slightly faster, and Jeff successfully blocks it once more. She suddenly spins on her heels and swings her sword toward him from the side as Jeff blocks her strike again.

"Excellent," she encourages as she lowers her sword to begin her lesson.

To Jeff's relief, the rest of the morning is spent focusing on stances and maneuvers rather than actually fighting. It turns out that he enjoys the broadswords more than he thought he would.

———

JEFF LOOKS at Genie as they walk the corridor afterward. "We had a good trip to CNAL on Saturday," he offers.

"Saw their spacecraft, did ye? It's uncanny how similar it is to ours; I would have assumed it to be one of our own Space Birds if I hadn't known the difference."

"That's true," Jeff agrees. "Dylen was the perfect spy. He had access to everything." Genie's eyes flare at the thought of Dylen, thinking of the lives lost because of his greed — especially Barry's life. Jeff notices the way she stiffens at the mention of his name. He gently nudges the conversation to talk about the ship itself.

"Bear and Brandish think we can use the similarity to our advan-

tage. Our engineers know those ships better than the Borgia do."
Genie nods, still fuming over Dylen's betrayal.

"Has Dylen said any more about what he shared with them?"

Genie stares straight ahead as she answers. The firm set of her jaw
reveals her opinion of the man. "He's only been partly cooperative. I
fear there are others he's protecting."

"Other spies?"

"Aye. It's a clear possibility. We still haven't heard from Seamus
Gill, the guard on duty the day y' arrived here."

"Do you think he left the island?"

"If he did, it wasn't by chopper or ship. Even a small boat would
have been detected by our satellite reconnaissance."

"What about a Dibjet — underwater?"

"We're certain he was not on any authorized departures. It'd be
awfully hard to sneak a Dibjet off the base unnoticed."

THAT GIVES JEFF AN IDEA. He uses his O-P — "ABBI, can you check the
flight simulator's logs? Have any unauthorized ships arrived or
departed in the past six weeks?"

> "No unauthorized ships have been detected in the undersea
> passage," ABBI reports.

Genie looks confused. "Why would the simulator know who's
come or gone?"

"Its virtual environment is constantly updated to mirror the real
world, especially here at Loch Harnan. Every arrival and departure is
used to scan for any changes."

"Ah...," Genie says, surprised that she hadn't known that. "Well
then, it appears we have a mystery on our hands."

"Add it to the list," Jeff says with a shrug before catching himself.
"That is, I mean... There are a lot of things here that are mysteries
to me."

Genie accepts his explanation, but Jeff can see in her eyes that she suspects there's more to his comment about mysteries than that.

Jeff stops walking and turns, looking at her anxiously. "This is why I have to find the Ring and Scepter. Dylen knows where they are — what if other spies have already stolen them?"

His words stir a look of deep concern on Genie. "You can't go after them — you can't try it." The fierceness in her reply broadcasts how serious she is. "The security is lethal!"

Jeff raises a hand to calm her down… "I-I know. Don't worry. I just know we have to get to them; we don't have much time!"

He can tell from the way that Genie is scrutinizing his expression that he has probably said too much. He draws a deep breath and releases it… "I'm sorry, I'm just worried, that's all. After all the recent attacks and espionage… I'm not used to any of this. It all makes me a little nuts."

Genie takes his hand. "You've got a good team here; there's none better." A sly smile lifts a corner of her mouth… "You've got a few surprising tricks of your own." She looks him closely in the eye, "We've got this."

JEFF IS FEELING anxious as he makes his way to the underground hangar. Piloting has become a welcome distraction from his worrisome quest, not to mention one of his favorite pastimes. He can't wait to get back in the pilot's seat again.

Brandish catches him as he emerges from the elevator.

"We've tracked the electronic signatures on those circuit boards from the Borgia ship. They belonged to a shell company that's part of an international consortium. The boards were shipped to a freight packaging facility in Malaysia. We're still looking into their computers to see where they went after that."

"Sounds like they've done a good job covering their tracks," Jeff admits.

"That they have. But we'll stay on it, I assure you."

"Thanks, Brandish. How are the defensive preparations coming along?"

"Progressing as quickly as possible. We've modified a few of our Dibjets to divert power from their reactors directly to the projection array. It should be enough power to support an AGC around the castle grounds."

Jeff recognizes the acronym; he's talking about casting an Anti-Gravity Curtain from the ground upward to protect the castle.

"What about the laser?" Jeff asks.

"We've managed to piece together one working laser cannon, which Klaus has ingeniously hidden inside the barrel of one of the old cannons on the castle wall," Brandish reports. He extends his arm toward Klaus in introduction. The young engineer nods in greeting.

"I'm afraid its targeting range is a bit limited," Klaus explains.

Jeff nods that he understands. "Please share my thanks with everyone working on this, and thank you as well."

"I will. Thank you, Sir."

ONCE AGAIN, Corporal Tanner has a Dibjet prepped and ready when Jeff arrives.

"Some more underwater maneuvers?" Jeff asks as he climbs in. His question is as much a request as it is a query.

"Yes, Sir," Tanner answers with a smile. "I thought we'd work on depth positioning and long-range scans. Unless you had something else in mind."

"Depth positioning it is," Jeff quickly agrees.

The ease with which Jeff navigates the precarious undersea passage is a testament to how quickly he has mastered his pilot train-ing. They emerge into the open ocean and coast slowly as Tanner gives Jeff a set of coordinates and waits for him to plug them into the ship's navigation. Once set, the ship starts off toward open water, descending as it goes.

"We'll start with a descent to fifteen hundred meters," Tanner explains. "The sea floor out here is at least twice that deep."

"Have you ever encountered any submarines — from other countries, I mean?" Jeff asks curiously. He is suddenly thinking of the huge Ohio class sub that arrived to pick up Azeem after the Borgia's invasion.

"None close enough for visual contact. Our long-range scanners give us plenty of time to avoid them."

That's reassuring news to Jeff. An encounter with a nuclear sub definitely sounds like a complication to be avoided. He watches the ship's steering yoke move by itself as the autopilot maneuvers past a pair of whales.

"It seems like the ship does a good job of driving all on its own," he observes, noting how their gradual descent is reflected in the console's gauges.

"Yes, it's quite good. As long as it's given proper coordinates," Tanner agrees.

"Does it have onboard maps for the entire planet — the same as the simulator?"

"It has the basic topography. More detail can be downloaded when it's needed."

The ship comes to a stop as they're speaking, registering a depth of exactly 1,500 meters.

"The ship can easily handle the pressure at this depth," Tanner points out, noting the ship's pressure gauge, which shows 150 atmospheres. "That's 2,190 pounds per square inch," he explains, pointing to the reading on the indicator below it.

Jeff's eyebrows rise, and he scans the craft's large windows for any sign of cracks. "That's a lot of pressure. What's this glass made of?"

"It's a ballistic material," Tanner does his best to explain. "From what I understand, it's molecularly similar to the metal used in the ship's surface. That's about the best I can do in explaining it."

"How deep is the ship rated for?"

"It's been certified for 300 atmospheres. It's uncertain how much it could take beyond that. I sure wouldn't want to test it."

"Right. I agree," Jeff quickly accepts, feeling a little queasy over the topic. "Why don't you show me more about the autopilot? How would you tell it to go around something — like circumnavigating the island, for example?"

Tanner begins to explain as the ship spins around and heads back toward base.

⌘

24

ESTONIA

TWO WEEKS LATER - MONDAY MORNING...

J eff glances at his bedside clock, noting that it's only 4:30 AM. He restlessly rolls out of bed; trying to sleep is useless. For the past two weeks, what little time he hasn't spent searching the Chamber and Archives has been spent pondering what Konnor told him about surrendering his quest to God.

Jeff is more determined than ever to locate the access code to his uncle's secret vault. He still doesn't know how to destroy the Ring and Scepter, but he no longer fears their power. Since he and Hunahpu read Arubija's ancient diary, he has become increasingly convinced that he has nothing to fear from the ancient objects. Admittedly, Hunahpu has adamantly warned him against such confidence.

Jeff is feeling more and more certain that if he could physically examine the Ring and Scepter, he could find the means to destroy them. He is keeping this conclusion to himself since Hunahpu and EB continue to insist that the means to destroy them must be found first. Even the avatar agrees with them on this point.

The avatar's agreement with them makes him wonder whether his uncle's AI program might be deliberately foiling his attempts to locate the secret vault. No matter how many lines of investigation he tries, nothing seems to lead to the vault's location, and he continues to come up empty in his search for the access code.

Jeff glances again at his bedside clock — there are a couple of hours to kill before breakfast. He decides to spend them in the Tower Lab.

"Good morning," the avatar greets as he enters the Lab.

"You are up early today. What can I assist you with?"

"ARE you aware of every message that my uncle left for me? How can I be sure that I've seen them all?" Jeff blurts out candidly.

"Your uncle created me to provide answers to all of your questions. What do you seek?"

"Well, that's just it," Jeff laments, "I don't know what I should be seeking. Where is the Secret Vault located? What is its access code?"

"Before locating the Ring and Scepter, you first must find the means for destroying them," CHET answers with maddening predictability.

Jeff runs a hand through his hair in frustration and paces across the room, then back again.

"Look, you're a logical program — you have to understand this. How can I be expected to destroy them without having the objects to test against? How would we know if our own theory is any more effective than everything else that's already been tried?"

"It has already been determined that nothing on earth can harm them," CHET states categorically. "The answer you seek will not be found with physical tests."

"How then?"

"Their secret lies in the Niergel."

"The Niergel... you mean the Mysteries — in the Secret Chamber?"

The avatar simply nods.

"But you said yourself that my uncle searched the Chamber for decades. How could he have missed it?"

"I said that the Secret Chamber had not revealed it to him."

Jeff stops and looks at the avatar in bewilderment. "I remember," he admits. "What does that even mean? How could the Chamber *decide* whether or not to reveal it? Even if it could, why withhold the answer from Uncle Barrymore?"

CHET remains silent.

Jeff paces again before finally taking a seat. He leans forward with his elbows on the desk and holds his head in his hands.

"Perhaps it is because the answer belongs to you," CHET suddenly answers, finally responding to his last question.

Jeff looks up at him, trying to digest what the avatar is saying.

"Why?" He stands and looks at the avatar with a challenging expression. "If the objects are that dangerous, why keep the means to destroy them from my uncle, of all people?"

"It is *your* Quest. You are the tenth."

Jeff stops and stares. He doesn't fully understand what the avatar means by that, but the words seem to roll over him with an undeniable ring of truth. Another thought strikes him as he considers it.

"Did Uncle Barry know what my Quest would be? Is that why he put them in his secret vault — to save them for me?" Jeff doesn't wait for the avatar to answer, rushing instead to the next thought that hits him...

"Then he must have wanted me to find them... if that's true, then he had to have left the access code!"

"Your logic is sound," CHET agrees.

Jeff wonders whether the avatar actually knows the secret code and is hiding it from him. He has never seen any reason to doubt its words. It seems likely to Jeff that his uncle either hadn't had time to give CHET the code or had a good reason for instructing him to withhold it. He doesn't like the second option.

As he ponders it, Hunahpu's words resurface in his mind:

"... Ask Him."

JEFF IS FORCED to concede that if no one else knows the answer — not even the avatar — then there is only one place left for him to go. The place that Huanhpu has been pointing to all along. He must go to God.

Without another word, he simply turns and walks to the elevator, returning to his room. Once inside it, with the secret passage safely sealed, he drops to his knees beside the bed and begins to pray.

JEFF REALIZES he has lost track of time when his watch alerts him that it is nearly time for his fight training session with Eugenia. It's already too late to stop for breakfast; Isabel chides him when he hurries downstairs and grabs a mug of coffee and one of her steaming, fresh muffins, then heads straight out the door. He has to admit that he looks forward more than ever to Genie's morning training sessions. They have become a welcome outlet for his stress in dealing with his uncle's Challenge, and he has become much more comfortable with his fighting skills.

Genie has fully recovered from her injury — although she still avoids flipping him over her shoulder, to his relief. Their weapons training has advanced steadily since the Dragon Pole. He has to admit he's done better with a Broadsword than he ever expected to; lately, he has been able to match her nearly move for move. He jokes that his improved skills are due to a healthy fear of being whacked in the head again, and it's a safe bet that a broadsword would be much more painful than a wooden poll.

GENIE THROWS him a weapon as soon as he enters, pointing to her watch with a displeased admonition for being late. He is defending himself from her assault before he even has a chance to set down his coffee cup. He not only defends his position but, as a matter of fact, he strikes back, driving Eugenia backward.

"Have you and EB had any luck locating the access codes to the vault?" he asks as he blocks her next sword thrust.

"You know I can't tell you that," she answers as she deflects his counterattack.

"Sooner or later, we're going to need a fallback plan," Jeff suggests. "What if we can't find the code? There has to be a way to tunnel in or something."

She drives him back several steps with an aggressive assault…. "Dylen said the vault is completely impregnable — attempting it would be certain death!" she yells through gritted teeth.

"What if he is lying?" Jeff counters, taking a swipe at her legs that makes her jump backward.

Eugenia spins aggressively, releasing what sounds like a loud battle cry as she catches Jeff's sword with hers and knocks it from his hand, then quickly follows up with an airborne kick that strikes him square in the chest, sending him flying backward. He has barely hit the mat when she plants both her knees in the center of his chest and leans into his face with an emphatic, angry growl through her gritted teeth: "**IT'S TOO RISKY!**" Jeff places his hands beside his head, palms up, in surrender.

EUGENIA JUMPS to her feet and turns away as Jeff gets up. Her outburst has concerned him; she is always aggressive when she fights, but not irritable like this.

"Is everything okay?" he asks carefully.

She sighs and grabs a towel, wiping her face, then drops down to sit on the mat without a word. Jeff waits quietly as he watches the wheels turning in her head. "I've been diggin' into my parents' last mission," she finally says, "— in Estonia."

Jeff sits beside her. "Did you find out what they were investigating?"

"It was part of a criminal investigation into Borgia's syndicate ties. They'd uncovered evidence of a parent organization, even bigger than Borgia and much more secretive."

"Why Estonia, of all places?" Jeff wonders.

"I don't know; that's just where the trail led. It seems that all the communications they'd intercepted originated there."

She looks at Jeff with a profoundly pained expression... "They didn't close th' case they'd been workin' on because the trail had gone cold," she reveals, "...it was because they encountered somethin' they couldn't fight."

Jeff looks at her, confused. She continues....

"All the agents who died... everyone on my parents' plane... their chests were crushed."

"Eljo!" Jeff reacts in realization. "Genie — I'm so sorry!" he adds, sensing her grief.

"It's alright," she quickly lies, shaking her head as she stares at the floor. Jeff can see her bottom lip quivering, revealing the depth of sorrow she is processing. She catches herself and climbs to her feet again, picking up her sword as she points to his: "Get your sword, come on, let's go!"

Jeff stands and approaches her instead, watching the hardness in her face melt with each step he takes closer to her. Finally, as he stands directly in front of her, she drops her sword to the floor and breaks down, leaning her face against his shoulder as she quietly begins to weep. Jeff wraps her tightly in both of his arms, feeling her body shudder as years of her bottled-up grief suddenly find release.

GENIE'S NEWS weighs on Jeff as he makes his way home. For one thing, he can't understand why the real reason for canceling the Estonian mission had been covered up — was it simply because it couldn't be explained, or was there a fear of panic? Furthermore, he wonders who knew about it — certainly his uncle Barry must have, and EB would most likely have been privy as well.

Jeff acknowledges that his older friend had sentimental reasons for keeping the details from his granddaughter; after all, she was only ten years old at the time. Yet a threat as significant as that could not have simply been ignored — Jeff needed to know what had been done about it. He finally decides to ask his great-grandfather.

AFTER SEARCHING for him in the castle for nearly an hour, he eventually finds Hunahpu on a bench in the castle gardens. He is quietly staring out over the ocean's horizon, with a solemn expression etched into his face. Jeff's approach seems to startle him.

"Is everything alright?" he asks Jeff, "You are normally in pilot training at this time of day."

"Everything's fine," Jeff assures him as he sits beside the kind old man. "I've been looking for you... I need to ask you a question."

"Ask anything, my son," Hunahpu invites sincerely.

"Did you know that Eljo killed Genie's parents?" he asks directly.

Hunahpu sighs and casts his eyes downward, unsurprised; he has been expecting the question sooner or later.

"I did," he confesses.

"Why was the Eljo's involvement covered up? Why was their mission aborted?" Jeff questions.

"Who said that it was aborted?" Hunahpu asks, looking at Jeff. He looks back at his hands folded in his lap and then gazes straight ahead at the ocean with a focused expression as he continues, "We knew we could not fight them; no one could before now... before you.

"Our surveillance had to become more secret — pursued from a greater distance," he explains. "We redoubled our research, deploying new satellites and stealth communications tracking. Barry developed software agents that spread through their networks, providing access to their core systems. We know a great deal about their plans."

He turns and looks at Jeff soberly: "This was how we discovered that they had learned of you."

Jeff processes what he is hearing... "Why wasn't Genie aware of this?"

"To maintain its secrecy, the efforts were confined to a small elite team of specialists. It reported directly to Barry himself... and now to EB. There was no need to reveal it to Eugenia... until now — he is briefing her as we speak."

"They've been reporting to EB...?"

Hunahpu can sense in Jeff's response that he feels hurt that they hadn't trusted him with this information sooner.

"All of this is new to you, my son. It was prudent that the strictest confidences be maintained... You must understand."

Jeff nods and looks down at his hands, conceding that Hunahpu is right.

"WHAT DO we know about the organization in Estonia?" He asks after a short silence. "How large is it?"

"It is quite large... global, in fact," Hunahpu reveals, motioning with an opening of his hands. "It is very old, predating Alexander's

Greece and likely reaching back to Babylon, or even further... to the time of Nimrod's tower."

"What kind of organization is it that could last for so long? What do they want?"

"Their mission is straightforward; they seek control of mankind — world domination. They have aligned with kings, dictators, and despots and used ideologies and government institutions. They have destroyed nations to advance their agenda. They care not how their grip is achieved, only that it is held fast upon the necks of men and women. They have battled for it incessantly for millennia and will not rest until total domination is achieved."

"The One World Government that Blandus spoke of...." Jeff says in realization. Hunahpu acknowledges his words with a simple nod of agreement.

"But what do the Borgia hope to gain by aligning themselves with such an organization?" Jeff wonders aloud.

"It is a long and intractable league," Hunahpu explains. "They cannot easily break their compact with such a partner, even if they wanted to. A deal with the Devil bears no expiration date.

"Nonetheless, they have much to gain in worldly terms: unlimited wealth and power are very great intoxicants."

A chill runs up Jeff's spine as he considers the horrendous bargain.

"What good is wealth or power to a dead man?" He asks rhetorically.

"That is sadly very true," Hunahpu agrees.

"What is the significance of Estonia in all of this?" Jeff asks, after a short pause, "And who is Koletis[1]?"

"We know only that Estonia seems to be the seat of their power at present."

"You mean the seat of power moves?"

"It has certainly moved over the generations," Hunahpu confirms. "Its power resides with its head... with its leader."

"You mean with Koletis," Jeff notes.

"Yes. We do not yet know who, but we know *what* he is," Hunahpu answers solemnly.

"Why is he called *The Beast?*"

HUNAHPU LOOKS AT JEFF — it doesn't surprise him that his capable great-grandson understands the meaning of the name, yet hearing its English meaning spoken by him has a jarring effect, nonetheless.

"There is more that you must learn; I sense in you that the time has now come for you to learn it.

"Come," Hunahpu says, standing up, "…we must go to the library."

Jeff understands that he is speaking of the Secret Chamber.

⌘

25

THE BOOK OF THE END

DE LIBRO IN FINEM

E ntering the Secret Chamber, they make their way to the golden bookstand. Jeff offers his great-grandfather his timepiece, but Hunahpu refuses it.

"It is your search," he explains to Jeff, "You must ask of it yourself."

"But, what should I ask?" Jeff wonders uncertainly.

"Ask for that which you seek," Hunahpu answers; his advice sounds simple, yet it could not be more profound.

Jeff stares back at him, then he turns his gaze to the timepiece in his hand and closes his eyes. After waiting for a moment, words begin to surface in his mind, soon forming with startling clarity. They are the words his uncle had written in his bedside Bible ...*find here all that your heart desires.* His eyes spring open as he realizes what he needs to ask.

He speaks to the timepiece:

"*Audire mihi votum meum* (Show me the desire of my heart,)"

...he requests, translating the urgent yearning into words, then places the timepiece into the bookstand's pedestal.

They stand aside as the Chamber's amazing retrieval system leaps to life, selecting a single golden volume from high above and lowering it to the bookstand. Jeff approaches it in awe as he sees its cover — overlaid with gold etched with intricate relief... an image of angels and demons in a great battle. Its title is emblazoned across the front as if it has been burned into its surface:

De libro in finem, ...The Book of the End.

"You have not seen this book before?" Hunahpu asks him. His voice jolts Jeff from his enthralled distraction as he stands staring at the fantastic volume.

"N-no... no, I haven't," Jeff answers with a distracted shake of his head.

"Your quest has led you to it," Hunahpu continues, watching Jeff carefully run his hand over its surface. "This book is among the oldest on earth; it speaks of the end of days."

"The end of whose days — the Niergel or everyone?" Jeff asks uncertainly.

"The end of man's reign upon the earth," Hunahpu explains.

"Who wrote it?" Jeff asks, feeling a chill as he considers the significance of Hunahpu's words.

"Ayud, the son of Gryff. He was the first to bear the Niergel mantle.

"*The first Mantle Bearer...,*" Jeff half-whispers to himself. "*...How?*" he asks, trying to understand, "*...how could he know what the end would be?*"

"It was a revelation, he wrote of prophetic visions."

"Do you honestly think it's true? I mean, is it really prophetic?" Jeff questions skeptically.

"The proof of any prophet is in whether his prophecies come true. Ayud wrote of many things, most of which have already happened,"

Hunahpu elaborates. "All of it, in fact, has been fulfilled — except for the last chapter... the final prophecy."

"What else did he write that's been fulfilled — what came true?"

"He wrote of the Niergel wars and some of the greatest kingdoms and nations of men, foretelling the Babylonian, Persian, Greek, and Roman empires and the rise of European powers — even the rise of America. He foresaw the death and resurrection of Christ and wrote of the spread of Christianity throughout the world. He described with chilling accuracy the World Wars of the twentieth Century, even giving accurate counts of casualties, along with a depiction of the horrible power of nuclear weapons.

His account appears to reach an optimistic state, with mankind exploring the universe and an explosion of knowledge and dramatic advances in medicine and science. Then comes the final chapter."

"And *everything* that he wrote has happened? All except the last chapter?"

Hunahpu nods soberly.

"Why do I get the feeling that the last chapter is not full of good news?" he asks cautiously. "What does it have to do with Koletus... the beast?"

"You must study it yourself, my son. God will show you what you need to know," Hunahpu answers enigmatically. With that, he places a hand on Jeff's arm with an encouraging grip, then turns to leave.

"Wait! ...How did you know?" Jeff asks, catching him. "How did you know the quest was leading me here... to this?"

Hunahpu's expression is kind but deeply serious, "When you read it, you will see," he answers mysteriously. "Time is growing short, my son."

Jeff watches the old man make his way out, feeling more anxious with each of the wise old man's steps. His final remark reminds Jeff in the starkest terms that he has only weeks left to complete the impossible Challenge. He turns his attention to the large ancient book before him and slowly opens it.

The distinctive text is recognizable from the writing in Arubija's

Diary. Jeff places the O-P on the first page and watches the translation being rendered ….

BOOK OF THE END

The Scroll of Ayud

The visions of Ayud, son of Gryf, Protector of the Mysteries of Arubija.

JEFF CAREFULLY SCANS AHEAD, skipping through the early chapters but reading enough to see the extent of Ayud's prophetic insights. His commentaries read like a history book, replete with tremendous detail about the lives of key characters — even obscure contributors whose actions affected history, describing not only their roles but even their thoughts and motivations. Yet they were written thousands of years before the events described.

Finally, he comes to the title of the final chapter. He places the O-P on it, catching his breath as he comprehends its opening words:

Prophetia Decima Signifer Pallium
(Prophecy of the Tenth Mantle Bearer)

Jeff feels his heart skip several beats as he recalls seeing that title before. In his uncle Barry's letter: '*...now it is your time; you are the tenth bearer of this great mantle;*' and more disturbingly, he remembers Semjaza's disdainful comment: '*the great prophecy of the Tenth Mantle Bearer was but a lie!*'

Jeff nervously begins to read...

AYUD'S REVELATION OF
THE TENTH MANTLE BEARER

I woke upon my bed, greatly troubled by the thoughts of my heart, when I saw one standing before me who was fear-

some in appearance — a mighty warrior, great in stature and strength. He held a sword as large as a weaver's beam, by which he had just dispatched a terrible foe.

Turning then toward me, he lowered his sword and bid me arise. I followed him into the night - beneath an open sky with a brightened moon of full face. Coming to the cliff's edge, we looked out upon the horizon where starry heavens and ocean meet, and then he drew my attention down upon the moonlit waves far below us. As we looked, I saw a great beast rising from the water.

Its appearance was like a fierce dragon, and it lifted its head toward the heavens in great defiance, shrieking in a terrible cry as it swept a large swath of stars from the sky with its mighty tail and cast them into the sea.

As I watched, the dragon was transformed, taking the form of a powerful lion with wings like an eagle's. The lion's appearance was like pure gold, and the sound of his fearsome roar shook the whole earth. I beheld him in great wonder as he trampled the cities of the earth, standing as a man and lifting himself above the earth. Then his wings shattered of their own accord, and he fell again into the sea.

Immediately in his place, there arose an enormous bear that raged in the earth, conquering kingdoms as it ripped its prey and devoured much flesh until its time was fulfilled. When this second beast had fallen, an even more frightful one appeared, having the form of a great leopard with four heads and four wings, like the wings of a bird. It conquered swiftly to rule the nations, and dominion was given to it to rule in regal splendor until its days were ended.

It was then that a beast more terrible than the others appeared. He was exceedingly strong, with great iron teeth, breaking the nations in pieces and trampling upon the residue of their destruction. This beast had ten horns. After a time, the beast became exhausted and fell, as if in the throes of death, yet it did not die but slept for an age as if it was dead. Then, as I watched, it began to awaken, and the beast's horns made war; three of them were plucked out by the roots and were replaced by a little horn that had eyes like a man's eyes and a mouth speaking great words. The little horn made peace in the earth for a time but smote the righteous saints throughout all the earth and prevailed against them.

I trembled at the sight of it and asked my guide what the meaning of the vision must be.

"It has been given to you to know the rising and falling of the kingdoms of men," he began to reveal.

"The golden lion is a great king who will rise in the east, in the ancient lands. He will be mighty, conquering nations and gathering their spoils.

"After this king's end will be another kingdom, fearsome in its brutality, subjugating nations and tearing its enemies to pieces. But God will judge these people, weighing them in a balance to show that their deeds are wholly evil.

"When that kingdom has fallen, a new king who is swift and cunning shall arise, falling upon his foes with great skill and unassailable might. Yet his reign will be cut short, and his kingdom will be divided into four rulers until the time appointed for their end.

"The beast that comes after this will be more powerful than the other beasts, consuming the whole earth. His ten horns are ten kings."

"What is the secret of the little horn?" I asked.

"God has shown you what will be in the latter times — at the end of days. The beast with ten horns is a government... at first, it is a mighty empire, filling the world, but it will fall, losing its power in the earth for an age, although the divided kingdoms of the ten kings will live on until the latter days. At the end of the age, the beast will rise again, stronger than before ...a confederacy of nations."

Jeff stops and rereads the passage, struck by the words: "...*a confederacy of nations,*" he shudders slightly before continuing to read.

"The little horn is a powerful king who will arise at the end of days — he will rule and prevail with a power that is not his own, but it is given to him by the dragon. With this power, he will cast down three kings and take their place, securing the allegiance of the rest, and will rule the whole earth in lawless defiance — railing even against the God of Heaven. In his ultimate defiance, he will conspire even to war against the Ancient of Days and His Great Prince, but then he will be swiftly cut off and cast alive into the lake of fire that has already been prepared.

"Yet know that in the latter days, there shall also arise a final son of Arubija — the tenth bearer of the defender's mantle — who will act nobly and save many souls from the dragon's fierce rage. He will know the strength of the Almighty more than his forebears so that he may prepare the way for the return of the Prince.

"He will stand against the Man of Sin before he is revealed... that Son of Perdition, who will magnify himself against the God of Heaven. In the wilderness, the Tenth Mantle Bearer will build a refuge deep within the earth. It is that refuge that God will use to preserve as many as He will save on that day. The implements that the Tenth Son prepares will give flight to God's Chosen — as the flight of a great eagle. Thus he will preserve as many as the Lord will save. When these things are fulfilled, then the coming of the great Prince will be near, even at the door.

"Write these things and seal them in a book, that those who bear the Niergel mantle may know the purpose of their calling. Let all who read them harken to the warnings they reveal... let those who harken guard these truths."

The familiar epigraph rings like a solemn oath as Jeff recognizes it from the Cronicis Niergel and its inscription on the golden bookstand. There is more written in the ancient book — much more, but Jeff's attention is fixed on what he has just read. He runs his fingers over the words describing *the tenth bearer of the defender's mantle* as a strange compulsion seems to come over him, drawing him into the description that follows about what the *tenth Mantel Bearer* would do *...so that he may prepare the way for the return of the Prince.*

HE NOTICES several notations written in the margins of the ancient text — it surprises him to see that someone would mar such an ancient manuscript. Yet he recognizes the handwriting; it is his uncle Barrymore's.

The notations are references... Jeff recognizes them as Bible verses:

Daniel 7, Revelation 12:14, Revelation 13.

He writes them down, pondering what they could mean as he turns to take a seat on the bench. To his surprise, his eye catches sight of Hunahpu's Bible lying there — he guesses that his Great Grandfather must have set it there for him to find.

Sitting down, Jeff quickly looks up the book of Daniel, finding chapter seven.

As he reads about Daniel's vision of the four beasts, he is amazed... the passages are nearly identical to what Ayud had seen. Yet, he knows that Ayud had written his account thousands of years before Daniel — and Daniel obviously couldn't have had any knowledge of Ayud's book, which remained hidden away in Loch Harnan's Secret Chamber.

Jeff then turns anxiously to the next reference: Revelation chapter twelve... he finds verse fourteen:

"The woman was given two wings of a great eagle so
that she could fly from the serpent's presence to her
place in the wilderness, where she was fed for a time."

Jeff considers the odd verse, comparing it with what Ayud had written about the tenth mantle bearer: ...the implements he prepares will give flight to God's Chosen — as the flight of a great eagle. He knows there is something important to be understood about it but isn't sure what it could be. The words resonate within him like a personal charge... a great mission. He also knows, however, that it is a mission for another day — right now, he needs to complete his Challenge. He needs to destroy the Ring and Scepter!

He flips to the next chapter in Revelation and reads a few verses, finding more references to beasts — he recognizes the same creatures named by Daniel, except Revelation combines them into a single creature. Jeff understands the symbolism... it is another way of describing the same thing. Although he has not studied them enough to gain any deep insights, he can tell that they speak of human governments and the earth's greatest ruling powers.

He considers Hunahpu's words: "We do not yet know who, but we know *what* he is." Jeff pieces together the emerging image. The visions of the Beasts, Dylen's mention of the Confederacy, and Blandus' description of a new World Government... are all the same thing. Koletus... *the beast*, has to be the ruler that the prophecies described... the *little horn speaking great words*.

He feels a great foreboding as he considers the connections that are already associated with him — the Borgia... and the sons of Maranish with their Eljo armies. It is a darkness far greater than Jeff has ever imagined before. A tinge of fear begins to rise, making his hands tremble, but he steels himself, pushing it back with a prayer for strength. Nevertheless, his heart is beating wildly, and his breathing is labored as he thinks about the implications of what has to be done ... what *he* has to do!

His O-P unexpectedly chimes with a calendar appointment, startling him. He glances at it and struggles for a moment to decipher its strange description: 'B. Brief...he soon realizes it is a shorthand description for a briefing with Uncle Barry's avatar. Maybe his AI tutor is exhibiting a little wit, after all.

Jeff retrieves the timepiece and watches the ancient book being tucked back into its place high above, then makes his way out, carrying Hunahpu's Bible with him.

⌘

26

A FINAL SON

J eff confronts the avatar urgently as he enters the Tower Lab: "There isn't much time - we have to find the Ring and Scepter now!"

"There remain twenty-two days to complete your challenge," the avatar answers him calmly as if that were an endless amount of time.

"You must know the location of my uncle's secret vault; tell me where it is!"

"I regret that I cannot. Nonetheless, the location is of no consequence as long as we do not have the access code," CHET answers pragmatically. "Even if we did, the means of destroying the artifacts have not yet been found."

Jeff squeezes his hands into fists and holds them to his head as his frustration boils over. "ARGH!" he exclaims through his gritted teeth. "...I'll never be able to do it... this is IMPOSSIBLE!"

The avatar looks at Jeff silently as it waits for his emotional outburst to subside, then speaks in a surprisingly understanding voice:

"Your frustration is understandable... this is a great burden for you."

Jeff studies the avatar's face — the level of emotional connection it has conveyed is as surprising as it is astonishing... it disarms him. He sinks into a chair and runs his hands through his hair, releasing a deep breath.

"I was just reading *De libro in finem,...The Book of the End*," Jeff reveals with detectable anxiety in his voice. "I read Ayud's prophecy about the Tenth Mantle Bearer. That's me; I'm the tenth."

The avatar doesn't speak but nods in confirmation.

"How can that be possible? I mean, how could I? I don't even know how to complete the Challenge ...h-how could I ever do what it says? How could *I* be the one to fight the Beast?"

"The prophecy tells how," CHET replies, somewhat mysteriously.

Jeff looks at him quizzically, not understanding. CHET recognizes Jeff's uncertainty:

"The Tenth mantle Bearer is different from his forebears," CHET coaches, "...what does it say of him?"

Jeff carefully replays the words of the prophecy in his mind: '*He will know the strength of the Almighty more than his forebears....*'

As Jeff considers that, he thinks about what he and Hunahpu learned from Arubija's diary... God Himself had protected him from Semjaza's Ring. Jeff can hear Hunahpu's words from that night as he saw the supernatural handwriting across the golden volumes; *God has made His choice.* Jeff knows he was saying he is the one God has chosen to protect. He struggles to comprehend it!

Another thought hits him, causing him to lean forward in his chair uncomfortably.

"If I fail the Challenge, then I won't be the Mantle Bearer, and the prophecy will be unfulfilled... what happens then? Can someone else take my place as the tenth?"

"Who?" CHET answers with sobering clarity.

Jeff understands the implied message — the bearer must be a descendant of Arubija, but there *are* no others. The prophecy's wording runs through his mind... *'there shall also arise a final son of Arubija....'*

A *final* son....

The words seem to reverberate inside him. Jeff remembers an exchange with Hunahpu from weeks before; it was in the Secret Chamber on the day of his uncle's Memorial Service, when they were discussing Cornelius' deal with the Borgia many years ago in Florence.

"I guess he never suspected that there would ever come a day when there were no more Hastleworths to lead it," Jeff recalls commenting.

He remembers how Hunahpu had looked at him then, as though he was about to answer, but then caught himself. Jeff had gotten the sense then that there was something more to his expression than just agreement; now, he knows what it was.

As Jeff sits down for breakfast the next morning, the prior day's revelations weigh heavily on him. The thought of being the last of his kind is burden enough, but adding to that the gargantuan responsibilities described in Ayud's prophecy has nearly been more than he can fathom. It makes the fact that he still has no clue how to fulfill his challenge even more terrifying and difficult to deal with.

Hanahpu seems to have anticipated the reaction. He sits quietly as Jeff settles into his seat and gratefully accepts a mug of coffee from Isabel. He can see in Jeff's eyes the evidence of another sleepless night and breathes a silent prayer as he waits for Jeff to speak first.

Jeff runs both hands through his hair in a familiar gesture Hunahpu has come to recognize as a sign he is struggling. He finally glances over his shoulder at Isabel before looking to his great-grand-father with a deeply discouraged expression and speaks quietly, using his great-grandfather's native tongue.

"AWKI (*GRANDFATHER*). Manaña tatasniypa yachankichu ruwayta (*I don't know what to do.*) Imaynatá noqa ruway ruwasqanqa allinchakuyta atinman karqa (*How can I do the impossible?*)"

Hunahpu leans forward, his gaze revealing how intimately he understands what Jeff is feeling, in a way Jeff has not expected; he can see his own pain reflected in the old man's eyes.

"Chaymanta, atillarqachu (*It is hard, I know*)," he sympathizes. "Allin kajta ruwanapaj mayta kallpachakuna (*at times it is a struggle to do what we must*)."

The wise old man leans back and releases a deep sigh, keeping his eyes fixed on Jeff's:

"Chaypaq ruwasqa kasqanchikrayku, chayqa chiqanpuni (*if you know that it is the right thing, then it is what you have been destined for*)."

His focused gaze bores into Jeff as he places one hand on the table, leaning forward slightly:

"Jina wakin yachakojkunaqa wasimanta wasi willayta qallar-erqanku (*you **will** accomplish what you have thought impossible*)."

Jeff studies his great-grandfather's eyes for a long moment; the strength and conviction they convey serve to bolster his soul, providing the boost to his confidence that he desperately needs. He nods silently in thanks and looks down into his coffee, absorbed in thought.

. . .

ISABEL HASN'T UNDERSTOOD what the men shared, but senses clearly that it has been a deeply meaningful exchange. She waits until it has ended before approaching the table with their plates, pretending not to have noticed. She is silent as she places the plates on the table and shares a concerned look with Hunahpu; he returns her glance with a warm expression and the glint of a smile, hinting that everything will be okay. She nods gratefully, then looks back at Jeff with a sympathetic expression before quietly leaving them.

Jeff remains absorbed in his thoughts as the two of them eat, finally speaking as he pushes back his empty plate and lifts his coffee mug.

"KONNOR TOLD me that his greatest lesson had been learning that nothing is impossible to God. It didn't seem like much of a revelation to me at the time - He *is* God, after all. But I'm beginning to understand what he meant by it. It's one thing to know that God is omnipotent *out there...*" he waves his hand toward the enormous kitchen windows, "...that He spoke everything into existence by the word of His power and all of that. It's something else entirely, though, to accept that same thing *in here,*" he places his hand on his chest as he makes the point. Why is it so hard for us to believe that He really takes such an interest in us personally? Why do we doubt that He cares enough to reach into our individual lives right here, to do what's really and truly *impossible?*

"It's funny," Jeff admits, "now that I get that, the trusting part almost seems easy. It's the *waiting,* now, that is hard to take."

Hunahpu's eyes smile, and he nods in agreement; then, he reaches across the table and places his hand on Jeff's arm. "It will be soon, my son. I feel it."

Jeff acknowledges his point cautiously, then lifts his eyebrows as he lets out a sigh.

. . .

"IT'D BETTER BE..." he says with a hint of returning wit, "...He's running out of time."

GENIE SEEMS preoccupied when Jeff arrives for the day's training session. Her mood is certainly melancholy, though he wouldn't describe her as sullen. He quickly notices the absence of her usual sly smile, and there is a noticeable sadness in her eyes.

"Hi," she simply says as he comes in.

"Hey," he answers quietly. "How're you doing?"

"I'm okay," she mutters quietly. She looks at Jeff standing a few feet away, meeting his eyes tentatively; the memory of the way he held her as she cried fills her mind... it clouds her thoughts.

"Sorry about yesterday," she apologizes, looking away.

"No... don't be," Jeff insists, "it was OK... more than OK... it was — nice." She glances at him momentarily, and a complex swirl of emotion sweeps across her face, then disappears behind her disciplined soldier facade. She nods as if to say thanks, then looks at the floor and clears her throat.

"I HAVE T' admit, I'm not completely organized this mornin'," she confesses. She studies Jeff's face and nods at him with a lift of her chin — "From the looks o' you, I'd say you didn't sleep much last night either. What was it that kept y' up?"

Jeff's discovery of Ayud's prophecy in the Secret Chamber and his conversations with Hunahpu flash across his mind in a blizzard of thought. He sees Genie tilt her head, as if she has detected the swirl of emotions they elicited in him.

"Me?" he says, feigning ignorance. "I guess I've just had a lot on my mind lately with the company; I suppose I worry too much about things."

"You're a horrid liar," she answers, cutting through his attempt in a way that reveals why she is such an expert interrogator.

"It's alright t' have secrets if there's a proper reason for 'em," she counsels, surprising him. "The key is t' know which is which. Those that protect a confidence or preserve a promise... or a sacred vow, those are the proper kind," she instructs, turning the exchange into a training lesson that shows wisdom beyond her years.

"It's a man who can keep a secret honestly, who's got integrity — that's a man who can be truly trusted," she adds, looking at Jeff closely — her eyes study his in a way that makes him nervous. "Yours is a vow," she says, surprising him yet again as she seems to see right through him; "...the sacred kind. If it's weighin' on you so heavily, then it must be a large one — somethin' bigger than yourself."

Jeff stares back at her silently, unable to answer.

"WELL THEN..." she says, wiping her palms together as if she is washing her hands of the subject. She glances over her shoulder at the rack of weapons behind her; "let's be on with it, shall we?"

She motions for him to follow as she walks to the weapons rack, then grabs the pair of broadswords and hands one of them to him.

"You were showin' me a few new moves yesterday as I recall," she says as her sly smile returns. "Let's see what else you've got."

With that, she swiftly swings her sword above her head and brings it down hard with a loud clang onto Jeff's. He blocks her strike and jumps backward; then he attacks her aggressively, driving her into the middle of the room. She nods at him approvingly as she smiles and bites her lip, then launches at him in a fierce attack of her own. They parlay furiously, holding nothing back as each tries to get the high ground against the other, jumping onto anything nearby and flipping in the air to dodge attacks.

At the end of the hour, the two of them sit together drying their faces with clean towels and catching their breath. Both of them are smiling from their energetic workout.

"Not bad," Genie commends, "you've come quite a way in a short time o' trainin'. That honestly wasn't bad."

"Coming from you, that's quite a compliment — It's thanks to you," he admits. "You're an excellent teacher." She nods in thanks as a smile fills her face, glancing down momentarily, before looking back at him with a friendly expression.

"It's been nice havin' a sparrin' partner," she answers quietly, "things were gettin' a bit lonely around here in recent times."

"Well, it's certainly been *eventful* since I got here, if nothing else. I get the feeling that waves of enemy attacks and supernatural horrors weren't quite as common before I arrived."

"Not quite as common, that's true," she answers with a loud laugh.

After a short silence, he picks up on something else from her comment. "*Partner* is awfully high praise; I don't know if I measure up to you just yet," Jeff confesses. "I think I have a lot more training to do."

"I'm countin' on it," she answers with her sly smile.

⌘

HIGH ALERT

It has been over two weeks since the Borgia attacked their satellite — far longer than anyone expected to go without another attack. Repeated messages in Dylen's secret email account have grown harder and harder for CHET to fend off. Their demands for the stolen energy shield plans have become increasingly threatening. CHET has warned EB and the others that an attack is now growing imminent.

EB opens Dylen's secret email inbox and taps the latest message, bringing it up on the large screen for them to read together. The subject line reads TOP SECRET:

MODIFICATIONS HAVE BEEN COMPLETED. ATTACK IMMINENT. AWAITING THE LATEST INTELLIGENCE REPORT...

"From the sound o' that, it certainly looks like they're plannin' a strike at any moment," EB observes.

A sobering thought suddenly occurs to Jeff, and he silently contemplates it — what if their actual intent is to uncover the Secret Vault?

He hears EB enlisting CHET's help, stirring him from his thoughts.

"CHET, respond on Dylen's behalf. We need to buy as much time as possible." He then turns to the others with a resigned expression. "I proposed that we raise the alert level to high."

Jeff and the others immediately agree.

HIGH ALERT...

Jeff forgoes his Dibjet training to assist Brandish and the others with the defensive preparations. EB and Hunahpu are already in the underground Lab when he arrives. Berenger and several top engineers from CNAL are on the conference call. Jeff listens quietly as they discuss status.

"The laser cannon is ready, although we're making modifications to it as we go along — it will be a bit stronger than our initial design," Brandish explains.

"How far along are we with the AGC deployment?" EB asks.

"The anti-gravity curtain is proving to be a bit more difficult. So far, the equipment is in place along most of the cliff's edge, protecting nearly half of the castle grounds. The grounds crews are working on the rest as fast as they can.

"There'll be no flyin' in or out once it's raised," he cautions.

"Understood," Berenger acknowledges. "Our fighters will remain outside. We've modified their tactical systems to avoid the curtain."

EUGENIA ENTERS the lab as he's speaking, disconnecting from the conference bridge with a tap to her earpiece.

"How are the ground security units doing?" EB asks her as she steps alongside him.

"We've expanded the number of troops with reinforcements from our team in London. Our munitions are at full strength. We're ready," she assures the group confidently.

"Let's hope it doesn't come t' needin' their help," EB says honestly.

He looks around the room at the faces of those present. Several of the engineers appear exhausted. "I don't have to tell any o' you what a grave threat we may be facin'. Thanks t' yer work, we'll have a fightin' chance against it. I pray that God be with us all. May He give us strength and cover us with His protection."

Several around the room respond quickly with sincere cries of "Amen," including Jeff.

"Let us know if there's anything else y' need," EB says to Brandish. "Feel free t' recruit any additional personnel needed." Everyone nods and agrees readily.

"Aye, we've got a good team on it," Brandish replies, sounding exhausted.

As the group is dismissed, EB places his hand on Brandish's shoulder. "Thank you fer all you're doin' Brandish, 'ol friend," EB says sincerely, "Yer work is all that's standin' between us and near certain death. I suppose you'll be wantin' a raise when this is over," he quips.

"No, sir, it'll suit me well enough just to avoid certain death."

Later that evening...

After a long day of preparations, the castle's new defenses have nearly been completed. The hour is approaching midnight as Hunahpu, EB, and Genie sit with Jeff in his office. Hunahpu finally excuses himself and heads to bed. Jeff and Genie are struggling to suppress their yawns as they scan for any clues. Genie has scanned the Northern Hemisphere a dozen times with meticulous scrutiny, and

Jeff has been busy poring over files from Dylen's laptop, finding nothing of significance. EB is monitoring the occasional cryptic messages that continue to appear in Dylen's secret email account, to which CHET expertly responds.

"They seem even more desperate for the stolen energy shield plans," he observes to the others.

"The surveillance airwaves are full of chatter, but nothing points just yet to an imminent attack," Genie confirms again.

EB STANDS and looks at Jeff and Genie for a moment, then holds out his hands for them to join him. "We've done all we can to prepare. It's time we asked the Lord for His hand of help."

They quickly agree, gathering together in the center of the room, bowing their heads as EB leads them.

> "Dear Father in Heaven, You have led and protected this work for generations. While we know that our lives may be in great peril, it is nonetheless an honor and privilege to serve Your great purpose. We can fight, but only You can truly defend this work. We surrender its defense into Your hands and ask that you use our efforts as You see fit. Give us wisdom and strength beyond our natural abilities and hearts filled with grateful praise, whatever the outcome.
> "Fill us with peace and confidence and give us rest tonight to renew our strength. We commit these things to You in the glorious name of Your beloved Son, at whose name every knee shall bow. The name of Jesus our Lord. Amen."

Jeff feels a sudden thrill in his soul as EB prays. It drives away much of the anxiety that has been plaguing him for the past few weeks, replacing it with an inner peace that he hasn't felt since the first day of his conversion. He gives EB an impromptu hug as they say amen, then turns to Genie and does the same.

. . .

"ABBI, continue full spectrum scanning for enemy crafts," EB instructs, turning to Jeff and Eugenia: "The two o'ye should be gettin' some sleep. Ye'll be no good for fightin' in the mornin'."

Genie smiles at her grandfather and touches his hand gratefully.

ABBI switches off the lights behind them as they make their way out. Jeff stands outside the office door for a moment, intending to say goodnight, but then he changes his mind.

"I'LL WALK YOU HOME… if you don't mind," he says, adding: "I've never actually seen where EB lives."

"Well now, I didn't want ye gettin' jealous o'my accommodations," EB replies with a grin. He offers his elbow to his granddaughter as he motions to leave.

Genie smiles and takes both of them by the arm, surprising Jeff as her elbow hooks into his as well. "It's not every day that a girl gets two eligible bachelors t'walk her home."

"I only promised to go as far as EB's place," Jeff jokes. Genie elbows him in the ribs, reminding him that he had better not get on the wrong side of his fight trainer.

EB's place, as it turns out, is just across the rotunda from Jeff's own. Genie kisses her grandfather on the cheek as he nods goodnight to them with a smile. As they turn to leave, Genie moves closer alongside Jeff and pulls his arm close, gripping it with her free hand.

Jeff is surprised by the move. "You're not going to flip me, are you?"

"Don't push it," she warns, "I just like to keep you on your toes… besides, I've already seen you go head over heels."

Jeff can't help but pick up on the double entendre in her words. He is beginning to wonder if there is more truth to them than he is ready to admit. He struggles to come up with a good comeback, finally settling for "Touché" in surrender.

· · ·

As IRRATIONAL AS it seems under the circumstances, he feels unusually happy. It is probably the happiest he has ever felt in his life, in fact. His conversation with Genie from their dinner runs through his mind, and he remembers with a smile how she and Isabel reacted to the news of his conversion. The events of that day with Hunahpu in the Secret Chamber still resonate in his thoughts, sending a thrill through his spirit.

Genie happens to notice the broad smile on his face. "You seem awfully happy about somethin'... is there a secret I don't know about?"

"Yes, ...I mean, no. No secret, ...but I am happy — I'm so happy I can't believe it! It's just that everything has been so different recently... everything is... NEW! Does that sound crazy?"

Genie looks him in the eyes, feeling a shared swell of rejoicing in her own heart, and leans her head against the side of his shoulder. "No, it's not... " It's not crazy at all," she assures him.

"Well, it *is* a little bit," Jeff admits. "After all, we're about to be attacked by who knows what, manned by indestructible supernatural evil forces intent on wiping us out."

"True," she agrees, "but we have a few tricks of our own... Brandish's laser and the anti-gravity curtain."

"For as long as they hold out," Jeff adds, "...who knows how long that will be."

"And... we have you," she offers. "We all saw what happened at the satellite attack."

Jeff suddenly feels awkward about the topic. "I... I'm not really...."

Genie interrupts him reassuringly, "It's OK; you don't have t'explain it." She stops walking and faces him: "Whatever that was, it was from God; we're not in this fight alone. It's certain that somehow or other you're part of His plan — whatever happens."

Jeff looks at his feet, struggling, "This is all so amazing to me ...I don't deserve any of this. Why should I be different from anyone else?"

Genie gently lifts his chin and looks into his eyes with a serious expression: "I can't answer that, but I know this. Your uncle Barry was the wisest man I've ever known; he would never have wasted a moment on somethin' that didn't matter. And if there's one thing I know about him, it's that he poured everythin' he had into preparin' for your arrival. Everything!"

The weight of her words hits Jeff with a sobering jolt. He thinks again about the overwhelming sacrifice that his uncle made to save him. A new thought strikes him as he considers it for the first time.

"At first, I couldn't understand his sacrifice," Jeff confesses, "but I can see it now so clearly... It's exactly like Jesus said," Jeff searches his memory of his Bible reading, "...*Greater love has no man than this, that a man lay down his life for his friends.*"

Genie looks him in the eyes and nods quietly. There's a brief sadness in her eyes as she presses her hand against the edge of his shoulder in a comforting gesture and then leans her head on it again while they silently walk the rest of the way to her door.

Standing in front of her door, they look at each other for a moment, and then Jeff clears his throat; "I guess ...I'd better be going ...it's getting late."

Genie nods.

"Well ...goodnight," Jeff says.

Just as he is speaking, Genie leans forward and gently kisses him on the cheek.

"That's a belated birthday kiss," she says, smiling coyly, "...for your new birth. Don't forget the date."

"Thanks..." Jeff says, his face reddening slightly. "I won't forget it for as long as I live."

Then he feigns a shrug and adds, "...which might not be long, depending on how things go in the morning."

"Stop it!" She scolds, pushing on his chest.

He smiles and glances at the floor, then looks at her again with a less flippant expression. "Goodnight."

He is suddenly contending with a barrage of complicated feelings. Her eyes tell him that she is as well. She just nods silently, then opens her front door, glancing back at him one more time before slipping inside. She leans back against the closed door as she releases a deep breath, trying to calm the storm of emotions swirling inside, then makes her way to her room.

JEFF FINDS himself staring at the closed door for a long moment before catching himself. His serious expression softens into a subtle smile as he considers his churning feelings and laughs at himself.

As he turns to walk home, he pulls out his O-P, slipping a headset into his ear: "CHET, what's our status?"

Four Dibjets have been positioned on the grounds surrounding the castle and wired to provide energy for the AGC. CHET reports.

"Does that mean that the curtain... uh... AGC... has been extended all the way around?"

Yes, with the exception of a few small gaps. The team is working to close those presently, CHET confirms.

"Is there anything new from Dylen's email accounts?

His contacts are expecting hourly updates. I've managed to convince them that a hasty departure by Dylen in the middle of the night would raise suspicions; they've agreed to wait until daybreak. That is to be the extent of their delay, I'm afraid.

"Let's hope it's enough," Jeff says. "We should alert Berenger to have his fighters standing by at dawn. The fewer who know, the better. We still don't know how many co-conspirators Dylen has.

"That reminds me, what did you see in your trace of the Borgia bank accounts?"

A cross-reference between the Borgia accounts and all personnel detected nothing. I'm now tracing all links to those accounts; unfortunately, the speed of my search is limited by the banks' systems.

"Alert EB and me the moment you detect anything."

JEFF WALKS QUIETLY the rest of the way home; his mind is racing through the past few weeks' events. The memory of the satellite attack brings a thrill as he recalls how the Staff's seed destroyed those Eljo creatures.

He remembers Hunahpu's description of the Eljo's origin and the ancient powers attributed to them, so much like the powers of the Ring and Scepter. The seed had been able to destroy the Eljo crew… just as the Staff had obliterated Semjaza's dark presence — that had to be the key to destroying the Ring and Scepter as well.

JEFF REACHES the door to his suite, thoroughly exhausted but still deep in thought. ABBI greets him and locks the door behind him while he makes his way upstairs, stifling a yawn.

A sound draws his notice when he passes Hunahpu's room, and he glances at the door, which is slightly ajar. The light of a bright full moon fills the room, letting Jeff see the old man kneeling beside his bed in prayer. It brings a warm feeling to Jeff's newly awakened heart, inspiring a natural response of thanksgiving deep within him. He breathes a prayer of his own as he passes by, thanking God for his Great Grandfather's prayers —and the wise counsel that led him to the greatest discovery of his life.

⌘

INVASION

Awakened by the shrill wailing of emergency sirens, Jeff is jolted to his feet. He is dressed and downstairs in minutes, already getting a briefing from ABBI on the state of the emergency.

An armada of at least 30 aircraft has been detected, with two dozen fighters escorting five larger aircraft that appear to be bombers. All of them are cloaked; they are approaching from the sea.

The ring of Jeff's phone draws his attention; it's EB.

"I'm with Brandish and Hun Hunahpu in the war room. You should join us here as soon as possible; it's best t' be below ground under the circumstances."

"Where are Genie and the others?" Jeff's tone reveals his concern.

"Eugenia and Zo are on the grounds inspecting our defenses," EB explains. "Christos is coordinating the general evacuation."

"Was *everyone* up an hour before me?" Jeff bemoans, "...why didn't anyone wake me?"

"I thought it best to allow y' yer rest," EB confesses. "The defensive preparations were already well in hand, thanks to your earlier direction."

Jeff can tell EB is exaggerating his contribution; the truth is that he wasn't needed. "Well, tell everyone thanks for their hard work," he says humbly, feeling slightly deflated. "I'll be right down."

As he ends his call, another thought strikes him: the castle is in real danger of being destroyed — including the Tower Lab, along with his uncle's fantastic avatar. He reaches for his O-P.

"CHET... what sort of redundancy is there for the servers that host your program — is the Tower's Avatar hosted off-site as well?"

You needn't worry about our redundancy, CHET assures him; our systems are underground and distributed across assets throughout the world... and off-world if you count those in orbit.

Jeff feels a small sigh of relief, although the risk to the castle still greatly troubles him. "What about the tower's research archives?"

Fully redundant as well, CHET confirms.

Jeff is about to head for the door to join EB when another thought suddenly hits him. If the approaching ships are piloted by Eljo as he expects, then he only knows one way to fight them — he needs a supply of the Staff's amazing seeds. He makes a spontaneous decision to visit the Secret Chamber.

ABBI is announcing the invading force's time-to-arrival as he bolts for the door — they will be in range in under ten minutes! He leaves his suite's door for ABBI to close behind him as he takes off, running across the upper promenade and down the marble staircase to the office suite. He makes his way quickly through the outer offices and into the library, locking the double doors urgently behind him. A quick calculation tells him that the elevator is his best bet for getting in and out as quickly as possible, and he rushes straight to the secret bookcase switch. Leaning heavily on the elevator's control lever, he descends as fast as it will carry him, then reenacts the secret combination he learned from Hunahpu to enter the Chamber.

Approaching the large urn where he deposited the amazing seeds, he scoops several dozen into his pockets, then suddenly stops and looks upward as a new inspiration strikes him. He pulls the golden timepiece from his pocket and raises it to his lips;

> *"Lego Vestibulum,"* he quietly speaks to it, then lets it lock
> into place on the bookstand.

The whirring sound overhead signals the Staff's retrieval, and he waits nervously as it lowers into reach.

Just as before, the Staff leaps from the remains of its shattered case the moment Jeff reaches for it. It is larger than he remembers -- when he stands it upright, the gnarly head is slightly higher than his own. Holding the huge ancient object in his hands, he wonders how the others will react to him carrying it with him; Hunahpu certainly knows its power, and he assumes EB has seen it before, but Jeff isn't sure who else knows about it. What's more, explaining its purpose will undoubtedly be difficult without revealing its ancient origins.

There isn't much time to worry about that now, however. A glance at his watch shows just minutes until the invasion's arrival. He anxiously checks his O-P, looking for a status update, but remembers that CHET can't be reached here due to the Secret Chamber's isolation. He hurries back to the elevator and heads for the surface as fast as he can.

THE SOUND of explosions can be heard outside as he emerges from the elevator, prompting him to run to the library windows. He can see an air battle raging just offshore as a squadron of Dibjets intercepts the enemy fighters. Jeff runs from the library into his office next door and stands in rapt attention, watching the scene outside the room's huge windows.

"ABBI! Put the satellite view on-screen — zoom in on the castle perimeter!" He can see the ghostly outlines of multiple enemy fighters swarming around the six large bombers; as he watches, two of their Dibjets are hit with fiery explosions and disappear beneath the cliff's edge.

"Open a channel to EB," Jeff instructs as he attaches a wireless headset to his ear. He sees his older friend's face appear in a window on the screen; EB looks at him briefly, recognizing Jeff's surroundings.

"You should be here below ground!…" he starts to argue.…

"Never mind that now — what's the status of the AGC?" Jeff asks.

Brandish steps into the image, "It's fully operational," he confirms, "but it remains untested."

"What about the laser canon?"

"Operational as well; we've connected the aiming controls to the satellite and radar arrays," Brandish adds.

"What's the effective range?"

"Under a mile, most likely," Brandish guesses, "but we'll need a clear shot; it won't do to have that cloud of fighters in the way!"

WHILE HE IS SPEAKING, a new explosion outside Jeff's windows signals the destruction of another one of the defending Dibjets. The two enemy fighters that had been chasing it immediately run into a rain of fire from four more defenders, exploding in spectacular blasts — their debris is sent crashing into the AGC field, which stops it like a solid wall and sends the pieces shooting into the stratosphere.

Almost immediately, two more attacking fighters clip the AGC barrier as well and are sent spinning wing-over-wing out of control; one of them crashes into the cliffside below while the other smashes into the underside of a third Eljo fighter, triggering fiery eruptions.

"Are you seeing this?" Jeff asks as he focuses on the satellite image, noticing that the bombers are grouping into a giant wedge formation. The Dibjet team's Mission Commander has also noticed it and is ordering a full attack; the squadron breaks away from the enemy fighters to engage the bombers directly.

Jeff studies the scene, realizing that the enemy fighters are scattering — moving *away* from the bombers.

"We have to pull back!" he shouts, "...Pull back NOW!"

"Berenger's voice echoes Jeff's command with extreme urgency: "FIGHTERS BREAK OFF, BREAK OFF, ...DO NOT ENGAGE! I REPEAT... DO NOT ENGAGE!"

WHILE HE IS STILL ISSUING the command, a gigantic blast of water explodes skyward, surrounding the wedge of bombers as they activate a harmonized anti-gravity weapon with a combined force that massively dwarfs the power of the last attack. Its outer ring smashes into the lead fighters — one of them is destroyed by a giant boulder thrown upward from the sea floor, and several others are shattered by the powerful wash of the airborne sea.

Most of the squadron breaks off in time, circling back in nose-over backflips.

"Bear... we need those enemy fighters cleared out of the way!" Jeff says urgently into his headset.

Within moments, a barrage of fiery explosions erupts all along the cliff's edge as the Dibjet squadron attacks the Eljo fighters from all directions, forcing several of them into the AGC field, where they are violently torn apart. With the skies sufficiently cleared, the Dibjets are ordered to retreat immediately and circle back to the other side of the island.

"Brandish — can you get a shot?" Jeff asks frantically, watching the enormous tsunami wave of destructive force move closer and closer.

"The castle's radar can't penetrate that blasted wall of water!" Brandish complains in frustration.

"We'll have to use the satellite!" EB says urgently, bringing the satellite's telemetry onto the screen.

"The odds of hitting all five bombers with that telemetry are astronomical!" Brandish objects. "It means triangulating the exact position of the moving satellite against the precise position, altitude, and speed of the moving bombers, not to mention calibrating the laser's oscillation to the frequency of their AG wave from five thousand miles up! We're talking about thousands of calculations per second... it would take days just to program it!"

"Give control to CHET!" Jeff immediately shouts.

"Chet? W-who on earth is...?" Brandish begins to stammer...

EB raises his O-P and asks CHET to join them on the lab's main screen.

Brandish looks on, aghast as CHET's image appears; "B-Barry?" he shudders in disbelief.

"It's Barry's avatar...." EB clarifies, "...we'll explain later." He speaks urgently to the computer...

"...CHET, we need you to target the approaching bombers...!"

"Yes, I see," CHET quickly responds. "A most ingenious design."

A chatter of short beeps can be heard as CHET scans the accompanying systems for a full second...

"Targeting...

...Five Targets acquired...," CHET announces calmly.

JEFF IS FACING THE WINDOWS, staring at the immense wall of vertical ocean moving closer—now only seconds away. "...FIRE!" he shouts.

The laser instantaneously flashes in five rapid bursts, each disappearing into the violent wall of churning water. A split second later, a massive shockwave erupts from inside of it, illuminating the entire expanse in a blinding flash of light and then blasting the airborne seawater outward in all directions, along with a thundering concussion that shatters the office windows and sends Jeff flying backward. The blasted water is caught in the castle's AGC field, which re-amplifies it skyward, allowing some to rain down onto the castle grounds like a torrential storm.

JEFF STAGGERS TO HIS FEET, brushing off piles of tiny beads from the windows' unique safety glass — they cover everything. Making his way back to the now-glassless window ledge, he surveys the scene outside. Huge waterfalls of seawater are falling from the sky; once they are finally exhausted, he confirms that the bombers are gone.

"Jeff... Report... What is your status?" he hears EB's voice on the commlink.

"...Fine ...I think," he responds, still slightly dazed. "We've made a mess of the place, though." He picks a smooth bead of glass from his sleeve and examines it... "You have to show me how this safety glass is made," he says curiously.

His distraction is suddenly interrupted by the sound of a man screaming on the grounds below. Jeff looks down to see one of the soldiers being choked by a familiar black mist. Two other soldiers run to him, trying to pull him free, only to be captured in the terrifying stranglehold.

"I'll call you back!" Jeff says as he kills his commlink.

IT IS ONLY THEN that he realizes he isn't holding the Staff. He looks around frantically, searching the room for it until he finally notices that it has become entangled in the chandelier high above him. He looks quickly back over his shoulder and sees a scene that makes his blood run cold — dozens of inky black figures are passing through the AGC field and making their way toward the castle.

Bands of soldiers open fire on them, but their bullets pass right through.

Jeff's heart is beating wildly as he searches for a plan, suddenly remembering the seeds in his pocket — several of them have begun to vibrate. He searches urgently through his pocket to grasp one of them, then holds it in his fist as he stretches his arm toward the menacing figure that is choking the soldiers. In a near panic, he fixes his gaze on the hideous black form and speaks through gritted teeth...

"PER VIRGAM DEI[1]!" The flash of light that blasts from his fist looks like a lightning bolt as it shoots downward to where the men lie gasping, engulfing the cruel black form in a bright glow that instantly vaporizes it, leaving only floating wisps of smoke.

In eerie unison, all of the other dark invaders immediately train their attention on the place where Jeff stands and begin to lift off the ground, heading straight for him!

Jeff finds several more vibrating seeds in his pocket and targets the closest entities, dispatching them in a bright flash, then grabs another seed and does the same, then a third and forth... but the creatures are moving too fast; they are upon him before he can stop them all. He feels their icy grip on his throat as others seem to grab his arms and legs, immobilizing him. He is able to break free using seeds already in his hand, only to be captured again and again by the vicious horde.

JUST THEN, the office door bursts open, and Genie rushes in, firing a pulse blaster that brightens the room like a flash grenade. Its pulses are bursts of bright light designed to disorient an enemy. It is enough to fool the creatures into scattering just long enough for Jeff to grab another handful of seeds, but when they realize they've been duped, they attack her in a rage.

Jeff fights them off her with blast after blast, alternately breaking himself free and then freeing her, but their numbers seem endless. He looks to the window and realizes that more are still arriving... dozens more! They are swarming over the castle grounds below like an angry black storm. A realization dawns on him that the ships must have been loaded with them — they carried an invading army!

There is no way he can fight them all, ...especially as he reaches into his pocket to find just a single seed remaining. He frees Genie one last time, only to watch as she is engulfed once again and slammed to the floor by her neck, where the cruel beasts begin to crush the air from her lungs; it looks like she is unconscious already. Jeff is being dragged down as he fights against them with all his might. He feels a tear run from the corner of his eye as his hope slips away — he is dizzy from asphyxiation and feels himself beginning to black out.

⌘

STRENGTH

J eff is nearly unconscious when words suddenly flood his thoughts... in his mind's eye, he can see them being written across the golden volumes and hears a voice inside his head speaking them with strong and powerful assurance:

...My strength is made perfect in weakness...

...*MY strength* ...the words reverberate in Jeff's mind. He suddenly knows he has been relying on the wrong power source! He had allowed himself to think that he had to defend *himself*, as if his own strength was needed! With a sudden and unnatural clarity of mind, he stretches out his hand and shouts the words that have suddenly been impressed upon his heart:

"*IMPERIUM CHRISTI, VENI VIRGAM DEI*[1] By the POWER OF GOD!"

In an instant, the Staff is once again in his hand, and a split second later, the room is filled with **a gigantic blast of intense light**. It expands in a blinding sphere that instantaneously consumes the evil beasts — not only in the office suite but all throughout Loch Harnan —purging the island of their presence completely!

———

JEFF AWAKENS HOURS LATER. He is in the Infirmary under the watchful eye of an attending doctor and an entourage of nurses. Hunahpu has not left his bedside since he arrived. When Jeff's eyes focus, he realizes where he is — a single thought comes to mind....

"Genie... how is...?"

"She's fine," Hunahpu assures him. "She's resting, the same as you; EB is with her now."

Jeff breathes a sigh of relief... "Thank God!" he exclaims sincerely. He looks around at the others in the room and tries to rise, realizing that he is pretty bruised up; it makes him wince in pain and hold his side.

One of the nurses comes alongside to help him, arranging his pillows and raising the hospital bed.

"You'll be sore for a few days, I'm afraid," the doctor cautions; "I'm Doctor Lebenberg," he introduces himself. "Please call me Aurick. You put up quite a fight; some around here are calling you a hero," he adds with a friendly smile.

Jeff shakes his head in disagreement and laughs at the comment, immediately wincing in pain again.

"Thanks, Doc. You, people, are the heroes. I'm afraid there's hardly anything heroic in being beaten half to death."

HE LOOKS at Hunahpu and back to the doctor; "Could we have a moment in private?" he asks.

"Certainly..." the doctor agrees with an understanding nod. He turns and motions to the others to accompany him outside.

Jeff lowers his voice as he speaks to Hunahpu, "The Staff... where is...?"

"...I returned it to its place," his great-grandfather says, interrupting Jeff's question with a reassuring hand on his arm. "Walej-pacha, allinta ruwaj kamachi *(well done, my son.)*"

"I made a mess of it, to be honest," Jeff confesses with a humble shake of his head. "If I'd been better prepared, Genie wouldn't have gotten hurt."

Jeff's expression changes as he remembers his unlikely victory, and he looks up at Hunahpu intently — "I know what it means now! Second Corinthians 12:9 — the words He wrote ...I know what He meant!"

Hunahpu smiles and nods, "I can see that you do, yes ...I see that you do indeed!"

IT IS several hours before Jeff can leave his hospital bed. The pain is a constant reminder of the day's harrowing events. The nurses insist that he use a wheelchair; it is plainly needed, whether he wants to admit it or not. His first stop is Genie's room, where he finds her characteristically bristling at being kept in bed.

"Would y' please tell 'em I'm perfectly fine?" she pleads, "I can't stand bein' cooped up in this stuffy room! I have work t'do!"

This is in spite of the fact that she is being treated for a recently collapsed lung, bruised rib, and dislocated collar bone. Jeff smiles at her complaints as he enters the room, recognizing them as a signal that she'll likely survive her injuries. EB greets him, winking at him with a glance toward his granddaughter as he shakes his hand.

"That was remarkable work, m'lad!" EB says in congratulations. "I dare say that Barry himself couldn't have done any better, though I must confess, I haven't a clue how you did it." Jeff stares at him uncomfortably, unsure how to respond. EB realizes Jeff's discomfort and lets him off the hook; "...But that's neither here nor there — the important thing is that Loch Harnan is safe and you're both alright."

Jeff nods gratefully; after a short, awkward silence, EB glances toward Hunahpu, standing in the doorway, and then excuses himself to speak with him.

. . .

JEFF LOOKS OVER AT GENIE, catching her eye as he sympathizes with the way she is feeling, and waits for her to finish another frustrated rant before trying to talk. He whispers something to the nurse pushing his chair, and she nods with a smile and leaves the room, leaving them alone. Jeff wheels himself closer to the bed.

"Look at us," he says with a disbelieving shake of his head, "...you'd think the two of us just fought off an army or something."

Genie smiles at his outrageous comment and exhales a deep breath. Her stress level seems to fall noticeably as she quietly reaches out her hand for Jeff's.

He accepts it with a smile. "Thanks for what you did," he says.

"Sure," she says with a nod as she looks him in the eye, "but you're th' one t'be thanked. I don't know how you did it; none of us would be here right now if it weren't for you."

"Yeah, at least not here in the hospital anyway," Jeff adds, borrowing a joke from Alpin Bannock. "That reminds me — I still owe Alpin a dinner," he confides to her.

The spontaneous smile on her face lifts his spirit.

"What were you thinking, by the way?" he asks her, "— a pulse blaster?"

She laughs, rolling her eyes. "It was a gamble... I was countin' on 'em bein' too ancient t'know the difference — it worked... at least for a few seconds."

"Yeah, before they almost killed you!" Jeff points out with a grateful smile. He grows more serious and adds, "The timing was pretty good though... You honestly saved my life."

"And then you saved everyone else's..." she adds quietly.

"That... that wasn't me," he confesses, "I was done for — I had nothing left." He catches himself, unsure whether he should reveal what happened with the ancient Staff. "...It was God's power — His strength is made perfect in our weakness."

She looks at him with a hint of admiration. "Ye've become quite th' theologian in one day, Mr. Sutherland," she commends him.

"Yeah, look at that day, though!" he exclaims.

DREYKEN SIDERO ENTERS his compound's command center, impatiently awaiting word on the attack; it has been hours since all communication with the assault team was lost. The command crew stands stiffly at attention as he enters, their faces etched with fear. The senior officer shakes his head reluctantly, signaling to Dreyken that they still have not made contact.

"Get Chesed on the line," Dreyken commands, clearly angry. A moment later, a raspy, hideous voice can be heard answering over the room's conference line.

"I'm waiting for you to tell me your team has completed their mission," Dreyken barks. "Need I remind you of the cost of failure?"

There is a short pause, and Chesed speaks in a slow and sinister tone, ignoring Dreyken's threat. "Our forces were invincible; no earthly power could vanquish them. Yet I sense a great upheaval in the dark powers," he admits with a hint of perplexed disbelief. "Only one power could have prevailed against the Eljo, yet it has not been seen in such measure — not for thousands of years."

"Is it a weapon?" Dreyken queries, trying to understand Chesed's strange reference. "I will remind you that that armada of aircraft cost me a huge fortune! This is the second time your ambitious anti-gravity weapons have failed! And you said those troops of yours couldn't be killed — well, what stopped them then?"

"As I have said," Chesed replies in a calm but disturbing voice, "only one power could have defeated them. The young one has learned of it."

"The young one? ...you mean Samuels? Learned of what?" Dreyken snarls, growing angrier by the minute over Chesed's vague riddles.

"He has used the Staff that his uncle once wielded... the Staff of the Ancient One — the Shepherd's Staff."

"Whatever it is," Dreyken answers sternly — clearly unconcerned about the details, "you had better find a way to beat it if you don't want to live out the rest of your miserable life back in an ice cave!

Dreyken turns to the control room's commander: "Alert me at once when contact has been made!" he commands sternly, then turns to leave, cutting off the call abruptly.

"You will be informed immediately, sir!" the control room's commanding officer vows adamantly to his superior, standing stiffly at attention.

One of the engineers in the room nods toward a nearby terminal screen displaying an urgent alert. The officer glances at it and subtly cautions the engineer to keep quiet, waiting for Dreyken to exit.

THE MOMENT HE IS GONE, the commander turns back to the terminal and reads the flashing message…

——< * URGENT * >——

TELEMETRY REPORT: RECONNAISSANCE CONFIRMED

    BOMBER ONE — DESTROYED

    BOMBER TWO — DESTROYED

    BOMBER THREE — DESTROYED

    BOMBER FOUR — DESTROYED

    BOMBER FIVE — DESTROYED

    FIGHTER SQUADRON:

    FIGHTERS DESTROYED: 20

    FIGHTERS REMAINING: 0

"Our surveillance drone is picking up the signals from their flight recorders, Sir," the engineer reports. "Should we dispatch a submarine to search for them?"

"No," the officer quickly instructs. "Hastleworth ships will be all over them. There is nothing to recover.

"What does the drone show of damage to the castle?" the officer asks.

"Some visible damage to the southern exposures, mostly broken windows, Sir. Nothing more."

The officer slams his fist on the desk, causing everyone in the room to stiffen in fear.

"Prepare a report for Commander Sidero," he finally says as he straightens, regaining his composure. "And then deliver it to him at once!"

"Y-yes, Sir," the young lieutenant acknowledges nervously as beads of sweat form on his brow.

⌘

RECOVERY

J eff and Eugenia make the best of their forced rest for the next five days, as difficult as it is for them. Genie is out of her hospital bed as soon as she can manage it, though she is still confined to a wheelchair, much to her chagrin. She introduces Jeff to the hospital's underground gardens, where they spend their free hours together. Jeff does his best to impress her by recognizing dozens of flower varieties and calling them by their Latin names. He begins to expound on the genetic history of each genus and species, tracing their traits through generations — until he notices her yawning and realizes he is boring her to death. He finally decides to just pick one and hand it to her, which seems to make a bigger impression.

While there, they spend the time in conversation, discussing their childhoods and career choices, as different from one another as they could be, and yet, in fundamental ways, strikingly similar. They recount and analyze all that has happened and debate theories about their enemies' plans.

. . .

EB JOINS them to provide a briefing on the aftermath of the attack.

"Dylen was found dead in his cell," he informs them on his first visit. "It happened during the invasion — his chest had been crushed."

"Has there been any sign of the Eljo that killed him?" Jeff asks with alarm.

"There has been an exhaustive search... apparently whatever you did to destroy the others took his killers as well."

Jeff grows quiet — not wanting to claim credit for the amazing deliverance but afraid to reveal more about what happened.

"What about his email account?" Genie asks, ignoring Jeff's discomfort. "Can it still be used for intelligence?"

"I'm afraid the email flow to his laptop abruptly ended around that same time. In fact, chatter on enemy channels, in general, has almost vanished. It's as if the enemy has been forced to retreat and lick their wounds."

OVER THE NEXT WEEK, EB continues to provide daily briefings, letting them know how the cleanup efforts are going and keeping them updated on the latest intelligence, as sparse as it may be.

Jeff and Eugenia make a point of visiting the soldiers who were wounded in the attack — relieved to see that all of them are making a quick recovery.

THEY FIND the three earliest attack casualties gathered in a hospital break room. They are watching a Scottish Rugby game on the large screen when Jeff and Eugenia wheel themselves through the door in their wheelchairs. All the men quickly rise from their seats to stand at attention as soon as they recognize the pair.

"At ease, soldiers," Eugenia quickly says in a friendly voice. She scans the trio of men, noticing that two of them have their arms in slings similar to hers while the other has one leg in a cast. "Please have a seat," she adds in a casual tone that is more of an invitation than a command. She looks over at Jeff as she introduces him: "I believe you know Jeff Sutherland."

The men quickly nod and salute.

"I'm Eason, Sir. Second Lieutenant Eason Barton," the first man introduces himself.

"Cooney Dolan, Guardsman Rifleman, Sir," the second man quickly adds.

"I'm Findley Portor; I'm a Rifleman as well, Sir," the third chimes in.

"It's Jeff, please," Jeff quickly corrects. He looks back at Eugenia with a nod as he continues, "We wanted to thank you for your service — it was a brave thing that you all did."

"I'm afraid I did nothin' more than let my guard down, Sir," Eason admits. "That thing came from nowhere — it was on me before I knew it."

"We didn't know what we were gettin' ourselves into either," the others confess.

"We're the ones who need to be thankin' you, Sir," Eason adds. "You saved our lives, as sure as we're standin' here."

"Sittin' here, you mean," Cooney corrects him.

Eason agrees with Cooney, looking briefly bewildered that his friend hadn't understood that he was using a figure of speech. Looking back at Jeff, he reemphasizes his point: "We don't know how you did it, Sir, but we owe our lives to you, there's no doubt."

Jeff looks down, obviously uncomfortable at taking the credit. "I think it's God who deserves our thanks," he offers.

"That's for sure, Sir," they each agree, "We've been doing little else besides thanking Him since it happened," Findley adds as the others nod.

They join the men in watching the rest of the game as Eugenia cheers and hollers at the screen with the others, while Jeff looks on with a smile. He is unaccustomed to the sport but quickly learns its finer points with help from the fans in the room.

AS THEY ARE LEAVING, Jeff catches sight of Alpin Bannock's room and decides to check in to see how he is doing. It has been more than a month since that first attack in which he had been swept off the roof while saving the castle's satellite dish. By now, Alpin has graduated from his bed to a wheelchair. Jeff finds him in his hospital suite's sitting room with one leg propped up stiffly in front of him and his left arm still in a long cast from the wrist to his neck. He is reading from a thick book, in which he is so engrossed that he fails to notice his visitors knocking on the open door.

Mrs. Bannock emerges from the bedroom carrying a basket of laundry.

"Oh, hello, Mr. Sutherland, Sir! What a nice surprise!

"Alpin m'dear, look who 'as come t'pay a visit — it's Mr. Sutherland an' Ms. Escutia, here t'see you!"

Turning back to Jeff and Genie in their wheelchairs, she invites them in.

"We all heard what happened — ye're both heroes, ever-one's sayin'," she gushes.

Jeff dismisses the label with a shake of his head; "There's a real hero," he says, nodding toward Alpin. "How are you feeling?"

Alpin grins with a wide smile and lowers his book. "Just fine, Mr. Sutherland, Sir! As well as can be expected," he replies. He motions toward Jeff's own wheelchair with his hand; "looks as though I aught'a be askin' you that same question."

"What are you reading there?" Jeff asks curiously. "It looked like you were pretty engrossed in it."

Alpin holds it up proudly, "It's a textbook on electrical engineerin'," he explains; "that's been my true hankerin' since I was a wee lad."

"Are you taking courses?" Jeff queries, growing more interested. His own love for learning makes any mention of it a favorite topic for him.

"Not formal-like," Alpin confesses. "Ain't never had the means for a true college education — not assumin' I could get into one even if I did."

Jeff glances at the book in his hands and is taken aback as he reads the book's title:

'Using Rhythmic Generators with Artificial Neural Networks in Microrobot Systems.'

"That's pretty advanced," Jeff says in surprise, "have you been studying neural networks and microrobot systems for long?"

"A few years, I guess," Alpin answers. "It seems to me that micro-robots could be great for medical uses, to avoid major surgery and the like, or for repairs inside complex machines. I was thinkin' that they could be linked with a neural network to give 'em enough intelligence and help 'em work together, y'know?" He continues to expand on the idea... speaking faster as his enthusiasm grows...

"...Usin' a hardware-based neuron model with microrobots has advantages because even if the circuit scale gets really large, it allows for nonlinear operations. O'course, they kin perform at higher speeds an' process work in parallel. The prototype design I've been workin' on uses a pulse-type hardware neuron model; it has the same basic traits as biological neurons, like the threshold, refractory period, and Spatio-temporal summation aspects, and it kin generate continuous action potentials...."

"Oh, there he goes again," Alpin's wife interrupts with a dismissive wave. "I swear I can't understand the first thing when he starts goin' on like that."

Jeff breaks into a wide smile as he shares a glance with Genie, who is staring wide-eyed. "How would you like an internship in our engineering research lab with Brandish Rushforth?" he asks.

"Seriously?" Alpin says, leaning forward in his seat so fast that it makes him wince in pain.

"Yes, I'm absolutely serious." Jeff assures him as he holds his hands up, signaling for Alpin to stay still, "After you've recovered, that is. It'll be waiting for you once you're back on your feet!"

. . .

WHILE THEY ARE STILL SPEAKING, a few members of the Grounds Crew happen to stop in for their daily visit with their fellow groundsmen.

"Ye ain't gonna believe it," Alpin announces excitedly, "— I jus' got an internship t'work in Rushforth's lab!"

"Oh great," Daire McCloskey jokes as he turns to the others, "we kin naer understand half o' what he says now as it is; soon, he'll be a bloody scientist!" The burly man's voice booms, filling the room and echoing down the hallway, along with the other men's laughter.

"Maybe then he'll learn why he can't fly!" Berk Fulton jokes, referring to the accident that put Alpin in the hospital.

Alpin laughs as loudly as any of them; "Flyin' wasn't th' problem — it was th' landin!" he yells as the room shakes with the men's boisterous laughing.

A nurse appears at the door, waving her arms and holding a raised index finger to her lips. "There are patients who need their rest — please do try to quiet yourselves," she pleads.

"Poor Nurse Cushley," Mrs. Bannock whispers to Eugenia, "she has to make that same plea every day at about this time." Genie holds her hand to her mouth, trying to hide her amused smile.

Jeff and Genie spend the rest of the hour enjoying the groundsmen's company before saying goodnight and wheeling themselves out. They decide to make a point of visiting Alpin each afternoon at about this time.

BY THE END of the week, the two of them are released and back on their feet, although Genie's shoulder is still in a sling, and her healing rib is tightly wrapped.

EB arrives to join Jeff and Huanhpu for breakfast on Jeff's first day back at home.

"I'VE BEEN WANTIN' t'thank y' fer the help you've been givin' Eugenia in her recovery," EB says as he takes a seat at the table.

"My help?" Jeff exclaims in surprise. "She hardly needs it; she's practically indestructible... I can barely keep up with her, even now."

"Oh, she presents herself that way, but under that tough facade's just a person, same as you an' me. It's in helpin' you that the healin' is worked in herself.

"She's become fairly fond o' ye," he adds, catching Jeff's eye encouragingly.

Jeff feels his face redden slightly, giving away the feelings he holds for her, although he wouldn't admit it, even to himself. Thoughts of the times they have spent together during their recovery in the hospital speed through his mind, bringing a smile to his face.

"It's mutual; we've become good friends," he confesses warmly. Isabel approaches the table behind Jeff and gives Hunahpu and EB a wink as she smiles at Jeff's comment. The men stifle their grins as they subtly agree with her unspoken point.

EB REPORTS on the latest intel, changing the subject. "Berenger's team has completed a full postmortem of the satellite logs and was able to verify that none of the Eljo ships survived to return to their base. The wreckage is still being located and retrieved. Not much remains of the obliterated bombers, but pieces of several hundred Eljo pressure suits have been discovered so far."

"What have we learned from CNAL's examination of the ship that was captured in space?" Jeff asks.

"They've confirmed that it is, in fact, an exact copy of one of our own designs — right down to the computer code in its control systems. Brandish and Berengar have discovered several ways to exploit that fact using their intimate knowledge of those systems."

"That's good," Jeff agrees. "The Borgia likely don't know that we have their ship, thanks to CHET's work with Dylen's secret email."

Jeff's expression saddens as he considers his next question... "What did the autopsies of their crewmen find?"

"Only that the suits' occupants had been dead for at least three to five years. It begs the question of why the ancient entities need corpses as hosts."

Jeff and EB look to Hunahpu for an answer to that question.

"There are mysteries in the world that we cannot easily understand," Hunahpu answers. He focuses his gaze on Jeff as he adds, "Perhaps it can be learned in searching."

⌘

RUNNING OUT OF TIME

E ntering the Tower Lab for the first time in over a week, Jeff settles into a seat as the avatar greets him.

"It's good to see you again.
"Looks like you've had a fairly interesting time over the past few weeks."

The avatar's words reveal a degree of subtle understatement that surprises Jeff. It appears that his virtual friend is learning to appreciate humor after all.

"I think my language habits are rubbing off on you," Jeff offers. "You're more like my uncle every day."

"In this lab, I most closely resemble Barrymore's human traits; that is true."

Jeff thinks about his comment for a moment.
"I need a better name for you. CHET is the name for your other

forms, but you're different here." An idea comes to him — he quietly contemplates it....

Barrymore Eldridge.... Jeff says, quietly repeating his uncle's name to himself.

"I've got it; I'll call you 'BE.'" Jeff decides, pronouncing it in a single word, as in, *to be.*

"It's an honor," the avatar answers. "Thank you, Jeff."

JEFF SIGHS as his thoughts return to the reason for his visit — his impossible challenge. He runs his hands through his hair, revealing the anxiety that seems to grow stronger each day. He gazes at BE with a look that borders on despair.

"Next week, we'll be at the end of my ninety-day challenge.... I still have no idea how to destroy the Ring and Scepter. I don't even know where they're hidden."

"The time that remains is enough."

BE's answer doesn't surprise Jeff, but he clearly doesn't share the avatar's optimism. He sighs as he takes a seat and tilts the nearest monitor screen for a closer look.

"Bring up the Objects' images. Have you come up with anything more on their origin?"

"Nothing new has been discovered." BE answers as the video of the rotating ring and scepter fills the screen.

Jeff considers the events of the Eljo invasion, especially the remarkable way that the Shepherd's Staff obliterated the ghostly army.

"You say the Ring and Scepter are from another dimension. Are the Eljo from that same dimension?"

BE appears to consider the question as he scans through a vast storehouse of data….

"Their supernatural essence bears many similarities to the Ring and Scepter. They, too, are impervious to physical harm."

"Yet they were destroyed by the Shepherd's Staff. That has to be the key to destroying the Ring and Scepter, also, doesn't it?"

"Barrymore thought the same but was unable to achieve it."

"Yeah, but he wasn't able to destroy the Eljo either. You said yourself that there's something different about the way the Staff works for me. Hunahpu said it's because of the joined bloodlines."

"Whether it be the bloodlines or your position among the Mantel Bearers, we cannot be certain."

"My position… you mean, being the Tenth." Jeff thinks about it for a moment. "Maybe that's the key — we need to test it!"

"Your uncle was clear in my instructions; you must not be permitted to face the Ring and Scepter until their means of destruction are certain."

"But how can we be certain of the means without testing them?" Jeff objects in frustration.

BE's answer is maddeningly predictable:

"They are too dangerous. The means to destroy them must be known first."

Jeff refrains from arguing the point. He realizes it's no use; the avatar won't be persuaded. Still, he can't help being reminded of what Hunahpu said after reading Arubija's ancient scroll. The wise old man had stared at the words inscribed across the golden volumes as he voiced his conclusion: *"It would appear that He has already made His choice."*

The inscription fills Jeff's thoughts — he repeats the words to himself... *"My strength is made perfect.... My protection."*

2,500 NAUTICAL MILES AWAY...

MONTAGNE BLANCHE ~ **The Maranish Brothers' Castle...**

IT IS EERILY calm around the Maranish brothers' seemingly tranquil island castle in the Mediterranean. Chesed, the eldest son of Maranish, looks more like a corpse than a living man as he leans close to his phone to address the mysterious caller on the other end of the line. His hideous voice speaks in raspy tones, muted by his advanced age.

"The young Mantle Bearer is gaining strength more quickly than we feared," he warns. "He has learned to use the Staff with great efficacy; our Eljo forces are already no match for him."

The caller is silent for a moment, then calmly replies, "You lack faith in our great master's schemes. His plan will not be stopped; our destiny is to rule all the earth."

"That is your destiny, my lord," Chesed agrees submissively. "Yet these Niergel remain a hindrance that must be removed... the Mantle Bearer must be eliminated."

"I agree," the stranger says in a smooth voice that seems to exude evil intent. "What do you propose?"

"We must retrieve the Ring and Scepter — it is our best hope."

"That has been tried to no avail — how do you expect to accomplish this great feat?"

"It would appear that it cannot be won with force. We must use the young heir himself for our ends; he must do our bidding for us," Chesed offers with sinister confidence.

There is a silent pause as the stranger considers his remark. "What makes you believe that he can be persuaded? Even Semjaza could not sway him."

"His pride will be his downfall," Chesed proposes. "We must make him believe he is doing what is necessary to achieve his quest — while he thinks he is relying on our Enemy's protection, we will cause him to forget the true source of that strength. By the time he realizes his error, it will be too late."

"You are deviously resourceful, my friend — I admire that in a man. Very well, I trust you will keep me apprised of your progress."

THE MYSTERIOUS STRANGER hangs up the call without another word. Chesed congratulates himself with an evil grin as he shares a look with his brother Eblis. "Our plan will not fail," he gloats confidently. "Our great victory will surely win Koletis' favor...."

Eblis grins widely — his smile deformed by the long scars that crisscross his hideous face. He grips his brother's shoulder in solidarity, "...and then **WE** will own the power of the Mysteries. The Ring and Scepter will soon be ours!"

⌘

THE END
OF BOOK THREE

THANK YOU FOR READING!

PLEASE TAKE A MOMENT TO LEAVE A REVIEW.

(Scan the QR code below)

Join the mailing list for updates on new releases and special offers at:
arkharbor.press and click on Contact.

Continue the Adventure in Book Four:
Niergel Chronicles
The Dragon's Tail

Niergel Chronicles - The Dragon's Tail

AUTHOR'S NOTE

Separating Fact from Fiction

The Niergel Chronicles is a fictional account, but like most fiction, it also contains many elements of truth. For readers who may not be familiar with the Bible or with what Christians believe, the summary below clarifies which is which to help distinguish between the two.

'Hastleworth Enterprises' is a fictional company; any resemblance to real companies is entirely unintended and coincidental.

The location named CNAL is an abbreviation for Cronk ny Arrey Laa, a real place on the Isle of Man. Its name means 'Hill of the Day Watch,' but it does not contain a secret underground aerospace base.

The Bible's account of Noah's Flood is not fictional. Everything else about the story of Arubija, his family, and their survival of Noah's flood is fictional.

There really is no secret Niergel organization.

'The Borgia Syndicate' is a fictional creation and is not meant to resemble or portray any real persons or organizations with or without similar names.

The depiction of smoky Eljo creatures is fictional. There actually are no smoky Eljo creatures. The Bible does make a reference to the Nephilim, saying simply that: "The Nephilim were in the earth in those days, ... when the sons of God came unto the daughters of men, and they bare children to them," Gen 6:4. Scholars commonly believe that "the sons of god" were the fallen angels described in the New Testament book of Jude: "And angels that kept not their own principality, but left their proper habitation, he hath kept in everlasting bonds under darkness unto the judgment of the great day." Jude 1:6. The Book of Enoch, which is not in the Bible, describes the Elioud race (Eljo) as the children of the Nephilim.

The Cylch o Awydd (The Ring of Desire) is fictional. Magical objects like Eternal Rings, Scepters, and Scrolls don't exist. Neither does the compass-like Stone of Hope.

The Shepherd's Staff is fictional. Its attributes are a metaphor for how God can choose ordinary people and use them to accomplish remarkable things.

The prophecy described in 'The Book of the End' is fictional. It is based on an actual prophecy that was already written in the book of Daniel, Chapter 7; that one is real.

The secret Estonian organization and references to Koletis (The Beast) are fictional creations of the author.

The story of Jeff's journey represents the real search that every man and woman confronts sooner or later in life. Jeff's most important discoveries are revelations about himself, especially his one greatest need, for a personal connection with his creator.

Thank you for reading!
D. I. Hennessey

BOOKS BY

D. I. HENNESSEY

Books in the Within & Without Time Series:

Book 1: Within and Without Time

Book 2: The Traveler

Book 3: The Secret Door

Book 4: Evil Ascendant - Deliverance

Book 5: The Time of His Choosing

Book 6: A Mission Rarely Given

Book 7: An Unexpected Hour

Books in the Niergel Chronicles Series:

Book 1: Niergel Chronicles - Last Hope

Book 2: Niergel Chronicles - Quest

Book 3: Niergel Chronicles - The Tenth Mantle Bearer

Book 4: Niergel Chronicles - The Dragon's Tail

Book 5: Niergel Chronicles - The White Castle

Available on Amazon

Within and Without Time Series:

"www.amazon.com/gp/product/B09DFDM364"

Niergel Chronicles Series:

"https://www.amazon.com/dp/B0BCHSRZ56"

END NOTES

5. UNCOVERED SECRETS

1. CAD is an abbreviation for Computer Aided Design. It is a format used for computer files containing schematics, architectural drawings, and 3D floor plans.

8. INTERROGATION

1. Koletis: "The Monster," Alt."The Beast", Estonian

13. REJOICING

1. French: Yes! I know!
2. French: Thank You Jesus!

21. CHAPEL GUEST

1. jamais vu, the opposite of déjà vu. — translates to "never seen" in French. It takes place when you're in a familiar situation but suddenly feel as if you're experiencing it for the first time.
2. Portions adapted from "Just Between Us",Copyright 2019, https://justbetweenus.org/faith/relationship-with-god/lessons-from-the-heart-of-god/

24. ESTONIA

1. Koletis: "The Monster," Alt."The Beast", Estonian

28. INVASION

1. By the Staff of God!

29. STRENGTH

1. Come Staff of God!

www.ingramcontent.com/pod-product-compliance
Lightning Source LLC
Chambersburg PA
CBHW072213170626
46813CB00003B/919